NOTES
ON
SURVIVING
THE
FIRE

CHRISTINE MURPHY

NOTES ON SURVIVING THE FIRE

WILDFIRE

The right of Christine Murphy to be identified as the Author
of the Work has been asserted by her in accordance with the
Copyright, Designs and Patents Act 1988.

First published in the United States by Alfred A. Knopf,
a division of Penguin Random House LLC

First published in the UK in 2025 by Wildfire
an imprint of Headline Publishing Group Limited

1

Cataloguing in Publication Data is available from the British Library

Hardback ISBN 9781035411399
Trade paperback ISBN 9781035411405

Offset in 12/16pt Garamond Premier Pro by Jouve (UK), Milton Keynes

Printed and bound in Great Britain by Clays Ltd, Elcograf S.p.A.

Headline's policy is to use papers that are natural, renewable and
recyclable products and made from wood grown in well-managed
forests and other controlled sources. The logging and manufacturing
processes are expected to conform to the environmental
regulations of the country of origin.

Headline Publishing Group Limited
An Hachette UK Company
Carmelite House
50 Victoria Embankment
London EC4Y 0DZ

The authorised representative in the EEA is Hachette Ireland,
8 Castlecourt Centre, Dublin 15, D15 XTP3, Ireland (email: info@hbgi.ie)

www.headline.co.uk
www.hachette.co.uk

After it happened, a woman told me
it doesn't have to fuck you over.
Her name was Betty.
We are all Betty.
This is for us.

I F SHE'S FEMALE, start between the legs. Dad taught me that, his hand on mine, the knife between us. Free the bottom of the colon. Be careful not to cut the intestines. The knife followed his words. The little black dog sat at our feet. Tie off the anus to prevent fecal matter from spilling out and damaging the meat. If she shits herself, she's ruined.

I park my truck on the side road that leads to the avocado farm at the end of the street. It's dark and it's hot, and Dad has been dead for years, buried under a tree back east. Nathan smokes weed in my passenger seat, passes it to me as I stare at the house across the road and think about how I am ruined. Fires dance along mountain edges. The air is thick with drugs and ash in the SoCal summer. June Gloom they call it, even though it's almost November. The heavy layer of damp, somehow both warm and cool, wet and dry, lingers over the town. Mixed with the ash, it forms a paste that sticks to your sticky parts—eyeballs, nostrils, mouth, and crotch. Or maybe it's something else in the truck, something else that sticks. Something like love between us, or the absence of sex. What grows when two people have nothing apart from each other.

I smoke the joint down to the end, hold the last inch between my lips, and breathe deep. He takes the remaining white stub, wet with our shared saliva, rolls down the window, and flicks it. It lands on the road in front of us, far enough that we can see it. My hand lingers on the horn as I watch movement inside the house across the street. Shadows behind windows. Men behind glass.

I am thinking about deer, but we are talking about love. Nathan says he loves me because I let him see me, and he knows how hard that is. He appreciates that I let him in. I say I love him because he is not a dick, in a world full of dicks.

"That is a definition based on negation, Sarah," he says. "You love me for what I am not, rather than for what I am. It is a comparison rooted in conceptions of the other, rather than a conception of the subject itself."

I roll my eyes, and Nathan rolls another joint. "I love you because you are nice," I say.

"I'm not nice." He licks the edge of the paper.

"I love drugs. You do drugs. Ergo, I love you."

"Post hoc fallacy."

I look back at the house, at the shadows inside, dark movements in dark waters. "I love you because I trust you."

He smiles. He admires the smooth, white shape of the blunt in the dark.

"I love you because you are good."

He puts the joint into his mouth and leans back, scalp against the metal edges of my gun rack. He lights the end. He shakes his head.

I take it from his mouth, slip it into my own, and watch the red end glow in front of my nose. "I love you because you're going to piss on that windowsill."

He opens his eyes. He looks at me. "That windowsill is kind of high." He opens the passenger door.

"I love you because you'll try," I stage-whisper around the joint in my mouth. On the ground in front of him, the previous one sparks, catches on something. It flickers, brighter than when Nathan flicked it. The man in the kitchen moves to the bedroom, the one near the bathroom. The man in the far bedroom, the bedroom I remember, is seated at a desk. A lamp shines like a halo behind his head.

Nathan crosses the street, slim limbs beneath Billy Idol hair, and reaches the shrub next to the window. Behind it, the man tilts his head. Perhaps he is reading, or writing. Preparing for his job talk. Nathan unzips his fly and waves, body tucked against the house, penis parallel to the earth.

I love you because you remind me of my father, I think but do not say.

I open the driver's side and step down. Nathan turns his back to me. He pushes his pelvis forward and aims upward. The moon shines, light scattered among clouds and smoke. The delicate splatter of piss against plastic siding, not quite reaching the windowsill, tinkles and twinkles in the light and the dark and the heat. Not far away, a British prince lives with his American wife. Newlyweds make love above vineyards. Tenured faculty watch the ocean from private balconies.

I walk to the street and crouch above Nathan's abandoned blunt. A fresh one dangles between my lips. On the ground, in front of the truck, the single ember sparks between my thighs. I think of bending down, growing a fire with my breath, filling it with my rage and my hate and watching it lunge across the street. I think of my father's knives.

The ash continues to fall, not at all like snow. My breath catches and I cough, loud enough for Nathan to turn. The smoke clogs my eyes, and tears streak through the dust on my cheeks. I hold the blunt in my hand and pull my shirt above my mouth. Beneath me, the ember flickers and sputters and dies.

Nathan tucks his penis inside his jeans. He ducks and scurries toward me. He grins and points over his shoulder.

I love you because you believe me.

Ash in my throat. Ash on my skin. He reaches me and holds out his hand. I stand. We move back toward the truck, away from the shadows across the street. We laugh in the dark and the smoke and the hate.

———

Nathan walks to the rear tire on the driver's side and reaches inside the wheelhouse. He pulls down my spare keys.

"What are you doing?" I ask after another inhale, eyes squinting.

He looks at his hand. "I want to drive."

"I drove here." I exhale. "Keys are still in the ignition."

He laughs. I snort. He puts the spares back.

I hand him the blunt and walk to the passenger side. "Try not to kill us."

"I don't know anyone else who keeps her extra keys attached to her car." He climbs in, one hand on the wheel, one on the door. He holds the cigarette between his lips on the right side of his mouth, exhaling on the left. He's tried to teach me how to do this, but I'm less ambidextrous with my lips.

"Which is precisely why it works." The joy of being a New Englander in California. You have so many practical skills in a state with none. "And it's not a car."

Nathan is from rich-bitch L.A. His parents make drugs. Sackler-adjacent, he likes to say. The opioid epidemic is the family business, but he prefers to teach coeds Intro to Zen in the second-most-expensive ZIP code in the country. His sister, Jessica, lives in Manhattan Beach. She's not in the business, either, I don't think. Maybe she fits it in around yoga and Hollywood parties, the ones in the big houses with the frozen faces. She invites us to them, up in the hills behind the gates, past the driveways that look like highways. Last time, Nathan and I stole an actor's E while Jessica flirted with him on a balcony next to the Hollywood sign. She left with a superhero. We left with his baggie and an Uber. I asked Nathan why we steal drugs when we could use his friends-and-family discount plan. He reminded me he takes nothing from his parents.

Jessica tolerates me because I'm the only friend her brother has, both of us former monastics. L.A. loves that about me. Tell a SoCal beefcake you study Buddhism and your chances of getting laid go up 30 percent. Tell the heiress at the smoothie bar you lived in a North Indian nunnery and suddenly you're worth talking to. They think I spent a month at a yoga center in Big Sur. They think I'm reading Deepak Chopra and Eckhart Tolle. They think I meditate. Pilates, someone explained to me once, is very Buddhist.

Nathan meditates, I tell them, you should talk to him. He lived in a Catholic monastery in the Dolomites. And he's a vegan. I suspect he does yoga, too, but he knows what I think about that shit. Catholics are perverts, people tell me, Buddhists are enlightened. Nathan has maintained vows of celibacy for over a decade, I used to argue, and my research focuses on violence within Buddhist traditions. (Nathan thinks I should title it *When Buddhists Kill,* bleach my hair, and make a career at Fox News.) SoCal doesn't want to hear that. In the land of whipped cream and garbage, image is everything. Buddhism is such a vibe, Catholicism not so much. So they explain our research to us, and Nathan and I steal their drugs.

He turns on the windshield wipers. The ash moves in streaks across the glass. I reach for the ice scraper in the door pocket and remember I am not in Maine. No one has one of those out here.

"When are you going to get this fixed?" He whacks the gun rack behind his head.

"Next year. When Colette has signed off on my dissertation and we have tenure-track jobs with matching houses in matching towns. A platonic spousal hire."

"Home ownership." He turns the key. The engine coughs. "Retirement plan."

Ash drifts across the house in front of us. I tuck my face inside my T-shirt. "I can't believe that pigfucker got an interview, and now a campus visit."

He pats my leg. "At least someone pissed on his house."

We leave the cover of the avocado trees. The shadows inside the house move in slow circles. I lift a middle finger to the window, and we drive down the silent street. Nathan's phone begins to jingle. The *Golden Girls* theme song. He hands it to me. I enter his password and open his messages.

"Jessica says you forgot your book at her place."

We join the freeway. The roads are crowded. The line that used to be green on digital maps now reads red from Mexico through San Diego, L.A., past us. It's not green until we're all the way up the stretch of brown mountains to your right, ocean to your left, toward Neverland Ranch, horse farms, retired tech bros. The occasional recovering attorney. We drive in silence. Nathan takes his exit and turns at the stop sign with "cunt" spray-painted across the bottom. Every week, someone washes it off. Every week, someone repaints it. Another stop sign, another road, and Nathan pulls into the driveway of the house behind which his studio is built. Suburbs of pleasant 3 and 2's that sell for over $3 million, each with a 250-square-foot studio in the back that the trust-fund-less, or the trust-fund-rejecting, rent for $4,500 a month.

He parks. He leaves the beams and wipers on.

I want to go inside and black out on a room-temperature handle of whatever he's got. We'll open our email and read Dear Applicant rejections and the perfunctory messages about another dead kid, OD'd on the beach, driving off the on ramp, from the Dean's office.

Both come with token condolences. Both express well wishes. The only difference is, the job rejections share the numbers: 800 applicants, 1,100 applicants. The dead-kid announcements don't. Every time a new name pops up—thoughts and prayers and a link to the Counseling Center—it is treated like we didn't get this email the week before. You'd think, at some point, the powers that be would address the suicides—"tragic loss"—across campus, just as you'd think, at some point, the powers that be would acknowledge there are no jobs, there is no funding, and $150,000 in student debt is not a compelling argument for why we should be hired outside of the ivory tower. Something needs to be done, you'd think they'd say, something more than hopes and prayers and the continued production of the overeducated and the underqualified.

Maybe we'll break out the Special K and the Van Damme and lie on the floor watching someone solve the world's problems by kicking really high. We try to limit ourselves to once a week, both for the drugs and the movies, but it's hard when everything sucks.

"I submit to Philippe next week." He sighs. "I wonder who in the department will kill me out of spite."

I try not to smile. I don't worry about the safety of straight white guys in straight white towns. I open my mouth beneath my shirt, listen to the swish of the wiper blades. I think of Rapist, tall and thin and nervous in a way that inspires both sympathy and alarm. Seated at his desk, the shadowy figure behind his window, preparing for a job talk. Or his roommate, Flopsy, his indignation and his rage, entitlement like body spray, doing dishes in the kitchen. Both so different from Nathan, his steady eyes and strong hands.

"You're doing OK, right?" I ask, and he laughs. Nathan and I are in Religious Studies, but our fieldwork relies on sociological methodology. That's a fancy way of saying you know how to ask questions. Open-ended: How are you? No lead. The subject comes up with their own response, the data collected is less influenced by the scholar's own biases. Closed-ended: You're doing OK, right? Lead. The subject is encouraged to answer in a prescribed manner, thereby invalidating the data. We promised each other only open-ended questions. Sometimes we slip.

He shrugs. "What about you?" Open-ended.

"I'm fine."

"Even though he's—"

"Submitted? Prepping for an Ivy League fellowship?" Closed-ended. I rub my finger across the skin of his forearm, watching a streak of gray follow its path. "I guess I should have expected this."

Ash falls in soft flakes across the truck beams. It does not look like falling snow, but West Coasters don't know that. They've never been where I've been. They think their ashy skies and brown hills are beautiful. He reaches for my hand.

"I'm so angry." I breathe in. The burn of the fires catches in my throat. "I can't remember what not-angry feels like."

His hand is warm in mine. He squeezes.

"And everybody knows, and nobody does anything." The ash comes in through the vents, swirls in front of my eyes. "I'll never understand that."

We don't do it because we want to, Dad said when I was nine, and blood matted the fur and pooled in the grass. We do it because we need to.

What if we didn't need to? I asked, cheeks cold in the frost. What if we just wanted to?

Nathan slides across the center seat and puts both arms around me. I don't know if I love him in spite of his celibacy or because of it. It's such a shame, someone said once, that you two can never really be together. I didn't know how to respond then. I don't know how to respond now. Sometimes I wonder if we love each other because fucking never got in the way.

I rest my head in the crook of his neck, press my cheek against his shoulder. He tucks a strand of hair behind my ear. "You wanna spend the night? Jessica sent me two bottles of mezcal."

My phone beeps. Tinder's familiar jingle. "Is she off the wagon again?"

"No, but people send her stuff." Another chirp. "Is that Brad?"

I shrug.

"Wasn't there a Craig last week? Or Greg?"

"What is this sudden interest in my sex life?"

"You never talk about your boyfriends. We talk about everything else. Why not this?"

"I don't have boyfriends."

"Whatever you call them. Since you got back from fieldwork, there's been a noticeable uptick."

"Want me to forward you my Excel sheet?"

"Sarah—"

"I could upload it to Dropbox. You could get real-time updates." My phone jingles again. I hand it to him. "Would you like to answer?"

He sighs. "Besides whoever that is, what are you doing this weekend?"

"I've got another postdoc application, and my forty-second attempt to get Colette to discuss my revisions."

"Is she still forbidding you from submitting to your committee?"

"Says I need her sign-off before I can have theirs."

"Just make sure she does sign off. How many of her students have quit in the last five years?"

"All of them." I poke him in the side. "But not me."

He closes his eyes and leans his head back. He swallows. His throat undulates in the dark of the truck. "God, I hate teaching." He opens the door to a blast of ash.

"Want to go for a run tomorrow?" I move to the driver's side. "I'll tell you all about my hookup."

He touches my cheek. "Tomorrow's Friday. Fridays at Four, right?"

"How about five-thirty?"

He keeps his hand on my cheek. "Call me if you start thinking about that fucker."

I roll my eyes.

He taps my nose, then reaches for the door. "You call me. Whenever. Whyever."

He goes into his house.

Does celibacy help with stress?

Maybe I should try it

It's the right choice for me

you'd struggle

rude

is it better than drugs?

Not even close

the drugs do help

you help

♥

OK, GUYS." I sit cross-legged on the table at the front of the classroom, a five-pound bag of candy beside me. "Who can summarize the reading?"

A senior raises his hand. I toss him a Snickers. "Buddha and five hundred merchants are on a boat. But there's another guy on the boat." He glances at his laptop. "'A doer of dark deeds.' This guy sees all the wealthy people, and decides to murder them and steal their stuff."

"Great. What happens next?"

Freshman in the front row. Twix bar. "Buddha has a dream, and in this dream all his Buddha buddies tell him this bad guy is on board. He knows this guy plans to kill everyone, but everyone is stuck on the boat. There are no bodyguards, no jail cell, no way to stop him."

I nod. "So—what's Buddha's dilemma?"

Freshman blinks. "He doesn't know what to do."

"OK." I hop down and approach the chalkboard. "But, according to this text, Buddha has three specific thoughts, each corresponding to a unique concern. Who remembers the first one?"

A hand in the back. "He thinks there's no way to stop the guy." Skittles.

"Yup, and why is that a problem?" I walk between the desks and place my hand on the shoulder of a tall, slim student scrolling through TikTok.

"Uh . . ." Phone fumbles. "Because people will die?"

"OK, and—"

"No!" A freshman interrupts me. "Buddha is worried that, if the bad guy kills everybody, he'll go to hell. That's his first concern."

I pivot and high-five the freshman. Three Musketeers. "Yes! And why does Buddha care about people going to hell?"

"Suffering." In the front row, turned sideways in his chair. "Hell is full of suffering, and Buddha doesn't want anyone to suffer." M&M's.

"Even a murderer?" Phone asks. Front Row nods.

"Awesome." I walk to the front and write "murder → hell → suffering" on the board. "What is Buddha's second thought?"

Hilary, doe-eyed, shaved head, next to the window. "He thinks, if he tells all the rich guys that this other guy wants to kill them, then they'll kill him." Snickers.

I nod. "And why's that a problem?"

"Suffering!" Front Row again, voice raised, bouncing in his chair. "If the rich guys kill the bad guy, then they'd go to hell and they'd suffer, too." He holds out his hand. Twix.

"Exactly." I circle my board notes, turn back to the class. "What is Buddha's final thought?"

A Chinese student in designer sweatpants: "Buddha thinks he could kill the bad man. Then neither the bad man nor the rich men would go to hell. And none of them would suffer."

"Excellent." Thumbs-up and a bag of Skittles. "What is the corresponding concern with this final thought?"

"Nothing." A redhead in the back, tattoos across her collarbones. "To prevent everyone else's suffering, Buddha doesn't mind going to hell." Baby Ruth.

"Wait a minute." Phone looks up. "Buddha kills a guy?"

"Sometimes the reading is interesting." I toss him peanut M&M's. "Maybe you should try it."

Phone shrugs.

"To minimize suffering!" Front Row shouts and points to the board. "He's not just killing people for fun."

"He took one for the team," Neck Tattoo adds.

I sit on the table. "So why are we reading a story about Buddha killing somebody?"

Silence.

"What does this story teach us about the relationship between Buddhism and violence?"

Freshman: "Last week, we talked about motivation, how the reason you do something in Buddhism is more important than what you actually do. This story is about that, right? Buddha killed the bad guy to prevent anyone else on the boat from going to hell, so, even though his actions are bad, his motivations are good."

Thumbs-up. Sour Patch Kids. "Anyone else?"

Bikini Top in the back: "Everybody talks about Buddhism like it's all peace and love, but this story shows that's not always the case." Milky Way.

I swing my legs. "Why does that matter?"

"Maybe sometimes what everybody thinks is true isn't actually true."

"Yes!" I hop off the desk and lob the remaining candy to the rest of the students. "Obviously, you're here to learn things to pass your exams." I point to Neck Tattoo. "But, sometimes, you also learn something useful."

"Like how Group Think sucks." Baseball Cap.

"Hell yes, it does." I slap my hands on the table. "Think for your-selves, guys. That's the lesson of this class." Front Row snaps his fingers. "And the relationship between motivation and karmic con-sequences in the later Mahayana tradition. Because that's definitely a question on the exam." Freshman nods. Phone is back to texting. The click of keys on keyboards, the crinkle of wrappers. There are no bells in this annex, or windows with a view of the clock tower.

"Papers are due before Thanksgiving. You've got three weeks, but I'm posting extra office hours, if anyone needs help or wants an early start." They pack their bags. I write my phone number on the board. "If anyone has a situation they need to discuss with me, reach out."

Out of the classroom, down the hallway, and across the parking lot. Some rush to their next classes, their jobs, their cars. Others stroll toward the boba-tea stall, the beach, the fitness center. There are two sides of UCST's campus. One has the official buildings, big beige blocks of Humanities, the glass and metal of Engineering and Accounting. The other has frat houses, sororities, three-bedroom apartments shared by nine students. Lecture halls for professors and coffee shops for adjuncts. Both sides share palm trees beneath a darkened sky and burritos priced at $25 each.

I walk through the bicycle tunnel that separates the two halves. It is lined with graffiti and protest posters. On one end, a list of indignations and reasons to rage, peppered with a-cappella and improv shows. Flyers taped on flyers, what you should boycott and where you should party. Tonight, there's a Halloween special, something for charity. On the other end, a list of names in black marker—students dead that year, the year before, the year before. Top to bottom. Various commentary. *Miss you. love you.* Some ear-nest and terrible poetry.

The university ignores the a-cappella announcements but cov-ers up the dead kids. They post their obligatory acknowledgments online, the email with a link to the Counseling Center. They never mention them again. And they literally cover them up. Every few weeks, some poor bastard in a uniform comes down here with a bucket and a brush and whitewashes the alcohol poisonings, the overdoses, an occasional meningitis. Washes it all away. Within a few days, the dead rise from their milky graves. Names, notes, poems rewritten. I read a few as I walk past. My students tell me about their debt, their family obligations, how, at the age of eighteen, they're medicated for anxiety, already on a path of financial burden. I can't get a job that pays without a degree, they say, but getting a degree means I can only get jobs that will pay off my debt. I teach Buddhist Studies and my kids major in Engineering and Accounting. They tell me they hate Engineering and Accounting. No wonder the list is long.

The tunnel leads from the parking garage, away from Global Studies and Music, into the Women's Center, a wide, cement building with advertisements for self-defense training and postcards of self-care methods. Punching men and eating vegetables. Today, someone has cut out a pumpkin from notebook paper, colored it in orange highlighter, and taped it to the front door. Bowls of candy-colored condoms adorn the welcome desk.

Through the entrance and the computer room, a left at the floor-to-ceiling glass windows, sign my name and open the metal double doors with the "Meeting in Progress" sign. Chairs in a circle. No desks. No windows. A small coffee table in the center with pens, notepads, and three boxes of tissues. Young women.

I sit.

Two therapists. Welcome breathing exercises. Sometimes a question. Sometimes a breakdown. Always an hour. Always Fridays at Four.

It's not a club anyone wants to be a member of, but it is a club plenty of people join. Group therapy is free, but you have to qualify—at least six months' work with an individual therapist on campus. Student Health Services provides eight free one-on-one sessions, after which enrolled students pay $75 per one-hour meeting. Student Health Services has nine full-time therapists, six of whom focus specifically on sexual assault. Scheduling an appointment requires a wait time of several months, qualification through the university insurance policy, referrals from the university primary-care physicians, and questionnaires—in person, over email—before and after appointments. I qualified in September, three years after the rape, after the one-on-ones with a nice lady in a small office in Student Health Services. I sat next to her dying plant, its withered leaves draped across my shoulders. She cleared her throat every time I mentioned my aptitude for anonymous sex. She recommended group therapy after I met my quota of individual sessions. Or maybe she was uncomfortable with my word choice and wanted to get rid of me. Perhaps you could refer to them as your colleagues, she suggested one sunny afternoon, instead of that other "c" word.

The University of California, Santa Teresa, handles suicide with emails and sexual violence with paperwork. By the time we qualify for group therapy, it's been years since our attacks. Maybe months, if parents threatened to sue. By the time we qualify for group therapy, we've been through police procedurals, the Academic Discipline Committee, the laughing and the eye rolling and the vigorous nods. You're OK, right? Dumb slut. He's such a great guy. By the time we qualify for group therapy, we are picking the meat off the bones.

But we're here now. At the front of the line.

There's a new girl today. A sophomore. She introduces herself and cries. Another, one of the freshmen who got in early, stares blankly ahead. She's been on campus less than two months.

"Title IX found him guilty." Sophomore shakes her head. "Responsible. That's the word they use. They found him responsible."

"That's great," Therapist 1 says.

"He has to leave campus for a semester. So I don't have to see him."

We nod. Crumbs from the banquet table.

"He won't be back until spring, but has two weeks to collect his stuff. I still have to see him for a while." She shrugs, fingers twisting the hem of her shirt. "I quit my job so I can load up on classes. It means more loans, but if I can skip senior year, then I'll only have to be around him next quarter and next year."

We nod.

"They're preparing take-home exams for him. He'll finish fall quarter remotely. He gets full credit and everything."

We nod.

"Someone told me that the punishment isn't counted on his transcripts, so it just looks like a leave of absence. I took a leave of absence, too. I guess our transcripts look the same."

We nod.

"But Title IX says he's guilty—well, responsible. I guess that's something." She looks up. She is small and freckled and reminds me of a girl I knew in eighth grade.

This is a success story.

"I called Title IX." Senior. Blond hair dyed blue at the tips, raped by her friend. "Wanted to know what the deal was. What was happening with my case. They said they were overloaded." She glances at the therapists. "They actually told me the numbers—two hundred and twenty-six new cases since the summer. Only six being investigated. Can they say that to me? Am I allowed to know that?"

The therapists maintain eye contact, shoulders down and spines straight. I admire their body language. The skill in not giving anything away.

"I'm not sure," Therapist 2 says. It's a lie, but it helps. The goal is to help.

"What's happening with all the others?" A Ph.D. in Chemistry leans forward, the only other graduate student in our group. Shaved head, tattoos. Her lab partner raped her at a conference. He was found on the beach, face blue, blood alcohol off the charts. His name is in the tunnel.

"Nothing's happening," I say. "Whoever files a report gets an email with an attachment titled 'Resources for Impacted Parties.'"

A woman across the circle, raped at a party while her friends played beer pong downstairs, nods. "That's what I got. Never opened it."

"It's a list of phone numbers," another woman says, this one large, lanky, sprawling across her chair, drugged by her boyfriend and raped by his friends. "Couple of websites."

"I'm still waiting to hear back." The other freshman, raped during her first week on campus, three days after her parents dropped her off.

We are silent. She's not hearing back. Well, apart from the email.

"If they don't do anything, does that mean they think he's innocent?" She looks at each of us, hoping.

"It means they have declined to pursue further investigation," Therapist 1 says. "And found him not responsible."

"So who is?"

If a tree falls in the woods.

"Who did you report to?" I ask.

"I don't remember."

"KKKathy?" Lanky asks. "Middle-aged blonde with Hitler hair?"

"That chick." Chemistry leans forward. "Before I'd even sat down, she gave me that 'office of record, nothing is confidential' speech. Then I watch her pull out that old phone on her desk and read her password off a notepad to log on. Jesus. At least make a hacker work for it."

Another new girl, a junior, wipes her eyes, takes a deep breath.

"I didn't file," she says, words soft. "I know people who have and nothing happened, or, well, you know how people act." She pauses. "Plus, he got one of those First Generation Scholarships. The newspaper did an interview."

We nod.

"My mom says I need to. She says I should report it, but when I do, I should lie. Tell the police I wasn't drunk." She crosses her arms and tucks her hands under her armpits. "My dad won't talk about it, but Mom told all my aunts and uncles. No one has called me. Isn't that weird? Like, if I had gotten in a car accident, they would ask how I'm doing. But this happens, and . . .'"

"When I told my mom what happened, she said she was going to the police," Lanky says. "She yelled at me when I said I didn't want her to do that. She said if I didn't report him and he raped somebody else, it would be my fault."

"Jesus *Christ,*" Chemistry and I say in unison.

"Well"—Lanky sits up—"not those exact words. More like, 'What if he does it again?'" She laughs. "Of course he's going to do it again. My report won't stop that."

We nod.

"I filed," I say, arms crossed, ankles crossed, "after I left campus for fieldwork. I had a Zoom interview with KKKathy. She made a joke that the ceiling light behind my head was shining like a halo. Said it made me look more innocent."

"She's a kkkunt."

"I read my rapist's statement," says a small girl in the corner. "He said I was mentally unstable." She stares at the coffee table in the center of the room. "He said he only had a one-night stand with me because he heard I was promiscuous, so he thought it was an OK thing to do, because he doesn't normally have one-night stands.

"He threatened to sue me, to sue the school. There was a note in the file from his father. He works at some big law firm." She smiles. "You can guess what it said."

Chemistry picks at the edge of her sleeve. "Litigation is just another way to fuck someone, so if you're a rapist I guess that makes sense."

"I didn't know we could read our rapists' statements," Sophomore says.

"If you filed with Title IX, you are entitled to read the report when the investigation is finished," Therapist 1 says.

"You guys who filed, do you wish you didn't?" Junior, no longer crying, asks.

Nods. Shrugs. One head shake. The usual responses.

Paper trail.

Harassment.

No point.

Worse than the rape.

Therapist 2 mentions the time. Another breathing exercise. We pack our items. Some leave quickly. Others are slow. Therapist 1 smiles as we head out the door. Therapist 2 moves the tables back to the center of the room.

They remove the "Meeting in Progress" sign and hand it to the student volunteer in the computer lab. We walk past the bowls of condoms, the self-defense posters. Someone holds open a door. We step into the heat and the haze and the gray. I watch the Fridays at Four crowd disperse. Toward the library, under reconstruction, with the windows overlooking the sunset. Toward the tunnel with the layers of dead kids, black ink on white wall. *Miss you. love you.* From a distance, we all look the same.

Early-evening sun drifts past, changes the smoke from gray to orange and yellow. Seasonally appropriate. Six months ago, a fire broke out fifty miles south. Nothing to see here, the Chancellor wrote in the university's proprietary font. Everything is fine.

The assumption was, it would all be over by the end of spring.

Summer. Fall quarter would be smoke free. Tomorrow is November and students still walk around campus with T-shirts pulled over their mouths, the closest thing to a turtleneck most of these kids have ever worn. Some are in costume for tonight—sexy kitten, sexy pumpkin, sparkly vampire twink—all with hands covering their mouths.

It's five-thirty, and Nathan's driveway is quiet. Jared, the furry little man who lives in the main house, complains if it isn't. When our paths cross, he holds his hands in front of his waist, elbows bent, as if protecting his belly. When I speak to him, one hand rises to his face, twirling the side of his mustache, fingers pinching and petting, lips pursed, eyes on mine. I avoid Jared.

I park on the road.

You ready?

I roll my shoulders and press against the faded headrest. The gun rack pokes against my temple.

I'm outside

I stretch my hands across the steering wheel. The sun is setting, and the orange and the gray turn darker, almost the colors of my childhood, autumn leaves under heavy boots. Dad, the little black dog, the woods. Almost. Dances of red line the mountain ridges. The birds are gone, flown elsewhere to breathe. I cut the engine, leave my keys in the ignition, and climb down. I prop one heel on a front tire and bend forward.

Don't make me come in there!

I switch legs.

A garbage truck rumbles. A parent tells a child to put on their seatbelt. I turn my head. Two princesses and one tiny dinosaur climb into an SUV, pumpkin buckets in hand. I glance at my sneakers, two years old, the cushioning shot. I reason that, because they're beach shoes and sand is soft, I'm not doing too much damage to my joints.

My battery is at 80 percent after being unplugged for three minutes. I check my email. Two responses to my ad offering essay-writing services. Both from UCST emails, one from one of my students from last year. He doesn't know who he's messaging. I respond and double my price. I open my texts. Nothing from Nathan.

> Fine. I'll drag your ass outside myself

I stick my phone in my sports bra and grab my keys from the ignition. The dinosaur waves as his car drives past. I walk up the driveway, past the entrance to the main house, where Jared and his mustache live, and around the back.

I reach my hand up and over the gate, lift the latch, and push through. The ground dips down on this side of the house, the line of concrete foundation rising to hip height. It creates a tunnel between the fencing and the side of the attachment in which Nathan lives. It's also a dead end, the backyard protected from renters with a sheet of vinyl siding slumped against the neighbors' chicken coop.

I enter the tunnel. Past the recycling bins and an empty tub of kitty litter. Past Nathan's bike. Past the side entrance to the main house, which Nathan uses to do laundry.

Nathan's place is one room with its own entrance. His bed is against the wall. There's one window on one side, just above my head, a microwave, mini-fridge, and plug-in single burner on the other. There is a tiny bathroom, walls and floor constructed from a single piece of plastic. The showerhead hangs above the toilet, a six-inch sink, and the drain in the floor. It reminds me of an upright coffin. No room to shave your legs, but you can puke and shit and wash your hair at the same time.

I reach my hand overhead and knock on the window.

"Nathan!" I hiss, mindful of Jared and his love of silence.

Nothing.

Yo!

"Nathan!"

Children scream and shout on the street behind me. I dial. It rings. His voicemail answers. "Hey, it's me. If you think that is a grammatically correct statement, don't bother leaving a message." Beep.

"You can't be bothered to pick up when I am standing outside your house?"

The dump truck passes on the other side of the fence. More giggles. The voice of an anxious parent. The sky is darker than it should be at quarter to six. I pull my shirt above my nose. Running in this is a joke, but it's perfect weather for Ellen Ripley and blow.

I turn back to his window, the sill above my head. It is open an inch. I stand on my tiptoes, tilt my head back, and speak toward the ledge. "If you are out somewhere else and didn't bother to tell me, you are officially a dick."

A cloud passes. The tunnel darkens, and goose bumps lift on my skin. The grate of the garbage truck down the road, screech of brakes, clank of a metal trash can inside its automated grip. A parent shouts to get back in the car. A child cries.

I dial again. Another sound, not the dump truck, not a trick-or-treater, comes from the other side of the window. I press my phone, still ringing, to my chest.

Thank you for being a friend.

"Nathan," I say. Full volume. I knock again. I stretch my arm and push the window open as far as I can, a few inches at most.

Traveled down a road and back again.

"Nathan." Louder this time, and I wave my hand overhead, just inside the window.

I grab the curtain and jerk it. The metal rings scrape across the rod.

His phone stops. His voicemail picks up. Nathan speaks into my breasts.

"Hey, it's me. If you think that is a grammatically correct statement—"

I hang up. I go around to the front of his house. I knock. I knock again. I pound my fist against the door.

Jared comes out in an oversized bathrobe, one finger on his mustache, the other tucked across his belly. He looks like an otter cosplaying Tony Soprano.

"Is Nathan home?"

He shrugs. At the end of the driveway, Pikachu holds hands with Princess Leia. Superman picks his nose.

"Is that a yes or a no?"

"I haven't seen him," Jared murmurs, eyes on me, finger on mustache. I honestly can't tell if he's in a costume or not.

"He's not answering his door."

"Maybe he's asleep." He pets his face.

"Can you let me in?"

Not even a nod or a shake of the head. This fucking guy.

"Nice outfit." I go back around the side of the building. I grab the kitty-litter tub and flip it over. I place it underneath the window and hop up, my fingers on the sill.

"Nathan." I shove the window farther up and swat at the stained curtains, the ones I spilled wine on when I was here for my birthday last year, trying to convince him Ecstasy had no effect on me.

Well, you just spilled wine down my curtain, so I think it does, he said at the time.

I'm *dyeing* it, I responded. The curtain is *dying.* I laughed and rubbed my face against the fabric, the way everyone does when they're high on E, until he moved me away from the curtains and brought me a glass of water.

I lean forward. The kitty-litter box sags beneath my weight. I jump, shoving the window as high as it will go. A line of pale skin. I jump again. One arm. Bare. Outstretched and straight. Reaching toward me, palm up. Fingers curled.

The kitty-litter box gives way. My chin slams against the metal windowsill, and I land on my ass, lip bleeding, my lower legs inside the broken container.

Jared has followed me. He stands inside the gate.

"Unlock the door." I kick the kitty-litter box off my legs, broken plastic slicing through my skin. Jared stares. "Jesus Christ, dude, unlock the fucking door!" I scramble up.

"I have to find the key," he says, at an almost normal volume.

"Then go find it!"

"It'll take a minute."

I shove past him and run to Nathan's front door. I grab the handle, pound on the wood, slam my shoulder against it.

"Call the police!" I shout over my shoulder, looking on either side of me for something to smash the door with, wishing I could kick it down like an eighties action hero. Halfway up the driveway, a middle-aged man in khakis hurries a donut and a dragon back toward the road.

Jared stands behind me; his lip bounces beneath his fingers, flashes of teeth and receding gum line.

"Call 911, you fucking moron. He's in there!" I grab the recycling bin, big and navy blue, and drag it through the gate. I flip it on its side; cat-food cans and soda bottles spill at my feet. I hoist myself up to the window, one foot on the bin, one on the siding.

The plastic cracks beneath me, but it's high enough that I can grab the sill and bring my upper body over the edge. Ass up, legs dangling, I worm myself forward until I tip. I tear the front of my shorts, scrape my thighs against the ledge, and land in a lump on the carpet.

His hand reaches toward me. Palm up. Fingers curled. The studio is small enough that I can see the details of his fingernails, a semicircle of faded blue. Not unlike the color he painted his toenails last year, when his sister gave him a bottle of nail polish she didn't like and he refused to waste it.

Anything that helps me be less of a typical dude, he said, as he finished his nails and turned toward mine. He held my hand, colored my ten tiny surfaces.

I reach for him, one finger touching one finger, like that painting, the one he saw as a child, when his parents were invited to the Vatican.

The ash follows me. The smoke follows me. Everything is cold.

A few feet separate the window from the bedside table, from the bed. The line of his arm is a horizon to my eyes, broken by a rubber band around the biceps, a needle in the crease of the elbow. I've never seen him naked before. Shirtless on the beach a few times, sure. The tops of his thighs, surprisingly white, when we stretch after a run.

Nathan's scrotum greets me as I crawl forward, his hair an unexpected shade of red. I was nine the first time I saw a scrotum. Balls ruin everything, Dad told me, the stag at our feet. Slice them off before you open the gut or they'll affect the meat. He watched as I severed the sack. It was covered in the same white pelt as the belly, shaped like a heart.

Dad always saved them, fried them, sliced them, and packed them for my lunch. Human balls are different. More wrinkled. Less furry. I was surprised by the first human testicles I saw, how coarse and thin the hair, how small the shape. Pretty underwhelming. Not nearly enough for a meal.

I expect him to jump up, shout at me, tell me to get the hell out. Jesus Christ, Sarah, don't you ever knock? But his thighs are silent, peachy pink with fur softening above the knee, becoming sparse on the inner flank. A line of muscle along the outer length of one, bent, knee in the same direction as his arm, reaching toward me. Hips open. Stomach concave. His penis is flaccid and light blue. It lies to one side. Uncircumcised. He told me about that, explained that it was because he was born in Europe.

A knock on the door, and I stand. Fabric pulls away from my torn skin, blood drying across my shins; kitty litter sticks to my ankles. I look down at naked Nathan. Dead Nathan. I've seen a lot of dead animals, but this one isn't right. Like a rifle with the safety on, this one isn't working.

Next to his outstretched arm, his laptop and his phone. Two missed calls, four unanswered texts, all from me. I pick up the phone and tuck it inside my bra.

More knocking. I unlock the deadbolt. Turn the handle.

Jared holds out his hand, a key in his palm, as if that's useful now. He's dressed, New Jersey mafia replaced by emo hipster. Behind him, a Prius pulls into the driveway, bright beneath the streetlight. A Santa Teresa police cruiser.

Across the street, Pokémons and princesses are replaced by devils and angels. They pass a vape pen and stare. I walk to the driveway. Earbuds wrapped around my neck, the old ones with the wire that attach to my phone. Both phones contain Nathan's voice, Nathan's messages. Both phones press together, spooning without shape, flat against my breasts.

The outer edges of my shoes are worn down more than the inner. Nathan says this is because I supinate. You have delicate dancer feet, he said, with high arches. I laughed when he said this, and looked at my feet, size ten like the rest of me, strong from a childhood of hunting and fishing and carrying carcasses. It was the first time, the only time, someone called me delicate.

The Prius parks and the passenger door opens. Rick Astley steps out. Glances at me, at Jared. He's young and slim and dressed like a cop, but, I swear, it's Rick Astley. Gig economy?

Driver door opens. Side profile—soft chin, soft belly, heavy brows.

I remember him. He sat across from me in the station. He ordered a copy of the report from the Title IX office. I told him I was raped. He asked why I took so long to file. I told him who did it. He said he'd get back to me. He's grayer now, with bulges across his middle. Rare to see a fat person around here. It almost makes me like him.

Sirens in the distance. The woman found the body, but the men confer among themselves. I walk over.

"What did you see?" Old Cop glances around, doesn't make eye contact.

"I found him in his room." The sun is gone; early-evening damp settles across my skin. Down the street, people laugh and shout. A bus screeches to a halt. Someone calls for Jenny. Someone tells Nick to hurry up.

My ankles hurt, and I realize I am moving side to side, swaying on the outer edges of my feet. Supinating. Jared stands across from me, next to the two policemen. I steeple my fingers together, dangling my arms in front. I press the pads of my thumbs together. The simple act requires enough concentration to still my swaying. A subtle way to stay awake in lectures, to distract myself from the loud men talking over each other. Nathan taught me this.

"What happened?" Rick Astley asks. His voice is soft. He looks at me.

"We had plans to go for a run." I avoid eye contact. Old Cop walks past. "I texted him a few times, but he didn't answer, so I knocked on his window and tried to poke my head in. When I saw him."

Nathan.

I shake my head. "I climbed through the window." Old Cop peers inside the doorway. "He's in there."

Rick Astley nods and takes notes on a pad of paper. Jared watches, fingers on mustache, pulling and pushing.

"Did you see anything unusual?" Old Cop is back, not looking at me.

"He—"

"There's a needle in his arm," Jared says.

Behind us, an ambulance pulls into the driveway. Old Cop looks to Rick Astley. Rick Astley nods. At the bottom of the driveway, a mother drags a butterfly toward a different house.

"Nathan didn't do heroin," I say. I bend one thumb and press the nail into the pad of the other, my fingers in the chapel.

Two young men in navy jumpsuits exit the ambulance. They're too old for trick-or-treating.

"How well did you know him?" Old Cop asks.

"He's my—"

Old Cop says something to the blue jumpsuits.

I start again, "He's—"

He jerks his head toward Nathan's door.

"We spend a lot of time together."

The men in blue walk past.

"Did he have a history of drug use?" Old Cop looks at me. No recognition. I can't say I blame him. Data shows University of California, Santa Teresa, has one of the highest rates of on-campus sexual violence across the UC system. That's a good thing, someone told me. It means women are reporting.

"Yes." I swallow. "But nothing like . . ."

The men in blue go into Nathan's room.

"Was he under stress?"

I laugh.

Rick Astley looks up.

I remember what civilians think of the ivory tower. "Of course."

Rick Astley glances at Old Cop.

"I know him." I shake my head. "I knew him. He would never, I mean, this isn't . . ."

A man in blue walks past.

"People can surprise us," Rick Astley says, so gently I want to hit him.

Man in blue opens the back of the vehicle, light shines in the night, and he pulls down a heavy metal gurney.

"We'd like to collect a statement, Ms. . . ."

"Common. Sarah Common."

Old Cop nods. A glint perhaps. A token. Maybe he remembers. Maybe not. There are so many.

Man in blue wheels past, over the step, and into Nathan's studio.

"We'll need you to come to the station tomorrow."

"What are you doing now?" My thumb pad stings. I pull my hands apart.

"Removing the body."

"What about photos? Evidence?" I press my hands together again. The other thumbnail into the other thumb.

"They'll take care of that."

"Is four p.m. OK?" Rick Astley is closer now, taller than I realized.

"For the station?" If he were Nathan, or Dad, I would lean into him and press my face against his chest. I would cover him with big, ugly sobs, not at all like the pretty people in the shiny films, with their shimmering eyes and single, perfect tears. I step back. "Sure."

Cameras click. The sound of a zipper.

Rick Astley tucks his notepad into his belt and moves toward me, arm out. "If you'd like to come with me," he says softly, like I'm a Southern debutante and he's a gentleman caller, like we are in the movies and this will all work out by the time the credits role.

I follow him, his hand on my arm. We move to the side of the driveway. He angles his torso to block my view as Old Cop talks with Jared.

I crane my neck at the sound of creaking wheels. Light spills from Nathan's open door. One man in blue unrolls a spool of yellow tape. The other pushes something, long and large. Thin mattress on metal sides. Tiny black tires roll down the driveway. Something big and thick and black on top, a rubber bag with a zipper down the front. I know what I'm looking at, but the safety's still on.

Rick Astley is asking questions. I am talking. He asks where I'm from. He asks about work. He asks, What kind of research? I know he doesn't care, and wouldn't understand if he did, but the men in blue are lifting the black bag into the ambulance. Fire dances on mountaintops and maybe we really are in a movie, because this can't be real. I tell him I study justifications of violence across Buddhist traditions. What kind of justifications? he asks. A three-part hierarchy of karmic consequence. He blinks and nods, and he doesn't get it, but I keep going, because the bag is inside the ambulance and Nathan is inside the bag.

The first is need, like hunting for food or self-defense. The ambulance door closes. A man in blue moves inside, the light shining on him.

The second is want, like revenge or anger. My teeth chatter. The man inside sits down. The man outside opens the driver's-side door.

The neighbors across the street stand by their mailbox, not coming over, not going away. Behind them, skeletons hang above a plastic graveyard. Pumpkins flicker on their front steps. Rick Astley places his hand on my arm. I feel his warmth through my shirt and realize I am shaking. He asks more questions. I keep talking. He gives me a pen, and I fill out a form and sign my name and promise I'll drive to the station tomorrow. He walks me to my truck, and the ambulance pulls out of the driveway. He asks me to finish, to tell him what the third justification is.

Moral imperative. He tilts his head, shifts his body so I can't watch it all go away. Nathan inside the bag inside the ambulance, down the street to wherever we go when we end up inside a bag inside an ambulance. What does that mean? he asks. When it's the right thing to do, I say, and he gives me a weird look, but Ph.D.'s are used to people giving us weird looks, and who gives a shit about his opinion anyway?

It's not until later, on my drive home, me in my truck, Nathan in his bag, killed by a drug he never did, that I understand why it doesn't work.

My friend, who is dead, had a needle in his left arm.

My friend, who is dead, was left-handed.

DRIVE TWENTY MILES up the 101, where the GPS goes from red to orange to green. The road is close to the cliffs as you get out of town, the hills higher on your right, ocean lower on your left. That's one good thing about California. Can't get lost on the highway.

I take the exit to the small town trying to sell itself as a home to wineries. Really, it's just the farmland capital of quasi-retired movie stars who show up on Hallmark and Netflix for a Christmas special; up the road is Neverland Ranch. I roll down the window and enter the seven-digit code at the entrance of the gated community. There are roads, private property made to look like a suburb. Horse trails cross the driveways, and wooden signs with "Blueberry Lane" and "Blackbird Way" gaze down at intersections marked with decorated wheelbarrows and potted lemon trees.

The air is clearer up here, colder, too. I wind my way around the bends and twists of the community. There is a three-thousand-acre cattle ranch on the right, owned by the guy who invented barcodes or QR codes or something, managed by Fred, who doesn't have many teeth but allows me to trespass when I run. On the left, twenty-acre estates behind iron gates. Olive trees, paddocks, and tennis courts. I enter another code for another gate. The fence swings forward, and I pull through. Gravel spins beneath my tires. I proceed up the curving driveway. The house is in front, a three-story behemoth with wraparound deck, porch, and tiered garden on three sides. The double-wide French doors overlook a barn with six Arabs for show and three Mexicans for work. Inside, the Empress and her wife, Elaine. Equally diminutive, inversely taciturn. Both Australian, and surprisingly cheap for a pair of castle dwellers. They've lived in the United States for twenty years, and, far as I can tell, hate everything about it.

My studio is off the second of three driveway offshoots, 250 square feet with a minibar fridge and a plug-in stovetop. It's cleaner up here, but the air still stings. The jasmine flowers along the brick patios and granite sidings are blooming, but I can't smell anything beneath the smoke.

The front of the studio has a set of double glass doors overlooking the designer lawn. Empress does not like footprints on the walkway around the side of the building, so I go in as I always do, through the small, attached garage. It's colder and wetter here—a problem in winter, when the lack of insulation means rain pools beneath the door and wind blows through the window that never fully closes. This garage door is manual, and the only way for me to get into the studio from the back is to hoist it overhead, jerking my body weight from toes to scalp. The other two garages on the property have air-conditioning, motion-detector spotlights, and surround-sound stereo.

This garage has a dog. Long and leggy and kept in a cage too small. Gray hair and sad eyes and a water bowl that is never full. I walk in, turn on the lights, and open her cage. She uncurls herself, sore from the folding necessary to accommodate her meager home, and hurries outside to piss and shit.

I reach into the cage and bring out the empty bowl. I open the door to my box and fill it from the sink, arm's reach from the entrance. Dog hears the faucet running and walks toward me, eager but stiff-hipped. I refill the bowl three times before she's finished. I open the minibar fridge and pull out a beer. I keep a bag of dog food under the sink. She consumes enough to tell me she hasn't eaten all day.

The other tenant just left her, Empress said when I moved in.

Elaine reassured me. We would never throw her out.

I used to bring her into the apartment, when it was raining and the garage flooded, or so hot her eyes rolled back, tongue long and limp. Empress threatened she'd make me pay to redo the place if it happened again. So I sleep with the garage shut, but the door into my box open, a Craigslist blanket on the threshold. Dog sleeps there, head in the studio, body on the concrete. Technically, she's not inside.

Empress is in her fifties and stays indoors, submitting local gossip to the local newspaper. She put me in there once, a lengthy complaint about work ethic and the privilege of student loans. Elaine is in her seventies and works full-time. They fight. Elaine sits on the lawn, visible through the designer doors I do not open, and stares across the brown-and-yellow hills to the distant glint of ocean.

I sit inside the door frame. Dog leans against me. The winds have changed, and the ash is thicker now. Too thick to open the single window in the box. Too thick to breathe comfortably. Neither of us will sleep in our cages tonight.

I run my hand over Dog's head, her gray curls springy beneath my palm. I think of the little black dog. I found her in a field and brought her home. Dad said we couldn't afford her. She licked his face and slept on my lap, and the next day there was kibble in the pantry. I close my eyes and hear the quiet shuffle of chickens not brought inside for the night.

Dog licks the blood on my leg. I reach behind me, pull the duvet off my bed, and lie back. Legs and Dog in the garage. Head and torso in the box. Nathan and me, our phones, our voices, our words and virtual selves, tucked against my breasts.

A coyote howls. A horse nickers. Empress is on the top floor, in the king bed in the main bedroom. Elaine is downstairs, in a single pullout in the home office. Eventually, the sky lightens and a bird makes noise. Dog is asleep. I am on the floor.

And Nathan is dead.

———

When the sun comes up, I take Dog for a walk across the billionaire's hills, copy and paste two contraband undergraduate essays in exchange for next week's groceries, sign off on an extension for a student who works three jobs, arrange a hookup, and put Dog back in her cage. Down the highway, mountains on my left, ocean on my right, I park at the top of Santa Teresa's only main street, across from a grassy area with dog walkers and homeless men.

At three-thirty, I climb down, stuff the keys in my pocket, and walk to the police station. A three-story Marshalls selling four-figure Prada bags, next to a Walgreens and a methadone clinic. One stoplight, Starbucks on either side, halfway between the freeway and the beach. Six-figure earrings hang in glass storefronts. Black men in uniform, the only black men you'll see, guard the entrances. Scientology center. Jewish news broadcast. Catholic church. Religions that can afford the rent.

One road, from the highway to the ocean, cuts through, scattered with homeless men and trophy wives, broken bottles, and brunch spots. At the end, where the road turns right or left and the beach stretches out in front, the ocean is pinned to the edges of the earth by oil rigs, big and black and outlined against the horizon. If you run on this beach, be sure to bring a spare pair of shoes. What look like strings of seaweed are stretches of tar. They trap the feet of seagulls, trip the wayward joggers, leave footsteps of black behind you.

The best places are off the road. The Four Seasons, where Kim and her sisters spend comped weekends. The vineyard where Gwyneth got married. Cafés, where starlets meet directors, are up the hillside, past the houses with the views, where Colette lives. Don't be impressed, she told me last year at eleven in the evening, after she texted she needed a book from the library and I brought it to her, we were only able to afford this place because of the disrupted view. I gazed out at her wraparound deck, 180 degrees of America's Riviera, a single telephone pole to the left. I drove home and looked up the sales history of the houses on her street, the ones with unobstructed views. I don't know which is more confusing—that Colette finds $2.5 million more affordable than $3.5 million, or that a telephone pole is worth a million dollars.

Downtown, there are needles in the parks. The world-famous Film Festival. Pelicans with plastic wrapped around their necks. Palm trees and mojitos.

"Tell us again what happened."

The police station is colder than I expected. The lights are harsh, and women of color are handcuffed. The only women of color you'll see.

Old Cop and Rick Astley, whose name, according to his badge, is Eric Hollis, sit across from me. He pours me a cup of coffee. Its flavor may explain Old Cop's attitude.

"I knocked on the window. He didn't answer. I opened the window. He didn't answer. I climbed through the window. He didn't answer." I take a sip. "Because he was dead."

"That window is pretty high off the ground," Rick Astley Eric says.

"It was a tough climb."

Old Cop lifts his eyebrows. "Why didn't you knock on the door?"

"I never knock on the door."

"Why not?"

I shrug.

Eric speaks up. His eyes are still and brown, like a deer after the bullet. "He was in the bed?"

I nod.

"Anything unusual?"

"Besides the needle? I don't think so."

"What—"

"He was left-handed." I cut him off. Old Cop sits back, makes a show of stirring his coffee. Fucker.

"He was trying to become ambidextrous." Because it's a useful skill, he said. Wouldn't it be nice to do something useful? "But his left hand was his dominant hand."

Eric makes a note. Old Cop drinks his coffee.

"Doesn't that matter?" I ask.

"What was the room like?" Old Cop asks.

"I didn't notice." I look at the men. "How does a left-handed man shoot himself up in his left arm?"

"You said he was ambidextrous." Old Cop yawns.

"I said he was trying." Double fucker.

"Addicts often look for different points of entry to avoid track marks." Eric speaks. Pity oozes from him. "It's not uncommon for an addict to use both arms as injection sites."

"He's not an addict."

Eric continues to look at me, really look at me, while that son of a whore returns to stirring his coffee. "Addicts hide their addiction, especially from loved ones."

I give one of those pointed looks I see rich women give in this town. "Any drugs he did, we did together. But heroin?" I lean back. "Jesus Christ."

"Lots of drugs are more dangerous than heroin."

I put the coffee on the desk and cross my arms.

Those goddamn eyes. "People keep secrets."

"Did you touch anything? Move anything?" Old Cop shifts in his seat like I've interrupted his nap.

"Just the tip of his finger, when I came through the window." I swallow. And his phone. I stole his phone.

"Anything else?"

Nathan. Dead in his bed. And these men couldn't give a shit.

"I didn't touch anything else." Except his phone. It's in my bra, literally right in front of you. Cocksuckers.

"Are you sure?"

"Oh, yeah." I stare at Old Cop. "I know the importance of preserving evidence on a body."

Eric pauses, pen in hand. Old Cop looks up. "Excuse me?"

"I was in here a few years ago."

"For illegal substances?"

I smile. "We've had this conversation before."

Old Cop raises an eyebrow.

"It was about my body. My body was the crime scene, and what were your words?" I tilt my head and tap my chin as if I haven't memorized them. "Oh, right. 'There's not much we can do, because you waited so long.'"

Eric writes slowly, head down. Old Cop doesn't. "Our job is to collect evidence."

"I thought your job was to solve crimes."

He exhales slowly, the way parents do to show their children they are losing patience. "We require evidence to assess criminal activity. Accusations aren't enough."

"That's convenient." I reach for the paper cup in front of me. "And when the nature of the crime precludes the possibility of evidence, I guess that makes your life easy. After all, if the only evidence is a first-person testimony of a physical assault on her own body . . ." I lift my hands and tip the coffee onto the floor.

Old Cop shifts forward. "Ms. Common—"

"You know, my job is to research and write and think and teach. When I can't do the research or find the thoughts or don't want to see the kids, I don't phone it in and blame it on things taking too long."

"Eric." Old Cop stands. "Take Ms. Common out. We will finish collecting her statement at another time."

"How long is too long, by the way? Do you absolve yourself of all professional responsibility when the clock strikes twelve?"

"Ms. Common, if you will follow me." Eric extends his arm. It is almost chivalrous.

"And he didn't do heroin!" I shout at Old Cop's retreating back. A homeless man watches from a bench. He nods.

Eric escorts me to the front of the station. Someone young and peppy steps up behind a desk and slides a chipped clipboard and dangling pen toward me.

"We'll have someone call to collect the rest of your statement this week. Do you have a time that works best?"

My writing is jagged across the page. "I teach on Mondays and Fridays, but I'm on campus the rest of the time." I pause. Pen in hand. Clipboard under my palm. "You or Cinderfuckingella should contact his sister. His parents are never around."

"We'll call her," Eric says, his voice gentle, "but you were his emergency contact."

I blink. I need to update my emergency contact. "Be careful. She's . . . fragile." A pair of eyes that look like Nathan's but aren't Nathan's. She doesn't climb out of a k-hole as easily as I do.

He nods and takes the clipboard from me. Between my breasts, Nathan's phone gives a low beep. Another dead battery. I reach into my pocket for my keys. I finger the jagged edge of the metal and wonder how to talk to someone about her dead brother when the cops just told her she's got a dead brother.

Eric remains in front of me.

"Are we done?" I ask.

His eyes are worried now. A blanket of something fatherly or brotherly or just plain kind is tucked around their edges. It's been so long since someone other than Nathan has worried about me. And Nathan is gone now. I want to cry, to curl up against something warm and soft and fall apart. I clutch the keys between my fingers like girls are taught in grade school.

"We'll reach out to her." Deer eyes. Like Nathan. Like Dad. But this man is neither, and I have been fooled by nice guys before.

He opens his mouth, and I bolt. Out the door, down the stairs, into the orange. The air is damp closer to the water. Palm trees sway, a seagull cries, and I scurry to my truck. Dog shit, human shit, May–December couples. People whisper and point to a shop where some dude from some film is buying his kid a frozen yogurt. My chest aches and my eyes burn and the jewelry stores blur. Thin Europeans, Chinese kids in groups, fat Americans, and a line of Teslas as I swim against the current to cut through the parking lot tucked behind the theater where the local symphony is performing Tchaikovsky. Again.

Across the road, up the hill, the grassy patch, the needles. I reach my truck, and it all comes up. Puke and grief and a burrito I don't remember eating. My dead friend, those fucking cops, and rape spray across the rusted red of the driver's side.

I'm sorry. I don't know who I'm speaking to, or if I'm speaking at all, but the words keep coming. I'm sorry. I slump against the truck, ass on concrete, back against the tire, insides outside. My fingers press against my mouth. I want to keep my body intact, to keep my insides inside. I tuck my head and press my lips against my knees, tight enough to bleed across my teeth. I close my eyes and breathe through my nose. I'm sorry.

Trees, shades of autumn, the scent of a woodstove. A different orange, a different smoke. Dad loading up the truck. The little black dog, our guns, our boots, skies of blue. I ignore the vomit. I ignore the ash. I ignore the cops and the rapist and the poverty. I pretend the ones I love aren't dead. I pretend the palm trees are maples, and the ash is snow.

I wipe a hand across my mouth, my neck. I'll be OK. I'll go back up the mountain. I'll shower. I'll do laundry. I'll buy painkillers and Band-Aids and numbing cream. I'll go to bed early. I know how to do this. I've done all this before. I climb into the truck and turn on the engine. I open a dating app.

Tonight, after I bang some random from the internet and get back in the box, after I leave a message for Nathan's sister and feed Dog and read whatever note Empress has taped to my door, after I watch Elaine sit on the lawn and stare into the night sky at the million-dollar view she cannot see behind the ash while her wife screams inside the multimillion-dollar house they cannot afford, after I shower off the unwanted fluids as I have showered them off before, after I brush my teeth and tuck myself into bed, I will not think of the men in the station, of the men in the house.

I will not think of Rapist and his hands, his teeth, the smooth line of his body as he glides through the hallways, circling the eighteen-year-old girls who depend on him to get their degrees. I will not think of the rumors that I am not the first, that I am not the last. I will not think of Colette, my unreturned emails, ignored edits, missed meetings. I will not think of Flopsy, who was there, who was so nice to me until I returned from fieldwork and filed the Title IX report, until the interviews began, and he realized that his friend didn't get away with it, even when he got away with it. I will not think of the police. I will not think of Nathan or Dad or the little black dog.

Tonight, I will say the words I wish they all said to me, the words only Nathan ever said to me. I will tell myself the bedtime story I want to hear, the story I will never hear, from the people who will never tell it.

I'm sorry.

———

Manhattan Beach is hot, the sun sharp. The air is cleaner in L.A. than up in Santa Teresa, which is as ridiculous a thing as can ever be said. More fires are happening between us, but the winds are driving them north. I spend thirty minutes looking for parking and find something a mile away. Jessica has two cars in her two-car garage and uses the driveway of her beach home for an outdoor Tibetan meditation spot, complete with Berber carpet and organic cotton teepee. My research has never connected Berber, Native American, and Tibetan meditation traditions, but maybe rich white women know something poor white women do not.

I said goodbye to Dan or Stan and left her a message on my way home. She called me Monday morning at five. She sobbed and said she wanted to see me, but there was no way she could drive. I'd have to come down. She told me she only had time at noon, between yoga sessions. I asked someone in the department to cover my class and put as much gas in the truck as I could afford. Jessica told me if she was late Frederick would let me in. I don't know who Frederick is.

Jessica greets me at the gate. Her eyes are red, her hair is long, and a slimmer, prettier Nathan, with eyelash extensions and gel-tipped nails, looks back at me.

"Come on in," she says, and turns around. The electric gate slides shut behind me.

She leads me past the teepee into the house, with its layers of beige and white and glass of varying transparencies. One wall, a window the height and length of the room, looks out on her private beach, unmarred by swimmers or sunbathers. Gentle waves lap at smooth sand, seagulls glide in the sky. A living painting framed by marble edges.

The first time I came here, when Nathan brought me after we spent the day at the Getty, I looked up the address on the drive home. She bought the place two years earlier under an LLC for $8.6 million. The HOA is $2,400 a month, for a monthly tax, mortgage, and insurance payment of $75,875. I make in a year half of what she pays per month. Then again, why would she have a mortgage?

"Have a seat." She waves to the white couch with the beige throw and decorative cushions, also white and beige. She pads barefoot to the kitchen, removes a carafe of sparkling water and cucumber slices from the stainless-steel refrigerator, and brings it on a tray, alongside handblown glassware, to the coffee table, a transparent crystal structure supported by sterling silver.

Jessica is twenty-eight years old.

I perch on the edge of the sofa, willing as little of me as possible to touch the pristine material. She sits next to me, slim thigh over slim thigh, perfect toenails on perfect feet, all elegance and drape beneath the soft folds of her casual and expensive clothing. I look at her in this room, her in these clothes with this tray, which, I now see, holds small plates of olives, watermelon radishes, and strawberries, and wonder if she designs her life around *Town & Country*, or if they design their spreads around her. To the right of the food is a sketchbook.

"Did you draw this?" I reach forward.

She hesitates, tucks a strand of hair behind her ear, and nods.

"I didn't know you drew." I flip through the pages.

"It helps to . . ." Slim hands like birds in the air. "It helps."

I stop. A series of images, a woman floating on her back, a woman beneath the water. "Drowning?"

"Addiction."

I turn another page. My truck.

"The police called," Jessica says, and hands me a glass.

I put the sketchbook on the table. Between us, my truck looks back. Everything except the gun rack. She takes a sip. The bubbles in the glassware reflect like the diamonds in her ears. Once, when I came here with Nathan, I wondered if she accessorized her kitchen items to match her clothing. She invited us in and served us tuna tartare the color of her nails. She and Nathan made small talk while I watched her sink into a chair the color of her skin and pull a shawl across her shoulders the color of her hair. Perhaps her clothing is designed to complement her home, and she changes décor as easily as I change underwear.

The last time I was here, I stared at the private beach behind the single pane of twelve-foot-high glass. I wondered if the woman and the surroundings were designed together, so perfectly did they fit. Stemware, pantsuit, beige furniture, and human female, born simultaneously, crafted interdependently, displayed like a collection of Fabergé eggs. Even her drawings, perfectly balanced, lightly sketched. My truck looks refined, classic. Something to display in a gallery, not the piece of shit I actually drive. Everything is Jessica, delicate and expensive. But that was before.

The cashmere, the sofa, the view—it feels on less even footing this time. As if the items in the house, the house itself, are not hers, but, rather, she is theirs. Today, everything in this room is holding her up. If we moved outside, she would crumple into a heap of couture and cosmetics. I wonder, if I keep flipping the pages of her sketchbook, past the drowning women and the sixteen-year-old

Ford, what her most recent drawings look like. The drawings she made after hanging up with the police. If the lines shake and waver, broken pencil tips embedded in paper.

I sip my imported water from my handblown glass and think, perhaps for the first time, I am glad some people are rich. Some people need to be rich.

"Thank you for coming," she says, and shakes her head. "I just can't believe it." Perfect hair falls in perfect waves. A single tear—an honest-to-God single fucking tear—rolls down a perfect cheek. The water, the diamonds, even the tear. Everything glitters.

"I'm so sorry." The words are tight and cold in my mouth. It's such a stupid thing to say. What am I apologizing for?

"I'm sorry, too." She presses her lips together. Her eyes shine with unshed tears, and if I didn't know any better, I'd say we were on camera and she was on track to win an Oscar. "I know how much you meant to each other."

The glass is tight in my hands. "Have you contacted your parents?"

She nods. She looks past me, across the beach and the waves and the seagulls, perfect sky on a perfect beach.

"What . . ." I pause. I know nothing about their parents apart from the occasional comment about Switzerland and helicopters and various ongoing investigations. "How are they?"

She shrugs. "They haven't gotten back to me yet."

"You told them what happened and they haven't gotten back to you yet?"

Another shrug, this one slower than the last, baring a slim shoulder. "I left a message with Zacchary, but I didn't go into details. Just told him it was about Nathan and we needed to talk." She sighs. "Mom is in Zurich, I think, and Dad is in Hong Kong. Nathan always did have the worst timing."

"About that." I lean forward, carefully placing my expensive glass on the expensive table, next to the sketchbook. My truck looks expensive, too. "What are your thoughts on what the police told you?"

She looks up. "What do you mean?"

"How they found him."

"I guess dying in your sleep is the best way to go."

The olives, the strawberries, the watermelon radish slices. This delicate and organized life. "That's what they told you?"

"Well, they said they hadn't finalized the report yet. Details would be forthcoming." She takes a sip.

My clipped, colorless nails. Small scars across fingers and palms from a youth spent chopping wood, chopping game, killing and gutting and skinning. I press my thumbs together. The pads turn white under the pressure.

"There was a needle in his arm, Jessica. And a rubber tie above his elbow."

"What?" She blinks.

"There was—" But she holds up one hand, as slim and graceful as a flower blossom.

I reach a hand forward, the tip of my finger on her knee, so delicate I wonder if she, too, is made of glass. She moves a hand to her face and she is crying, slim shoulders shaking, back hunched. I don't know what to do with this crystalline figure, so like and unlike her brother. I remain seated next to her. My fingers on her knee. I hear a soft noise and I realize it is my own. I reach into my pocket and find a tissue that I think is clean and hand it to her. She accepts it and presses it to her eyes.

"Jessica, I don't mean to upset you"—my voice alternates between words and an instinctual murmur—"but do you believe that? That he did heroin?"

She cries harder.

I pull her to me, wrap my arms around her. She is half the

size of me, and I worry this news may actually break her. That expression—to break someone—as if there are some people who shatter and are never remade. "Jess." I use the name Nathan used. "We don't have to talk about this."

She stiffens and pulls away, face pressed into the tissue in her hands, back toward me. We sit in silence. Two women, one dead man, on the perfect white couch. I keep my hand on her shoulder and look out the window. The sun is bright. The sky is clear down here. Even the ocean seems still. Down the beach, someone is putting up a volleyball net. On the other side, far to the right, a family spreads a blanket and unfolds chairs. No oil rigs on the horizon.

She stands and looks down at me. "I'm sorry, Sarah." She swallows. "I can't talk about this with you. I need you to leave."

"I didn't mean to—"

"Please." She swallows again. I wonder if she is going to throw up. If she is so frail that doctors refer to her health as her constitution. I can't imagine Jessica throwing up. I can't imagine her doing a lot of things—puking, shitting, fucking. Maybe she is this delicate. Or maybe I make her sick.

"I'm sorry, Jessica." I stand, awkward and surprised at our similar height. She seems so small compared to me. "But I also think it's really weird. I mean, I can't believe that he—"

"You need to go now," she says, firmer this time, moving away from me and toward the corner, her back toward the window. For the first time, I realize there's a man in the room, pale and broad and silent against the back wall. He watches me. Frederick, I presume.

I walk away from the couch, past the crystal table and toward the dining area, across the sea of neutral. I turn back when I get to the door. Her silhouette against the window, the ocean in the background. She looks like she could walk through the glass and beneath the waves, a lot like drowning.

I head out of L.A. The sky is darkening. I text that I am driving back and will be able to teach my sections after all. The fire zone is 10 percent contained. My A/C died years ago, but I shut the vents. The smoke gets in anyway. The mountains are less steep down here, rolling hillsides that plateau across the highway, then sweep down into a rocky coastline. Parked vans, surfing bodies, the occasional swimmer. I guess they don't mind the gray.

California is different from Maine in so many ways, not just because the ocean is on the wrong side. Similar, too, with the taxes and the holiday homes. Beach towns and weekend retreats. My seventh year here, on and off, but I've never liked it.

At first, I thought it was my lack of interest in sunbathing, in surfer culture. Then I figured it was PTSD. Trauma taints perception. Or the yoga I don't do. The organic produce I don't eat. Every conversation a reference to the interstate. The famous people I don't know from the movies I don't watch, so thin their veins pop and their heads wobble. Maybe some places are good for some people and bad for others, like a plant in the wrong ecosystem. Maybe Nathan was genetically programmed for this region, and if I moved him eastward, he would wither and fade in the frost, just as I have been uprooted and replanted in a soil inhospitable to my chemical composition.

Or maybe it's overrated as shit.

I park on campus and walk through the tunnel, past the dead kids. *Miss you. love you.* The names are thick and dark and stand out against the pale backdrop. I should write Nathan's name down. I keep walking.

I reach the classroom. Students are already seated. Some smile, some mutter, some don't look up. We discuss the paper topics. I remind them I'm setting up extra office hours. We go over Colette's lecture from last week, the one with the decade-old PowerPoint about the Four Noble Truths that only lists three.

Colette lectures twice a week in a lecture hall with not enough seats. Students sit in fire-escape routes, stairs, each other's laps. Some stand for the full seventy-five minutes, holding their laptops and typing with one hand. No questions asked. No questions answered. This is not an environment conducive to learning, so, to prevent everyone from flunking, graduate students are brought in as Teaching Assistants. TAs have four sections every week, groups of fifteen students that are twenty-five students because, regardless of union demands, professors want as many students to enroll in their classes as possible. Enrollment numbers are factored into annual salary assessments.

Once I make sure the kids have memorized enough of Colette's ten-year-old lecture in order to pass her ten-year-old exam, I try to teach something. I guess I'm an old-fashioned romantic, but I always thought the purpose of education was to learn. Most of the undergrads are smart. Some less so. Some pay attention, some don't, but what matters is the money: Who can attend office hours and who has to scoop ice cream. Who can pull an all-nighter and who has to return their rented laptop. Who can pay for tutors, extra books, internet hustlers to write their papers. Who has to send money home, pay their own rent, pay their own tuition. One question— Who pays for your life?—answers everything.

Or, as was the case last summer, two seniors were found dead on the beach. Everyone assumed alcohol poisoning and hypothermia, but nothing was official. The rich kid had a scholarship created in his name. The newspaper ran a full-page article. What a tragedy. The poor one—well, we never heard anything else. I wouldn't remember him if he wasn't listed in the tunnel. Sometimes the question is, who pays to remember your life?

Parents tour the campus, thrilled there are eight Nobel laureates on staff, their names and faces printed on flags across the quad. I never have the heart to tell them that "on staff" doesn't mean "on campus," and "on campus" doesn't mean Professor Nobel gives a shit about Karen's grades in AP Chem. The truth is, AP Karen won't even get into the same classroom as Professor Nobel. Karen will show up to the lecture hall, along with six hundred other Beckys, Chads, and Zhous. She will lean against the back wall and use that shiny new laptop to take online quizzes and watch TikTok videos. And it doesn't matter how well you raised her, or if AP Karen really wants to learn. Professor Nobel doesn't know she exists, and AP Karen can't find a seat.

Don't get me wrong—I like AP Karen. I even know her name. But neither of those things has any bearing on my Ph.D. conferral, my employability, my career prospects. I need to research, publish papers, apply for grants. I teach her. I listen to her. I care about her, Mom and Dad, I do. But I'm one of the rare ones, and when I have to make a choice between AP Karen and anything else, she gets the cut. In an institution of higher learning, education is the lowest rung on the ladder.

Last week was the boat story, from the "Upayakausalya," the "Skillful Means Sutra." This week is the *Chetva-vaggo* of the *Samyutta Nikaya*. The "Slaughter Sutra" from *The Book of Kindred Sayings*. We're discussing killing again, but this time in an allegorical sense—what must we slay in order to be happy? The students are finishing a freewriting exercise. They hand it in when they're done, and I let them out early.

I would slay my debt.

I would slay my diabetes.

I would slay my depression.

A tall girl in the back, sporty and leggy and tanned, approaches the table at the front of the classroom. She hands me a lined paper.

I used to want to slay my brain and my body, so I couldn't remember and I couldn't feel. Then I learned that there are between 50 and 75 trillion cells in the human body and each cell has its own life span. The cells of your skin are replaced every two to three weeks. Red blood cells can last four months. The cells of your bones regenerate about every ten years. Some cells never regrow—teeth, eyes, and brain.

I've changed my mind. No matter what anyone else says, I will always know what happened because the cells of my brain will always be the same. And I like that the cells of my body will regrow. Every few days, weeks, months, or years, there is a new part of me. A part he never touched.

A few smile and wave goodbye. Others are on their phones before they've left the room. The last one, tall, dark, and nervous, approaches me.

"Dr. Common?"

"Yes?" I love the title, even though it's not official yet.

He stands in front of me, one hand on a backpack, the other in his pocket. He has never spoken in class or introduced himself, but I still feel bad I don't know his name.

"Raymond." He points to himself.

"Sarah." I point to myself.

"I was hoping I could talk to you." He hunches forward. "I have a situation."

"Sure." I nod. "About your paper?"

"I need to take a leave of absence." He blinks. "Can I come to your office hours?"

"Of course."

"Thanks." He clears his throat. He hurries out.

A small brunette waits for me by the door. I know her name. Cindy. She walks with me. I like the ones who walk with me, who talk with me and ask about graduate school. A part of me wants to warn them, to wave Dante's sign in their face. A part of me enjoys it, the optimism and the interest. It's all new to them, it's still interesting. Their shining faces, their attention to the books and the ideas contained within. The magic of seeing their own thoughts and questions written down by someone else, somewhere else, millennia ago. Teaching Cindy is why I'm here. Being Cindy is how I got here in the first place.

She laughs at something I say, and I am about to tell the story of my high-school Vice Principal bribing me with brownies to complete my college applications when I look up.

Jessica. In the hallway.

I look at my phone. Two missed calls from her number. One text.

I'm coming.

I interrupt Cindy. "I've got to catch up with someone." I nod in Jessica's direction. "I'll be in my office most of this week if you want to swing by."

She grins—"Great!"—and skips off, light and sweet and smiling.

"Hey." I step forward.

Delicate hands clutch a shoulder satchel like a lifeline. High heels and jewelry. She looks around the hallway. The flow of foot traffic, bumping backpacks, loud conversations. Her fingers tighten on the bag.

"Come on." I place a hand under her elbow.

She follows me into the swarm, down the stairs, people pushing from the back and from the front, upward and downward, laughter and high fives. Someone throws a soda can overhead, and another someone catches it one floor below.

Out in the daylight, muted beneath the haze, I walk her across the pedestrian areas, dodging skateboarders and cyclists, couples and throuples, hands in each other's pockets.

We walk to a coffee cart behind the Chemistry and Engineering buildings. It is shaded and quiet. No one comes here, because material scientists work in buildings with free espresso. And I've never seen one socialize.

She stands behind me as I order two coffees. The bored guy behind the cart, bandanna over his mouth, hands me two empty cups and points me toward the carafes. $9.50.

"I'm sorry about this morning," she says, and sits on the cement bench a few yards to the left. I place the cups between us and reach into my bag to silence my phone. Greg or Craig says I left my underwear behind. I delete it. No messages from Nathan, of course. I don't erase my texts from him. Alive in some small way, tucked between the circuit board and the memory chips. I look down at my hands. Thumbs pressed together, fingers intertwined.

"Nathan taught me to do that." She nods toward my hands. "For concentration." She picks up a coffee. Delicate fingers tap against the side of the cup. She takes a sip, her eyes straight ahead. We sit in silence. I look at her legs. Leather pumps, real crocodile as far as I can tell, and dark denim.

"You're wearing jeans." It slips out. It is odd to see her in anything similar to what I would wear, no matter how much more expensive her versions are. As illogical as my truck on her crystal table. Jessica strikes me as a woman people design jeans for, not a woman who wears them.

Jessica looks at herself, then back at me. "Isn't this what people wear at college?"

"This afternoon, I had someone in pajamas and two girls in bikinis." I take a sip. "Last year, a guy came to every class in a hula skirt."

She pats her knee. A diamond the size of an ice cube winks back at me. "I tried to fit in."

I choke on my coffee, just a bit.

She sighs. "I realize I don't."

"No, no, I just—"

"I know what you think of me. You don't exactly hide it."

"Jessica, I don't—"

"It's what everyone thinks of me."

I pause, cup to my lips. Ash wafts into my nose. I should have brought her to the Engineering building. They have air filters.

Her finger traces a circle across the lid. "She's so rich. She lives on the beach. She doesn't work. Daddy pays for everything." She turns to me. "For the record, Mom started the company."

"I never meant to—"

"You're not wrong." She blows across the top of her cup. "But you could be a little less cunty."

"I'm not—" I pause. I want to tell her the truth. "I'm not trying to be cunty."

"Most people who are cunty aren't trying to be cunty."

"I don't mean to be," I say, surprised her opinion means so much to me.

"And I don't mean to be a spoiled, rich bitch, but here we are." She tilts her head backward, and that hot, tall guy is there. "Frederick drove me after you left. I figured out where you were when someone pointed me to the Religious Studies Department. Someone there knew your schedule and took me to the building." She looks up. "Wherever this is."

"Chemistry." I look around. "Or Economics."

"I can't believe you didn't know."

"I never come out here." I point back the way we came. "I teach over there."

"About Nathan." She takes a sip. "I can't believe you didn't know he was using."

What do I say? Your brother is dead and a junkie and neither of us can believe it and neither of us knew it and we both feel like fucking idiots. A left-handed man with a right-handed overdose. "You didn't know, either." I look at her. "Right?"

She shakes her head. "I never thought anyone could hide heroin. You think you can, but you can't."

I glance at her silhouette. Hollowed cheekbones. Pronounced clavicle. Veins visible on her forearms. Nathan said she was clean, but it's hard to distinguish idealized femininity from the consequences of addiction.

The times we passed out on his floor. Ecstasy, Molly, Special K, an ocean of booze, and a mountain of pills. "I never saw him shoot up."

She shrugs and smooths her palms across her thighs, heels tapping against the concrete. "Most of us try to hide it. Shoot between our toes. Pretend we've got the flu for, like, years." She laughs. "But no one can hide it. It's so obvious when you know what to look for."

I nod. It's uncomfortable, being a drug user around a drug addict. Like a sommelier in an AA meeting.

"Every month, my parents deposit money in his account. Every month, he sends it back. They bought him a house. He sold it and wrote them a check. He enrolled in this ridiculous program. Wouldn't even let them pay the tuition bills. Whereas, me . . ." She looks down, tiny hands pressed against tiny thighs. "God, I can't count the number of times I've been in rehab."

I rest my hand on her shoulder.

"The last time"—her fingers intertwined around the cup, thumbs pressed together over the top—"he came to the hospital. He made me promise." Her voice cracks, her back hunches. "He said, if I wanted to kill myself so badly, he'd do it with me. But neither of us got to do it alone."

I remember Nathan telling me about that. The late-night call. He took an Uber to L.A., stayed for four days. I covered his classes.

"I've never made it more than a year. Every holiday season, ho-ho-ho." She reaches for her bag, finds a tissue, and presses it to her face. "But he's the one who's dead."

"What if he didn't do it?" The words are out before I can stop them, before I think about their impact on this woman on the brink of self-destruction. Less than two months before her annual death dance. I glance at Frederick. Amazing how someone can watch you without looking at you.

She blinks.

"What if someone shot him up?"

She folds the tissue on her leg. "Addicts always look for excuses, and family members often enable—"

"How can I enable him? He's dead." Her sharp intake of breath. "Sorry."

"Sarah—"

"Just listen, OK?" I pivot to face her. I put my coffee on the cement near my feet. Behind us, someone giggles. Someone swears. Frederick stands. He blends in unless you know he's there, all blue-eyed and mysterious. "You just said no one can hide heroin. So what are the odds that his best friend"—I point to myself—"and his sister"—I point to her—"wouldn't know he was doing it?"

"Well—"

"I spent all my time with him." My throat tightens and I swallow. It has nothing to do with the smoke. "I slept over at his apartment, I have the passwords to his phone, his computer. I was his fucking drug buddy, for God's sake. Why would he hide this?"

"But why—"

"And he was left-handed. The needle was in his left arm."

She rolls her eyes. "Trust me, when you need a fix, you can—"

"Can you spot a heroin addict?"

"I thought I could. Like a secret handshake."

"But you didn't spot it in him?"

We sit on the concrete bench. Eyes on each other. She shakes her head.

"I think someone did this to him," I say. Voice low. Another impossible thought. The words crackle between us like electric fencing. Sparking beneath the ash and the heat.

"The police said there was no foul play."

"Do you trust the police?"

"Depends how much we've paid them."

"In a case like this, a man with a history of drug use found in his own home with a needle in his arm, do you think they're going to investigate a homicide?" She opens her mouth, but I keep talking. "Do you think, in this town, with nothing but underage driving and parking tickets, anyone even knows how to investigate a homicide? And do you think some Santa Teresa cop wants your family's lawyers up his ass?"

"They said the door was locked."

"The window was open."

"Nathan doesn't have a lot of money. He's not connected with the business. Why would anyone—"

"I don't know, but that doesn't mean it didn't happen."

She swallows again. "I told him to keep security. I told him to pay for someone to . . ." She trails off. She starts to cry. Frederick doesn't move.

"Look, it might be nothing. Maybe Nathan secretly shot up, maybe it was a one-time thing." I take both of her hands in mine. "But maybe it wasn't. And I want to make sure we at least look into it."

She hiccups.

"I don't know if you and Nathan talked about me, but I know how incompetent the police are in this town. I won't let them blow this off." I squeeze her hands.

"How?"

"I stole his phone, and I'm going back to his apartment tonight. The cops told you it's not a crime scene, right? I should be able to get in."

"What are you looking for?"

"I don't know."

She is skeptical. Who wouldn't be? I'm a Buddhologist. The most useless Ph.D. on the planet, and I don't even have it yet. What do I know about solving crimes? Then again, Old Cop solves crimes for a living, and I know how skilled he is. The undergraduate disciplinary committee. KKKathy and Title IX. If these are the experts, I'll be detective of the fucking year.

She takes a deep breath, coughs. Her eyes water. "Can I help?"

"Take care of yourself." I smile. "And pick up the phone when I call. I might have a question."

She nods. Jessica is one of those women that people worry about, a woman men rescue. I wish I were delicate, I said once to Nathan, sitting on the beach, my head in his lap. Small and fragile, like your sister. I passed Nathan the bottle. Maybe people would be gentler with me. Don't. He ran his fingers through my hair, one finger across my lips. Delicate people don't survive this world, and the world is better with you in it.

I take both our coffee cups and throw them in the covered bin next to the drink cart. I lead Jessica back toward the Humanities building. We walk through the tunnel.

"What's this?" She points to the names.

"We get a lot of dead kids around here. This is an unofficial memorial."

"Where's Nathan?"

I haven't checked my email today. His name isn't here, so perhaps the university hasn't yet sent their thoughts and prayers. Perhaps I'm still the only one who knows. "I'll add it."

She studies the list. Her eyebrows go up. "It's only November."

We walk toward her car, something large and shiny. Frederick walks past us to wait beside the door.

"You stole his phone?"

I nod.

"You have his passwords?"

"Yeah."

She smiles. "He never gave me those."

I blink, and it has nothing to do with the ash. Nathan's eyes look into mine, and I lean forward, give her a quick hug before I can remember she's not Nathan. She stiffens, then softens, then pats my back.

I pull back and turn. I am halfway across the parking lot when she calls out, just loud enough for me to hear:

"Nathan said you grew up hunting."

I stop. Across the campus, bodies walk inside the gray, shadows in the air. "That's right."

She walks toward me. "So you know how to track and find and . . ."

I look over my shoulder. I nod.

"If you find out he didn't do this to himself, what are you going to do?"

I shrug.

"My family prefers to avoid the police."

I face the other way. Gray people with gray faces, shirts pulled over noses. "I can imagine."

She doesn't say anything else. I take two steps forward.

"Were you any good at it?" she calls behind me, louder this time. I think of the guns and the knives. The deer, the moose, the bear, and once, even when they said it was impossible, when they said we didn't have any on the East Coast, the wild boar, trapped in a cage built by my dad. How large and still after the bullet between the bars. She's a hell of a shot, John, the old men in the old bar used to say when we drove in, carcass in the back, blood pooling on the tarp. How many bullets this time? they'd ask, and offer to buy me a drink even though I was barely a teenager when I said what I always said: One. I think of the man in the woods, that time another hunter snuck up on me, how surprised I was that someone could sneak up on me.

I tap one shoe against the other; dust shakes off. "Yeah."

"Are you still good at it?"

I tap my other shoe. More dust. "Yeah."

She doesn't say anything else. I turn, and she nods, and Frederick opens the door. The car pulls out of the lot, sleek and dark and silent. I walk back to the tunnel. I stand in front of the names. *Miss you. love you.* Next to one, someone has drawn a small heart. I take out a pen and write his name. Thin, shaky letters. I trace them with my finger, the whitewash coming off on the tip. I pull out my phone and take a photo, his name and all the others.

Fuck you, Nathan. Fuck you for dying. Fuck you for going away.

———

I pull into Nathan's driveway and look at my phone. The perfunctory email from the Dean regarding Nathan's death, copied and pasted from the other emails and the other deaths. Tragedy. Community. A link to the Counseling Center.

A calendar notification pops up for the Welcome Reception tonight. Nathan and I volunteered to set up the drinks station. No one from the department has reached out to say that, because my best friend just died, I don't need to organize Costco sodas for people I hate. No one has reached out to say, because we had a recent death in the department, maybe now isn't the best time to throw a mediocre get-together full of bologna and despair.

I stuff my phone in my bra and step down from my truck. I

knock on the door of the main house. A shuffle on the other side. Jared opens it.

"Hi," I say. He stands there, one arm bent, hand resting on his stomach. The other reaches for his mustache. I wish I were holding something large I could hand over, a bag of groceries or a box of books, to force both of his hands away from his body. I imagine asking him stressful questions with his hands full, how his eyes would widen and mouth twitch under the strain of not touching himself.

He says nothing. Of course. It's not like we have anything to talk about.

"You busy?"

He stares. Feet planted inside his doorway. Mustache fully engaged.

"Nathan's sister said I could pick up some things from his apartment."

That gets a nod.

"So . . ." I take a step back, gesturing to the studio.

He remains in the doorway.

"The key?" I ask. This man is a postdoc. A fully employed member of staff at the university, selected from over a thousand applicants to do whatever it is he does, with access to the State of California's government pension, full health care, and paid leave.

Computers, Nathan said. Something with computers. A three-year position.

Jared continues to look at me. Pets himself.

Definitely computers.

"I need the key," I say, emphasizing each word, "so I can get into the apartment to collect his—"

"I have to find it," he says, words muffled beneath the twisting, twirling fingers. Seriously, Jared, we're doing this again?

He backs up.

I step forward.

He looks at me.

I step forward again.

"I have to find it," he repeats.

"I heard you." I step forward a third time. I am inside the house. I look down. Four pairs of shoes are lined up at the door, in order of height and color, gradations of gray. He turns and disappears down a hallway.

The air smells of cleaning products. I take two more steps, aware that my shoes, both in size and color, in no way match his collection. The pillows on his couch, three squares, each slightly larger than the next, arranged in order, lavender, purple, indigo. At the far end of the couch, a cat. Sphinx. There's a joke there, something about bald pussy and hairy mustache, but I'm not in the mood to make it.

It feels deliciously subversive to enter this compulsive domain in my bedraggled state. Faded shoes beneath torn jeans and ten-year-old T-shirt with a history of red wine and frozen yogurt across the front.

I walk to the couch and pet the cat. Jared is down the hallway. Cupboards open and close.

I pick up the smallest pillow and move it next to the largest.

I walk to the kitchen. Five succulents line the windows, arranged according to height and color. He comes out and shuffles forward, hand on mustache. The hand at his waist opens like a fern. Inside lies a key.

"Thanks." I reach for it, making sure to press as much skin of my palm against as much skin of his as possible. I enjoy the recoil.

I walk toward the door and look again at the shoes. I want to move the lefts to the other side of the rights.

"Did Nathan ever come over here?" I ask.

He shrugs.

"What did you two do together?"

"Sometimes I cook."

That clocks. Nathan would do anything for a free meal.

"What about last Friday? Or the night before?" I ask, staring at the finger on the upper lip, the small repetitive movement. "Did you two get together?"

He shakes his head. Twirl. Pet. "I thought you spent the night again."

"I dropped him off, but I didn't stay over." I walk back toward him, away from the door, my clothing and body language an affront to his ordered life. "Why did you think I stayed over?"

"There was noise." Twirl.

"What kind of noise?"

"Like he was taking out the trash really late." Tug.

He moves into the kitchen. I follow.

"You mean, you heard someone rifling through your trash? By the side of his apartment?"

He shrugs.

"Why would that make you think I had been over?"

"You drink a lot." He stares at me. I stare back. "I figured he was taking out the bottles."

Flipping the recycling container to climb inside Nathan's window. The sound of glass spilling. I keep my eyes on Jared and lift my hand to my right. I rearrange the succulents. Just the end two, the ones I can reach from across the counter. I reach down and press my fingers across his countertops. My nails are dirty. He stares at my hands. I rub them back and forth. "That wasn't me."

"Maybe it was a raccoon."

"Maybe." I head for the door. The scratch of planted pots moving against the windowsill.

I walk across the driveway and am about to open the door to the side entrance, to the alley with Nathan's window, when I remember

I have a key. Because he's not inside. Because he's dead. I pivot and step onto the concrete slab at his door.

We first met in student housing. I was in Building B and he was in Building G, and everyone else was from China or doing their undergraduate degree, because we were the only two Ph.D. students dumb enough to think that the fairly priced accommodations advertised for Ph.D. students would be (a) fairly priced and (b) for Ph.D. students. We later learned that the university prices their graduate housing 20 percent higher than the going rate in town and only advertises it to international students. Parking not included.

I saw him in the laundry room. He saw me in our first class. We bumped into each other at the library. Within a week, we were sharing a beer next to the dryers, waving books under the smoke alarm and laughing around our cigarettes. It was fun and flirty, and back then I had boyfriends and thought I knew how men worked. When he told me about his celibacy, I nodded, but I didn't understand, because it was fun and flirty and I figured it would change. I figured he would change.

He had a car in the beginning, some old dumpster fire that needed its tires checked every time we got in. We took turns driving, to the mountains, to the ocean. Picnics and long walks. It was almost romantic. We attended open houses of eight-figure homes in Oprah's neighborhood, pilfering organic snacks and laughing at the bowling alleys. Why do rich people always have bowling alleys? Nathan grew up with a bowling alley. Why do they never build libraries? I asked in an eight-bedroom house, staring into a toilet with lilies floating in the bowl. To get this rich, either you don't have time to read, or you grew up never needing to, he said.

The rape happened near the end of our third year. We were planning our fieldwork, back to the Dolomites, back to the steppe. Between qualifying exams, visa applications, and the offloading of my meager possessions, I tried to forget about it, the inconvenience of it. I graded finals and sold my mattress and bought my flights. Until June, on the beach with celebratory champagne a week before we were leaving, when he asked what was wrong, why I had been so different the last few months. He held my hand in his lap, petted it like a small bird while the words, questions more than statements, fell from my lips.

He messaged me daily, but cell reception was limited in the Gobi. His photos and messages came sporadically—silence for a week, then a rush of anecdotes from his archives when I went into town. I couldn't afford to visit him and he couldn't afford to visit me, but we spent our year together, 4,250 miles apart. When we returned to campus, to our respective boxes, beer and cigarettes became Molly, cocaine, ketamine, and Fridays became therapy. Reading for class was grading papers, and discussions on texts was job-market prep. Men became fuck buddies, and dating was a hop-on, hop-off bus pass. One night, alongside Stallone or Van Damme, fully dressed and spooning, he pressed against my back and told me how sorry he was—that it had happened, that he hadn't been there, that he couldn't do anything to make it go away.

The crime-scene tape is gone. I insert the key and turn the handle. The room is dark, and I flick on the light. A single bulb hangs from the ceiling. They rolled him out while I watched. I cross the room and turn on the small light on the bedside table. The bed is rumpled. No little numbers on plastic stands like you see in lobster shacks or detective shows. Nothing in boxes. Maybe Jessica paid an extra month's rent. Since she and I are the only people who give a shit, I guess there's no rush.

I tap my hands against my thighs. I told Jessica I would find evidence, but what the hell is evidence? I go into his bathroom and turn on the light. My face stares back at me from the six-inch mirror between the showerhead and the dollhouse sink. I glance at the toilet. Nathan used to laugh at me when I threw up in here, before I accepted that wine comes out the way it goes in. I offered to bring him up to my box in the mountains, but he always shook his head. Rich people and large houses made him uncomfortable. Big money is never ethical, he said. My place isn't big and I'm not rich, I reminded him, face down in his toilet. But you live near them, he said, holding my hair and rubbing my back. You're contaminated.

I turn around. The faint yellow of the bathroom light spills into the studio. His pots are stacked in the corner of his countertop burner. I cross the room and open the cabinet beneath the microwave. A stack of canned vegan meatballs. I let him watch me vomit, but I never let him feed me one of those.

The bed. The duvet is where it was when I found him, kicked to the side. We used to lie here and watch movies on his computer. I introduced him to Ellen Ripley, Sarah Connor, and the Johns (McClane, Rambo, Wick). Why do you like these movies? he asked, chewing his canned monstrosities. The good guy always wins, I said around my jerky. Aristotelian notions of justice are best understood through action films. Plus, the *Alien* franchise is a basic morality tale: when you don't believe the smart woman, you die. *Deus ex femina,* he said, and smiled.

I move to the window and drop to my knees. The bed is a few feet away, eye-level. I crawl toward it, remember his fingers, cold and blue and curled upward. I stop where I stopped that night. His nightstand is to my left, the light of the small lamp casting a glow in the late-afternoon sun. Next to the lamp is his music. He still played CDs—Tori Amos, Kesha, Fiona Apple. The glory days of Lilith Fair.

I look around. The cops must have taken his laptop. I open the nightstand drawer. Colorful pieces of folded paper. Inside, white pills, blue pills, yellow pills. Small baggies with white powders. I bought half, but we kept them here. Empress has a tendency to rifle through my things, and I don't want any more details about me showing up in her weekly gossip column.

The collection of colors reminds me of Mrs. Sanghera, a Sikh woman who found her way to Northern Maine and looked after me while my father worked. When I was a child, he deposited me each morning in her arms and picked me up every evening, carrying me across the street in the dark. Her house was small and warm, like ours, with oil lamps for light and bathwater heated on the stove, but her kitchen smelled of spice and beans and fermented things, while ours was meat and fat and bread. Mrs. Sanghera draped herself in sunsets, yards across her neck and down her back. Even in winter, when she worked on fencing and farming and shoveling snow, the heavy jackets and workman's boots could not hide the glimpses of citrus and rose and summer sky, her rainbow vibrant in our small town. Mrs. Sanghera married Mr. Todd, a man poor and tall and bearded like my father, and went with him to Boston once a year for fabric. The little black dog and I spent hours in her home, staring at the rhythm of her feet, as they pressed the pedals of her mechanical sewing machine. She drew for me the curving letters of the Devanagari, each hanging below a vine like fruit. I sang for her my father's nursery rhymes. We both practiced our English.

I stuff the drugs into my pockets and reach toward the back of the drawer. I pull out a newspaper article and a notebook. The article is from the summer. I tore it out of the local paper and brought it to him—Nathan's face featured in a write-up on volunteers in the community. His work with the women's shelter. It was posted online; the comments asked if his name meant he was part of that family and, if so, demanded that he needed to do a hell of a lot more than volunteer with beat-up chicks to make up for his family's impact. Ironic, an anonymous user posted, that he cleans up the shit his parents created.

The notebook is cheap, something for $7.99 at the Prada Marshalls downtown. Fake leather cover with wide-lined pages. Nathan's penmanship is tidy and compressed, too small for the white space. My hands shake and I flip through. He wrote daily. A few lines at a time.

Derrida has ruined me. How am I expected to enjoy anything now?

Spinoza is nuts, but I salute his optimism.

Everything is neat. His spelling is excellent.

Flopsy tried to push me into a wall today. You know in the news, when someone opens fire on a classroom of preschoolers and everyone who knew him says, we had no idea? I have an idea.

I tap my fingers against my thigh. Flopsy is Rapist's roommate and all-around pigfucker. The bleach blond with the DUI and the assault record, who uploaded revenge porn of an ex-girlfriend after face-fucking her so hard she threw up in the shower. When she threatened him with litigation, she received a phone call from his mother, a star member of the Google legal team, who assured her that the alleged photos on the supposed website were taken down. Oh, and he was back in therapy. He's still around Santa Teresa, still enrolled, still applying for jobs. The girlfriend quit. I didn't realize Flopsy ever targeted Nathan. Evidence?

I flip to a page with three sentences. The date in the corner, in his short, steady writing. Six weeks ago.

Overheard Carl making jokes about his wife again. Shouldn't be surprised. Cocksucker.

Feminist Carl, a loud, off-the-wagon alcoholic, is one year ahead of us and lives in his in-laws' basement. He was at the party. He drove drunk back to family housing. He called the morning after to make amends. Step Nine. When I met him that afternoon, he looked at my face and asked what I tripped on. When I mentioned sex with Rapist, he congratulated me. When I tried to tell him the other thing, the impossible thing, he laughed and shook his head. No way. No way. He's such a great guy. There's just no way. He had known Rapist for years. I only knew Rapist from passing him in the hallway. Feminist Carl wasn't in the room, but Feminist Carl was sure, so I said nothing else, told no one else until Nathan asked me on the beach.

I told Nathan about Feminist Carl when I told Nathan about Rapist. He said *"cocksucker"* then, like he wrote *"cocksucker"* here. I never understand that one, he muttered once, on his back, while I read him Foucault in French. Nathan didn't speak French and came from the world in which it was the language of the educated. Why is being a cocksucker a bad thing? he asked. Have people stopped enjoying oral sex?

It's rooted in patriarchal understandings of gender roles. I sipped my Mountain Dew/tequila blend and flipped a page. It's a misogynistic and homophobic slur against people who suck cocks, as opposed to people whose cocks get sucked.

No one wants their cock sucked anymore?

Everyone wants their cock sucked. I tipped the glass toward his lips. But they hate the people who do the sucking.

From that day forward, "cocksucker" became Nathan's favorite word. Insulting someone for sucking cock in a world obsessed with getting their cocks sucked was, for Nathan, never not funny.

My eyes fill and my breath catches. His writing dissolves in front of me. I close the journal and turn my head. I'm close enough that the edge of the mattress greets my eyes. The puckered tuck of his bedsheet pulls away from the corner. His pillow, still cradling the shape of his skull, is pushed upward, wedged in the corner of the mattress and the wall.

I climb onto the bed. Destroying evidence, I suppose. I lay my head in this hollow. My eyes see his ceiling. My legs stretch where his were. My pelvis, the warm, bloody heart of me, in the center. I drape one arm outward, over the side of the bed, just in front of the table and where the pills were. My fingers curl toward the ceiling. My palm dips away from my wrist. The baggies and envelopes crinkle inside my pockets. I could take something, a pill from the packets of color, and lie here, staring at his ceiling, seeing what he saw. I could take two something. Blow off the department event this evening, get back in my truck, and drive up the coast, smooth black snake of highway blurred beneath me, sparkle of oil water on my left, and fire mountain on my right. I could take more and not get up at all.

I lie in his bed, our drugs in my pocket, our heads on his pillow. The ceiling looks down at me. A single, naked bulb. I think of what Jared said. The noise Thursday night. After I dropped him off. Nathan's window, still open, to my right. I think of my efforts to climb through the window. The noise I made. No one could sleep through that. I take my phone out of my bra.

> Did you do it Nathan?

> Did you do it to yourself?

I think of the pills and the powders. The nights I don't remember, the mornings with a movie on loop, good guys righting the world. The mornings I slept through Elaine and Empress pounding on the garage. Dog barking. Trucks moving. All the noise you do not hear when you are buried in the deep and the dark.

> Did someone do it to you?

I look across my arm to the window, the cheap curtains stained with wine.

> Why didn't you tell me, Nathan? I would have helped.

But that last question is a lie.

> Why didn't you tell me, Nathan? I would have come too.

THE RELIGIOUS STUDIES DEPARTMENT'S annual social event is inside one of those formal rooms on campus for rich parents, complete with air filtration systems and windows facing the lagoon. The building is shaped like a two-story turret, with the fancy room on top. I'm surprised they let us in, but I guess the Alumni Foundation keeps an eye on Humanities Ph.D.'s as potential revenue sources. Hilarious. We were supposed to do this in September, when everyone was fresh from fieldwork, a summer studying for qualifying exams, or gearing up for job applications, but so many professors were attending conferences or finishing up sabbaticals, they decided to wait. If we had done this in September, Nathan would be here. Instead, Nathan is dead and I am standing in front of the buffet table.

Next to me, a first-year is organizing soda cans according to color. I peel back the plastic wrap on a platter of rolled meats. First Year has stacked the drinks next to the day's local newspaper. The trial is canceled. The one about the missing girl, sixteen years old and kidnapped while walking her dog. Police found her naked and drugged in a forty-seven-year-old's apartment in Bakersfield. "OMG," people wrote on social media when she was found and the man arrested, "I can't believe someone would do this." I can't believe their disbelief.

First Year rearranges cookies. She takes them out of the packaging and creates mosaics across the plastic platters. People are coming in. First- and second-year graduate students show up because they think people care that they show up. Later years are here for the food. Allison Stevens, Professor of Christianity and the Ancient World, militant vegan and macrobiotic fanatic, walks in. Michael Riscasse, Endowed Chair of Tibetoloy and Buddhology, follows her, shakes his head at the food.

"Do you think he doesn't like these?" First Year asks me, holding a bag of chips. "I could run out and get something else."

"I wouldn't worry about it."

Last year, Nathan and I manned the buffet table at the same party, in the same room. We took turns dubbing the attendees.

Can somebody drive me to work? I refuse to retire. I had mimicked the high-pitched voice of Professor Okawa, an eighty-two-year-old woman in charge of the department's hiring committee.

Do you like my fake British accent? Nathan had whispered, watching the tight, nervous movements of a visiting lecturer from Nebraska.

First Year changes the cookie mosaics, and I think of that children's book I loved as a kid. Dad read it to me every night when he tucked me in. A thick, dusty novel with a green cover. Stories of a woodland princess, a girl born among the trees, who befriended animals and spoke to the sky. After a teacher told him I was good at reading, he began driving me to the library two towns over. Dad looked down at his torn shirt and dirty jeans and sent me in by myself. I looked for the book, but the librarian had never heard of it. I settled on the children's story *Frog and Toad*. I borrowed it so often that the librarian, hearing I got accepted for seventh grade into the private school an hour away, bought me a copy. *Frog and Toad*. The two of them. Nathan was Frog, all kind eyes and patient words. I, with the swearing and the fucking and the history of violence, I am Toad.

Anthony Runner is a new Assistant Professor who won something for studying born-agains. I have seen him cry twice this year. He holds the door open behind him. Flopsy walks in, then Ann with no "e." She smiles at Flopsy and flips her extensions. She doesn't know about the revenge porn, the DUI, the strangulation, and the head kicking of a classmate in a bar downtown. Ann with no "e" is getting her Ph.D. in History, not Religious Studies, but her adviser told her to apply for our jobs because he has friends in our field. Ann with no "e" is married to an ophthalmologist. Ann with no "e" was my friend until I mentioned the rape and she said, Oh, that's too bad. Can you proofread my paper for this panel I'm putting together?

And then there is he.

If Nathan were here, he would block my view. Tell me a joke. Of course Rapist is here. One year ahead, with Flopsy and Feminist Carl. He does textual work—old white guys and their theories. No languages, no fieldwork. Pussy. There were rumors, when I came back from Mongolia, about him and another woman, a blonde from Anthropology. She quit. He has a campus visit.

Rapist doesn't make eye contact with me. Flopsy does. Flopsy always does. He mouths words that would embarrass someone else. I grab two cookies from the table and stuff them into my mouth. They taste like shit, nothing like Mrs. Sanghera's rose water and cardamom. Flopsy stares at me. I lick my lips.

Flopsy is angry and awkward, the slow, stilted movements of the self-pitying. Nathan saw him as a predator. I told Nathan that was impossible. Predators are smooth. They wait in the underbrush, in the dark water. They see you before you see them. The man in the woods, dark eyes above his balaclava. They kill a squirrel at the age of eight, father behind them, supporting the rifle. My weekends back home, away from the private school with the shiny kids, their straight hair and straighter teeth, I walked through the woods, one gun, one bullet, but I didn't feel like a predator. I look around. The relaxed smiles and tweed jackets of the faculty. The clean jeans of the graduate students married to nine-to-fivers. The tans and the tattoos and the iPads and the confidence. I don't feel like a predator here, either.

At some point, seventh- and eighth-years gather around the buffet table. They discuss the upcoming conference. I am cornered by Eye Contact Austin.

"Sorry about Nathan. Do you have any interviews?" His nostrils flare.

"I have one paper and one interview," I mutter.

"I have two papers, one panel, and four interviews." Ann with no "e" appears, summoned by the subject of career advancement. Her orthodontic excellence reminds me of the *Jaws* theme, and I take a step back. "I don't know how I'll manage with so much to do."

"You could skip the interviews," I say. Beside me, someone coughs into their drink.

"What?" She blinks.

"Are you talking about AAR?" A furry hipster, with round glasses and hair gathered in a bun, materializes to my right. I don't know if he's new or just someone I don't care about. I would bet my $1,900 teaching stipend he studies Heidegger.

"We are. Will you be attending?" Aysel, the only brown person and the only one with social skills.

"Of course. I published a biography last year, so I feel it's my responsibility to help progress the dialogue."

Jesus.

"You published a biography? Out of your master's thesis?" Ann with no "e" asks. Aysel shoots her a warning look.

"Yeah. My professors were really pleased with it, so I thought, Why not?" Bun reaches for a cookie off the buffet table. First Year frantically rearranges the color scheme.

"Where did you publish it?" Ann with no "e" tilts her head. "OUP? Yale? Chicago?"

"Well . . ." He glances down, mouth full. "I mean—"

"Is it forthcoming in print?" She looks at Aysel, who is looking at the floor.

"It was only online, but—"

"Oh." She draws out the vowel. "I suppose it's hard for someone at your level to have a real publication." Ann with no "e" has two peer-reviewed articles, both in the journal her adviser edits. She looks over Bun's shoulder. She walks off.

"I'm working on another one," he says quickly. His topknot jiggles. "I'm planning on using my seminar papers as chapters, so I should have my second book out after my coursework is done."

Sure, dude.

"I hope that works out." I smile. I try to force it to my eyes. I never know if I should tell the new ones. It feels like shooting something I don't need to kill. Or putting something out of its misery.

Eye Contact coughs, and Aysel places a hand on Bun's shoulder. "Why don't I introduce you to some of the newer faculty?"

He nods and looks back at us. He doesn't understand. He's only been here two months. Big fish, he thinks.

Eye Contact counts prime numbers under his breath. First Year re-creates her mosaic. Colette is speaking with new students. She has not returned my last round of edits, my last email. How many of her students have finished in the last five years? Nathan asked me. Haven't all of them quit?

I walk to the exit. Behind me, Rapist leans toward a master's student, twenty-three, in a tank top. She is thinking of staying on to do a Ph.D. A professor says, What a good idea. The department doesn't guarantee funding, but student-loan rates are lower than ever. Rapist leans closer. What a good idea. He'd love to talk about this with her. Their movements are smooth. Flopsy leans against the wall, clumsy and stilted.

Do you see, Nathan? Do you see who the predators are?

I push open the door. The bathroom is down the hallway, away from the party. The overhead lights are motion-activated. They illuminate as I walk. Floor-to-ceiling windows on my right; the sun has set but swirls of ash dance beneath the parking-lot lights. I follow the signs for the bathroom. The windows stop, replaced by office doors. Small names on brown plastic tags. Metal handles. Behind me, the lights click off as the ones above me click on. Behind me, the party noises.

I reach the bathroom. Gender-neutral. I try the handle. Above me, the light clicks off.

Out comes Ann with no "e." The light clicks on.

"Oh my God, hey!" Those teeth.

"Hi."

"I'm so happy you have an interview!"

"And you have four. That's great."

"I know, right? So stressful."

"Yeah."

"I'm just glad things are working out for you after . . ." She tilts her head.

Dead Nathan? So far, only Austin has said anything. Rape? She likes to talk about my rape, tell me a statistic or forward me an article. My students would say she's performing her allyship.

"That was a long time ago," she says. Ah, more rape talk.

I nod.

"And it's so sad about—"

"Would you excuse me?" I brush past and shut the door.

I pull down my pants and sit on the seat, still warm from Ann with no "e"'s ass. This surprises me. I would assume she hovers, no concern for the splatter. My jeans are faded, and a hole is growing in the crotch. My shoes squeak when I walk, and the hand-sewn repair job I did on my underwire isn't holding up.

They said, Get therapy, so I did. They said, Get a journal. I did that, too. I brought it to a café one day and watched Rapist walk in, order a coffee, extra milk, extra sugar. After he left, I drew lines on every page, my pen slicing through the paper, into the smooth wood of the tabletop.

You do the therapy, you do the journaling, maybe you go on antidepressants or join a group and read long books about sad statistics, but it doesn't go away. You report it. Someone takes a statement. Nothing happens. Rinse and repeat. Police, Dean, department chair, nurse. Friends who become no longer friends. Whether you're in the station or in the stirrups, interrogated with words or lube, you have to retell, relive, and it's always the same. Awkward silence and change of subject. No way, no way, there's just no way. If you're lucky, a sympathetic head tilt. Or maybe they start to cry and you have to make them feel better. Then nothing. An email, typed in bureaucratic code. A link to Counseling Services. Thoughts and prayers.

Flopsy found out I reported Rapist. They've always been roommates, so I guess it was really upsetting for him. Bros before hos. Now he whispers *"Bitch"* when I pass him in the hallway. Gives me the finger. Calls me a liar and a whore. I tap one hand against my bare thigh. Flopsy hated Nathan and pushed him into a wall. Evidence?

I adjust my ass cheeks and bear down. When I see Rapist, I always need to take a dump. Therapist 1 says this is a common response to fear. Some people actually scare the shit out of us.

I wipe, I stand, I wash my hands and dry them on my jeans. My phone is in my bag upstairs, next to no-name soda and rolls of warm meat. Everyone from my year is still here. They can't get jobs, so where else would they be? My throat tightens. Almost everyone.

I open the door. The hallway is dark. I step out, and the overhead light turns on. Flopsy stares at me.

I stare back. We are alone. The hallway on either side of us is dark. Above us, the light shines. Down the hallway, the party sounds. I know what it's like to be alone with a man with party sounds in the background.

"Nathan got what he had coming." Flopsy leans forward. "And I don't feel bad about it." A wad of spit lands on my neck. He shoves past. My shoulder hits the concrete wall, and the bathroom door closes. Behind the closed door, the sound of his zipper. I regain my balance. His saliva drips down my body.

When I enrolled in the private school an hour away, Dad took another job to cover the gas from the drive. He left me with Mrs. Sanghera on Friday nights. She and her husband had gotten electricity the year before, and bought a television. I sat between them on the couch and watched how the rest of the world sees killing. Movies taught me people kill because they want to, because it makes the world a better place. Guns, I learned, are not for feeding yourself, but for restoring order. Somebody kills your wife. You kill the somebody. Credits roll. Everything is better. Well, except for the wife.

Hollywood doesn't know much about killing. Neither did the tourists. Loud and drinking and trampling down the snow like it, too, needed to be shot. They paid a lot of money for Dad to take them into the woods, me tagging along. They drove up from Boston, flew in from Connecticut. Told us they had come here when they were kids. Really knew the area. Dad smiled and packed the guns. They said they knew what they were doing. Said they had a range back home. They swung the guns, pointed them where they shouldn't. Hunting is fun, they said. I collected the checks. Dad kept the bullets in his pocket.

What movies don't get, what tourists don't get, is: You can't want it. Wanting throws your aim off. Your heart rate goes up. Your breath gets loud. You shift your weight and move your shoulders. You lose your sightline. Don't get so excited, Dad used to say to the anesthesiologists and the lawyers and the dot-com guys, in their brand-new, brand-name snow pants. Desk-job thighs rubbing together beneath the crinkling, crackling fabric as loud as their jokes about *nailing her*. Don't get so excited, he said, his accent thick, but they didn't listen. The excitement was why they were there. He steadied their hands, steadied their arms. I stood off to the side and watched their bullets fly into the woods, every possible direction. The deer fell. Got her! They laughed and high-fived. I stood behind them, cardamom cookies in my pocket, the little black dog at my feet. One bullet. One deer. Got her.

The light above me clicks off, and it is dark outside the bathroom. I wonder what I should do to this tall, thin animal. I have no gun or knives or bow, but he has no claws, no hooves, no jaw strength. I know what you can get away with in the dark with a party down the hall. I know the damage you can inflict, one body on another.

He doesn't feel bad about it. My hands shake. Nothing to do with paying bills or filling the freezer. Something I never felt in the woods.

I walk back to the party. First Year rearranges the cookies. Rapist laughs with the young woman in the tank top. Flopsy follows me. He moves to the side of the room. He leans against the wall. I

almost smile at him, at the limp hair, the revenge porn, the DUI, the
assault charges. The sallow face and the skinny legs. I almost smile,
because it's almost funny—all of that, and he's still here. Still teaching, still in a position of authority over barely-legals, still a burgeon-
ing expert in his field.

He stares at me. "Fuck you," he mouths from the side of the
room. People around him chat. I lift my hand to my neck. Rapist
circles the master's student. She tilts her head, exposes her throat.
Professors encourage the first-years—more coursework, don't rush
it, stay longer. Professors encourage the eighth-years—another year,
another loan, don't rush it. I lift my fingers to my mouth and rub
Flopsy's juices across my lips.

I almost smile, my mouth wet with him. Almost the smile of the
doctors and the lawyers, heart rate up, breath too loud. When they
laughed and cheered and thought they had killed the thing they
didn't need to kill. I look at Rapist. I look at Flopsy. What would it
be like, to do it because I want to? My hands shake. I would need
more than one bullet.

My cheeks lift, my lips separate, I bare my teeth. Perhaps it is a
smile. Perhaps it is something else.

———

Through the tunnel and the dead kids. Colette is not in her office.
Nathan's phone is charged, next to his journal, in my bag. I have
stared at both the last few days, unwilling to open either. Most of
the library is closed for refurbishments, and there aren't enough
seats for asses in my TA office, so I walk to the back of campus. I
follow an undergraduate into the Engineering Department, make
myself an espresso from one of the stainless-steel machines, take a
pastry from one of the baskets, and look for an empty classroom.
Sweat and ash cool on my skin as I walk down a polished hallway

and breathe deep the filtered air. The elevator, like the front doors, requires security access, so I enter an empty lecture theater on the first floor. Each seat has fresh cushions and working outlets and a tiny table that comes out of the padded armrest and pivots for maximum comfort. The windows look out onto the lagoon. On the door, an announcement for Professor Chris's forthcoming book on civil engineering in the public sector.

I take a seat in the back and pull out Nathan's journal. I text Jessica and ask if she knew he kept a journal, if he has any others in her house.

Which house?

May 15

Students late with papers. Excuses range from "I forgot" to "You didn't tell me" to "It's only an elective."

Nathan never enjoyed teaching. He loved his research, burying himself in thoughts and archives and specialty books, dustings of green across their covers of flesh. It made sense when you got to know him, the celibacy, the monkhood, even the drugs. Nathan enjoyed observing the world, but he did not want to be a part of it. Interesting that he would choose to spend time with a woman as comfortable with Tibetan hagiographies as with the beating hearts of bloody things. I flip the page.

Philippe tells me my chapter needs to be revised. Again. Recommends I reconsider my use of Derrida if I'm going to focus on Heideggerian phenomenology. I told him I was so exhausted I was having trouble being in the world. He didn't get the joke.

I sip my espresso. I've decided I'm over deconstructionism, Nathan said. How can we build anything when all we know what to do is tear shit apart? Buddhism rejects the notion of inherent existence, I said. So, if it helps, the only thing you're deconstructing is your own ignorance. That does help, he said.

Sarah has a conference in Virginia next week. I'll miss her.

Tightness in my chest. Tightness in my throat. At that conference, I sent him a photo of two bottles of iced tea in the airport— sweet and sweeter. Order a beer, he wrote back.

I pick up his phone. I enter the password and look at the home screen. The wallpaper is my hand giving the middle finger to a sunset. I open the notes app. Empty except for a two-year-old grocery list. I open maps. Instructions to a restaurant in L.A. from two weekends ago. I text Jessica to double-check they went to that restaurant.

How did you know that?

His phone

Oh, right. You steal.

His photos are of me, of him, the occasional beach or tree. A few pictures of Jessica. Books is empty. Wallet isn't set up. Calendar is blank. I click on Health. He averaged two thousand steps a day. Such is the life of an academic who can't afford a gym membership and doesn't want to work out next to his students. Podcasts. Calculator. Some bullshit translation app. Venmo. NYT Cooking (that must be a joke). CandyCrush and Solitaire.

I swipe left and the app library opens. Nathan didn't use social media, but I see a small pink square hidden from the home screen.

Instagram opens, and one account pops up. A goat farm selling soap. Cute photos of baby goats. Nathan probably scrolled it for stress relief.

I go back to the home screen. There is a black box between Clock and Calendar. I click on it. A bank page opens up. His user ID, in italics, already entered. His password is blank.

> Any idea what his bank password would be?

> Why would you need that?

> I'm looking for clues

> In his bank?

I wait. She doesn't text anything else.

I enter his phone password. Incorrect.

I enter his university-account password. Incorrect.

I tap my foot and finish my espresso. I stretch backward. Even the armrests have padding. I enter his Gmail password. Incorrect. The screen switches and says I've been locked out.

"Fuck."

"Excuse me." A young man pokes his head in. He looks like Matt Lauer. I cross my legs. "What are you doing in here?"

"Hi." Customer Service smile. "Can I help you?"

"I asked what you're doing in here," he repeats. He's wearing a buttoned shirt, tucked into clean khakis. Engineering student. Or Mormon. Virgin? Christ, what if it's all three?

"I was looking for a quiet place to work."

He continues to lean, not stepping in. "Only Engineering students are allowed in the Engineering Department." He looks at the empty espresso cup, the pastry crumbs. How dare I?

"I am in the Engineering Department."

He looks at me. I look at him.

"Which field?"

"Civil," I say, after the briefest of pauses.

He straightens. "Which professor?"

"Chris."

He looks at me. I look at him.

"Well, OK, then."

He leaves. I give the doorway the bird.

I pick up the journal. The second half is blank. I turn the pages back, one at a time, until I reach his writing. Two pages facing each other. Thursday, October 30, and Friday, October 31. The last night he wrote in it. The night he died.

October 30
I hate job applications. And post-structuralism.

October 31
She must never go away.

I close the journal, and my eyes fill. If that virgin Mormon Engineering son of a bitch comes back in here, I won't be able to lie again, and he'll call Campus Security or, more likely, remind me of university policy and stand awkwardly while I break down in front of him. I tap my hands on my thighs. No evidence in the journal, except for Flopsy pushing Nathan into a wall. Flopsy pushing me into a wall. Flopsy saying Nathan deserved it. Flopsy saying he doesn't feel bad about it.

I stand, throw the espresso cup in a covered silver trash can in the corner of the lecture theater, and walk out. I look at my phone. Quarter to noon. Another student has requested I write their paper, says they can only pay half-price. I delete the message. Colette has emailed me. Nothing in response to my dissertation. Instead, she has forwarded me and ten other students a message about a dissertation completion fellowship. The application is due in a week and is limited to doctoral candidates in their fourth year or earlier. I delete the message. Another email—a department-wide reminder that Rapist is giving his job talk in ten minutes.

The Disenchantment of the World:
An Examination of Weber's Process of Rationalization:
A New Hermeneutic of Modern Visible Enchantment That Yields
Care for All Beings,
Thus Challenging the Domination of Nature

I eat another pastry. What a load of shit.

I delete the message and walk to my truck. I climb inside and toss my bag onto the seat. Flopsy, blond hair swaying, walks across the parking lot, late to his BFF's job talk. He reaches the double doors. He pulls twice, then goes through.

Rapist and Flopsy are in the Humanities building.

Rapist and Flopsy are roommates.

How are you doing?

"a displacement of a part or organ of the body from its normal position"

?

definition of prolapse

Want me to take you to the doctor?

No

Want to talk about it?

No

Want to come over?

Yeah

THE WORST THING about shitting your pants is shitting your pants. The worst thing about thinking about shitting your pants is remembering the time you shit your pants. The time you did it repeatedly, for a two-week stretch, and had to buy pads for your underwear like your dad did when you were eleven and you woke him up crying because there was blood on your sheets and knives in your stomach.

I press my hand to the horn. No movement across the street. Flopsy and Rapist are on campus. There is a third roommate, someone told me, a second- or third-year. I wait inside my truck. No movement in the house. I look at my phone. Ten past twelve. Rapist must be introducing himself. He is telling the faculty and graduate students about the job, about the teaching load, the focus of the department. He is explaining the directions he received, if any, and asking for feedback. Be brutal, he is saying with a smile. The master's student will show up. She wants to learn more about the job market for Ph.D.'s. She will smile at him. Rapist will smile at her. He will approach her afterward. He will seem shy. He will invite her for a drink. Let's go someplace quiet, he will say, someplace we can be alone.

I toss my bag under the passenger seat. I grab a dirty sweatshirt off the floor and put it on, pull the hood over my head, and climb out of my truck. I tuck my keys into my pocket. I stand there, hidden behind the avocado tree that blocks the parking spot from the house. No cars in the driveway. My stomach gurgles. The noise it makes after espresso. The noise it makes when Rapist is near, in the room or in my thoughts.

I walk across the street, head down, hood up. I go up the driveway and look through the tall, narrow windows on either side of the door. I remember this door. No lights on inside. No movement. I try the handle. Locked. I walk to my left and stand on my toes, peering into the kitchen. I walk farther left, toward the room I remember, where Nathan pissed on the windowsill. I push my hands up the glass. Locked.

I walk around the side of the house, behind the shrubs and tall trees. The neighbors won't see me. The neighbors won't care. Santa Teresa has two kinds of neighborhoods: rented and owned. No one asks questions in the rented neighborhoods. No one can afford to live here, so whatever needs to be done to make living possible is what gets done. I poke my head around the back corner and into the yard. The fence sags, cheap metal across rotted wood. It wouldn't keep a cow out, but suburban fences aren't for cows. The houses on the other side, their backyards scattered with plastic toys and cracked lawn chairs around tilted tables, are quiet. Not even a dog.

I press my body against the plastic siding. The backyard is empty. Slabs of cement across dust and wilted grass. At one point, perhaps the landlord thought to put in a patio or barbecue area, but ran out of money. The slabs lie in stacks and odd angles, only flat in front of the sliding glass doors and the hot tub. I don't know why he put in a hot tub when he can't put in grass, but whatever.

I walk along the back of the house. Bathroom window. Hot tub. Sliding doors. I remember the bathroom. I remember standing there, pulling my clothes on, wiping away the blood and the shit. I remember the hot tub. The lid is thick gray Styrofoam covered in plastic, clipped to each corner. We were in the hot tub. Feminist Carl. Flopsy's former girlfriend. Even that little guy from Buddhist Studies who makes snide comments and rude jokes, whose mother killed herself. I never tell him to fuck off, no matter what he says. I never tell him to fuck off because, no matter what he says, when your mother has killed herself, no one should tell you to fuck off.

I was in the water. Naked. Laughing. Drunk. Bottle of beer floating. Rapist in the kitchen. Music playing. People dancing. Sliding doors open. Pills on countertops and powders on laptops. Rolls of one-dollar bills. Laughing.

I walk past the hot tub and grip the door handle. A plate with crumbs on the low table in front of the low couch. Empty beer cans on the counter next to the sink. It opens. No alarm, no voices. The smell of dirty laundry and old milk. The weight of silence when you are expecting noise. I step inside and slide the door closed behind me. The tile floor sticky beneath my feet.

When I was here, it was loud and bright. Someone brought a floor lamp from a bedroom and tilted it toward the ceiling. The fridge door opened and closed. People smashed ice against countertops. Booze from back shelves. Bowls of chips. Salsa spilled. Rapist laughed. My hair was wet. Feminist Carl complimented Flopsy's girlfriend on her nice, tight ass. She laughed. Flopsy laughed. Rapist put his arm around me. I put my arm around him.

The kitchen has three doors. Where I just came in, the front door straight ahead, and, to my left, the attached garage. To my right, the hallway leading to three bedrooms and one bathroom.

The front door is where I walked out, the morning after. I did not understand what had happened. I did not understand what was happening. I did not want to ask. The front door is where I stood when I hugged Rapist goodbye, where I paused so I didn't throw up in the bushes, where I turned, keys clutched in my hand, pressed to my stomach. The front door is where I first felt it, the gurgling and the razor blades.

I step into the hallway to my right. Another smell. Damp carpet and mildew. Dirty clothes and sweaty bodies. That night, the chlorine and cheap beer, stale chips and warm dip, and, later, the puking and the shitting and the blood, each its own pungent flavor. Something else, too. The warm, heavy smell of men. I take three steps. The carpet sinks beneath my feet.

Behind me, the sliding doors open.

***

I slip inside the room closest to me and hold the door to the frame. The bathroom. When I was in here, my eyes were red and my lip was bleeding. Jeans on. Feet bare. Razor blades. Another smell. Coconut and almonds. On top of me. Behind me. My stomach gurgles.

The sun is bright through the window behind the shower curtain. I breathe out, lips apart, and peer through the slit of light between the door and the frame. On the other side, a young man stands. I've seen him before. Second-year. He smiles a lot. Sweaty and huffing, small white earbuds. Music playing loud enough for me to hear. He kicks off both shoes and reaches for the handle with one hand, looking at his phone with the other. He mutters and turns, walks down the end of the hallway.

The first time we went hunting, Dad pointed to the leaves. See the sunlight? I looked at the shifting patterns across the branches. See how it moves? You never aim at something moving, Sarah. When an animal knows you're near, they freeze. Look for the unmoving things. He picked up the rifle and double-checked the safety. Beginners think they will see them before they see us. It doesn't work that way. He handed me the gun. He stood behind me, held the rifle to my shoulder, showed me where to aim. We stood, legs planted, arms still, turning at the waist. Open mouths, breath white in the air. Always look for the stillness, he whispered above me, the back of my head beneath his chin, our orange caps hand-knit by Mrs. Sanghera. When something is hiding, it is still. When something is moving, it is not hiding.

I open the door and stick my head into the hallway. The door on the right is open; sounds of drawers opening and closing. He is singing to himself. Two steps and I am out of the bathroom and inside the room directly across the hall. I saw him before he saw me. I shut the door and press against it, mouth open, breath quiet. The bathroom door closes. The shower turns on. I look around. This is not Rapist's room.

Hello, Flopsy.

Behind me, the shower rains down on the man, still singing. To my right is a double bed, low to the floor. No headboard. Wrinkled sheets. To my left, a two-layer shoe rack next to a closet. Two shoe boxes with two pairs of dress shoes, the lids fitted underneath as if they are on display. Shiny and unworn. Flopsy is preparing for interviews. I heard he has one for a small school outside Seattle, the city of his mother. American corporations bought American universities long ago. She wants to keep an eye on him.

In front of me, in front of the window, a desk. Papers. Stacks of books on the floor. A bedside table, chipped and decorated with rings from cold beers on warm nights. A tilted lamp. Next to the closet, a rack for clothing. Two suits. Tags on. Flopsy knows he will get a job.

I work quickly. The bedside drawer is open. Inside, bong pipe, pencils, condoms, and lube. A small packet of tissues. Bottle opener. Starbucks gift card. The floor is covered in unwashed clothing. Everything smells of body spray and dried cum. Gym shorts folded beneath hanging shirts and a collection of ties in the closet. No computer. I open the books, skim the papers. Printed copies of articles from JSTOR. Outlined feedback on his dissertation from his adviser. A stack of Chuck Palahniuk.

Everything back where it was. This is the boring room of a boring man. I was hoping to find something exciting. A collection of Dexter slides. A collage of revenge porn. Maybe a hit list? Instead, there are old sheets, old clothes. Body odor and takeout. I pick up one of the paper piles from the desk. It is clipped at the corner. Green pen at the bottom. "Work on basic sentence construction. Simple errors detract from the impact of your research." His adviser, kind and gentle and gay, tells a thirty-six-year-old Ph.D. candidate applying to be a Professor that he don't write so good.

I remove the clip and shuffle the papers. The shower continues behind me. He hasn't numbered them. I move them around. This on top of that. That on top of this. The professor's edits across every page. No notes, just edits. A semicolon where there should be a comma. New paragraphs. Spelling. Mom keeps you out of jail, and adviser is your spellcheck. What a support system, preventing the stupid from knowing how stupid they are.

I squat and look beneath the chair in front of the desk. Nothing. I turn my head and look under the bed. I pull forward a small plastic bag. I sit on the ground, next to a pile of dirty underwear. In my hand, in a ziplock bag, are a spoon, a lighter, a thick rubber band.

A needle.

There are two tragedies in life. Not getting what you want, and getting it. Not finding what you're looking for, and finding it. I stare at the bag. I should be angry, I suppose. Or smug. Vindicated. Since I broke in, I guess this is inadmissible evidence, and would never hold up in court. I think of Jessica, of Frederick. I doubt her family pays attention to what holds up in court.

The shower stops. I stand up. I hold the bag and open my mouth, my breath soft. I listen at the door. The sound of an electric razor. He is still moving.

To my right, the kitchen, the sliding doors, the backyard. I can be out and away in thirty seconds. He is singing again. I can close the door behind me. Leave the shoes and the notes. Steal the weapon and bring it to the police. Bring it to Jessica and let her family do whatever it is they do when they want to avoid the police. Maybe Flopsy will see it's missing and think it's me, come after me. Maybe then I won't need Jessica or the police. Maybe I can keep my hands steady and my aim straight and claim it as self-defense.

I close the door behind me. My stomach cramps. I walk to the left. Away from the kitchen, away from the bathroom. I breathe soft and wide and silent at the end of the hallway. On my right, Second Year left his door open. On the left is the third bedroom. The bedroom I remember.

———◆———

If the worst part of shitting your pants is shitting your pants, then the worst part of remembering shitting your pants is not remembering exactly why you shit your pants. The memories come in flashes. Postcards and photos.

You retrace your steps. You were in the bathroom. You looked in the mirror. Water on your face. Blood and shit between your legs.

You remember the party. The hot tub. The laughing.

The beer.

The wine.

The pills.

The hands. The mouth. The shirt off, the pants off, the condom.

His room is similar to Flopsy's. Same size. Same window place-
ment. The bed is closer to the wall. Sideways. I guess he likes to look
out the window when he's lying down. Maybe the natural light helps
him wake up. The desk is tidier. No paper piles. No clothes on the
floor. I open the closet. He is organized. Shirts on the left. Pants on
the right. Sweaters stacked up top. Shoes lined up below. I crouch.
Imported leather. Made in Chile. Soft soles and leather sides. No
sneakers for Rapist. No need to sneak.

A hanger with ties and belts. Flopsy's belts are new, with the tags
still on. He bought them for his interview. These are worn. Aged and
elegant. Brown. Black. A blue one. A green one. His shoes match.
Brown. Black. One pair with blue trim. One pair with green soles.
I wonder which pair he will wear to his campus visit, to show he is
the best fit for a position of power over thousands of young women.

His bed is tidy. It has a headboard. I bend forward. Light citrus scent. On his bedside table, a dog-eared copy of *Being and
Time*. Unlike Nathan, Rapist has no trouble being in the world. A
notebook, leather-bound. A pen next to it, diagonal and deliberate. I open the notebook. Notes on his reading. Page numbers and
quotes. Insightful commentary. Nice penmanship.

I don't remember coming in here, but I remember being in here.
His body on mine. Coconut and almonds. Razor blades. Later that
day, my right hip bloomed purple, a series of bruises on my side.
From his fingers. A larger smudge just behind. From his thumb.

When breeding horses, live cover has fallen out of fashion. It's
too dangerous. The stallions are aggressive. The mares are fragile.
Large, padded mounts are built. If you don't know what you're looking at, you'd wonder why a barn has oversized gymnastics equipment on display. Why the stallions stay in their stalls, kicking at the
doors, while the mares walk past. Why the handler leads the stallion out of the stall, over to the mount. Why the stallion rears up,
why the handler holds the big baby bottle, with its rubber opening,

and the stallion fucks it. The mounts don't last long. They are torn and shredded from teeth and hooves. The handlers get hurt. Broken arms. Broken faces. But the mares would have it worse. Legs broken. Backs broken. Necks bleeding from where he bites down and holds on. Mares can be aggressive. They kick. They buck. It's dangerous for the stallion, too. That's why they have the mount.

Certain industries require live cover. The Jockey Club forbids registering foals conceived by artificial insemination or embryo transfer. This is not to protect the mares. Live cover justifies the stud fees and guarantees the quality of the mares. Inferior mares can't have access to premium semen. It would dilute the bloodline. Live cover guarantees only the highest-quality mares get fucked. Where I grew up, live cover was standard, but it had nothing to do with bloodlines. Live cover is free and easy. Sell the babies, make some money. Bit or kicked or broken, everyone survives. Or they don't.

I place my hand on my hip, the corner between my thumb and forefinger at my waist. Like keys on a piano, I lay each finger over where the bruises were. It's a stretch for me. My hands are smaller than his. The day after, I found another bloom on the top of my left thigh. No fingerprints, but a thick, swollen violet. The bedrail, maybe. Or a fist.

I lift the pillows. He has three. One on either side of the bed. The third on top, forward and reclining against the two behind. The duvet is folded back, dark blue. One clean sheet, light blue, pulled down on top. The colors coordinate. It looks inviting.

I may be an inferior mare. No South American shoes in my closet. No citrus scents on my sheets. But I could never dilute his bloodline. Not the way he did it. That explains the shit and the blood in the bathroom, the razors when I walked, when I sat, when I stood. When I discussed Foucault and the panopticon two days later, in a classroom full of men, full of people who had been at the party. When Feminist Carl laughed and shook his head. No way, no way. He's such a great guy. There's just no way.

I didn't know him, and the memories were blurry, so I hugged Rapist in the morning, by the front door with the narrow windows. I ran back to my truck. I threw up when I was behind the avocado tree, and patterns of purple tattooed themselves across my body. When Flopsy's girlfriend, the one with the nice, tight ass, texted that I left a ring in Rapist's room, a ring he found under the bed when he was cleaning the house after the party, I responded she should put it in my mailbox. I didn't know rings just fell off fingers, but when you are pinned beneath a man, when there is no handler and he fucks you up the ass so hard you spend the next two weeks holding the bottom inch of your intestines inside your body, actually holding your body together with both your index fingers because anytime you sit on a toilet the force of gravity pulls your body outside of your body so that your flesh hangs outside your flesh—well, I guess it's possible then.

The room is boring. Cleaner than Flopsy's. Smells better than Flopsy's. Rapist's clothes are nicer. His books more organized. He does not have green-inked feedback on basic punctuation. Amazing, how it all tidies up. Wash the sheets, run the vacuum, shut the door behind her. It's like nothing ever happened. He doesn't even have a bedside drawer filled with lube. He doesn't use lube.

I move to the door. The electric razor has stopped. Second Year continues to sing. Something popular and dated. My stomach churns. Espresso and Rapist and whatever I managed for breakfast.

I walk to the bed. I hold Flopsy's drug bag in one hand, and pull down the duvet with the other. The sheet. I move the third pillow on top of the two pillows, a tidy stack. I step onto the bed.

I unzip my pants with one hand. My stomach gurgles. I remember what Therapist 1 said.

I squat.

When I'm done, I use the bottom of the third pillow to wipe and place it neatly back against the other two, at an angle. I step off the bed. I remake the duvet, folding the sheet over the top, with both hands, needle and spoon and rubber band in the plastic bag, held under my chin. I tuck in the side. It looks inviting.

I move the desk and open the window. I slide one leg over, mount the windowsill, but gently. No teeth. Nothing broken. The other leg. I jump and land next to where Nathan stood in his effort to piss on the windowsill.

Maybe he'll know it was me. Maybe he'll drive up the mountain with Flopsy. Maybe it will be like in the movies and, afterward, everything will be better.

Walking back to my truck, I smile at the plastic bag in my hand. I pull the hood of my sweatshirt off my head. The sky is gray, but all I feel is sunlight.

I LIE IN BED. Dog is on the sheets next to me. Flopsy's baggie is on the table next to the bed. The sun is down. There is less ash tonight, and the moon is bright. It is time for my routine.

When I was eight, Mrs. Sanghera packed us sandwiches and juice boxes, and my father drove up the coast, all the way up and east to the Canadian border. He was born out there, and his brother still lived in a small town overlooking the water. Does he hunt like us? I asked. Sort of, Dad said. He lobsters. It is a different way to hunt.

We arrived with the little black dog, and everyone spoke French. I wasn't used to people speaking French. I thought it was the language of my father and myself and a handful of neighbors. The Bay of Fundy moved like the ocean, Dad told me. I was used to rivers, but had never seen the sea. I stared at the sands, bare and dry, then wet and full. Back and forth, throughout the day.

My father and uncle laughed and drank beer. We went out in his boat, large and yellow and smelling of guts and salt and men. My uncle introduced me to my cousins, gangly boys with rumpled hair and stained T-shirts. Lobster is not always the food of the rich. The boys laughed at me when I said I didn't know how to swim. They laughed at me when I asked where the cows were. They looked at each other when I asked where the guns were.

One handed me a lobster. Avoid the claws, he said. I reached for the tail. Blood splattered across the deck when the incisor shells on either side snapped and sliced my fingers. My father yelled, and the boys gaped with broken teeth. Maybe it was a prank. Maybe they did not understand someone who did not understand lobsters. My uncle apologized, slapped both children across the face until their cheeks were red and their eyes ran. He turned the boat back to shore. That night, he boiled lobsters outside the house in a giant pot with a gas tank and a hose. I stayed in the room I was sharing with my father. I said I wasn't hungry. I held my hand to my chest, bandaged by the woman my uncle was living with. Everything wet and salty. I missed the woods.

That evening, Dad read to me a story from the old green book. He didn't have it with him, but he said he had memorized it. The woodland princess had gone on an adventure, had visited the ocean, and was very brave, and would return home soon. When Dad was asleep and the boys silent on the sofa, I crept into the kitchen and pulled a jar of peanut butter from the shelf. I ate in the dark, the little black dog licking the spoon. It, too, tasted wet and salty. The rest of the trip, I watched the tide through the window. I avoided my cousins. She's so quiet, said my uncle. Boys will be boys, said the woman.

I have a routine for my box. It starts with panic. My chest tightens, my breath catches. I think of men outside, men trying to come in. I do my rounds. I shut the garage door and check the lock. I close the window next to the bed and fit a stick inside the slider. I check the small window in the small bathroom. Another piece of wood wedged inside the tracks. I close the curtains. I draw down the shades on the front door with the glass panels. On the bedside table, I keep a kitchen knife tucked inside a book. I am enclosed. An oyster firmly sealed. Any noise and I wake up. Dog barks and I wake up. Voices, engines, a coyote, or the scratch of a possum and I wake up. I didn't used to be like this, but I've been like this for a long time.

We left the town after a week. When we returned home, school started. My teacher, sweet and soft with dimples in both cheeks, said we were studying the ocean that year. Students had to choose a sea creature and prepare a report for the class. We trekked down the hall in single file to the library, where Mrs. Flanagan sat us around a table with picture books and pop-up books and a few plastic-coated posters. The girls chose dolphins and turtles. The boys, sharks and electric eels. A few branched off into manta rays or sea urchins.

What do you want to study? Mrs. Flanagan asked me. I sat by myself, my fingers bandaged. I don't know, I mumbled. How about the lobster? She smiled. We all love lobster. I shook my head.

Sunfish?

Jellyfish?

Well, she said, what kind of fish do you want to learn about? An angry fish, I said. She tilted her head. I don't think fish get angry. I shrugged. How about a scary fish? I nodded. She pulled a book from the table and opened it for me. The anglerfish. Perfect.

Tonight, the lights are off and I lie in my bed. The garage is open. I sit up and lean over Dog. The window next to the bed is unlocked. I remove the piece of wood and slide the window open. The curtains do not sway, because there is no breeze. I open them, and a slice of moon cuts through. I unlock the front doors. I roll up the blinds. I kick off my jeans. Moonlight from the garage opening, the window, the front doors. It pours in, a spotlight on everything in its path. The studio is a square box. No secret corners. Dog snores, soft curls pressed against a faded blanket. Her lips drool across a crumpled T-shirt.

My presentation on anglerfish got an A. They are dangerous, I told the class, holding my poster, on which I had glued a cutout.

Bulbous chin beneath protruding teeth. Tiny eyes on a head of jaws. Slick black flesh with tentacles and gaping maw illuminated by a dangling light protruding from its forehead.

They hide in the dark, I said. They have a small light that shines in the water at night. Other fish come close. The anglerfish kills them. The anglerfish is a hunter. Mrs. Flanagan smiled. Sometimes they eat each other. Mrs. Flanagan nodded. The girl fish are bigger than the boy fish.

It's so ugly, said a girl in the front row. Two boys behind her nodded.

I like it, I said.

I pull off my shirt. I roll down my underwear. I run my fingers through Dog's scrunchy fur. I stretch beside her. Above the sheets. Doors unlocked. Window open. Curtains open. Blinds rolled up. Moonlight from all sides. An oyster on a plate.

I reach both arms above my head and stretch. Breasts rise white and round in the dark. Flopsy will look for his needle, Rapist will find my scat. Maybe Second Year saw me. Maybe they will find my address on the department contact sheet. Maybe they will drive here, climb over the fence, bypass the security codes. Maybe they will come tonight.

I smile and bring both knees to my chest. I hook each index finger around each big toe and hold myself open, ready to be shucked. Beside me, Flopsy's needle. My knife.

I started my routine out of fear, years ago. I still have fear, but it's different now. I fear they will not take the bait. They will stay below the surface, swim past this worm on a hook, all soft and wet and wiggling. Past the moonlight glinting off my flesh, the light that dangles in front of my gaping maw.

It is a different way to hunt.

With Dog's head in my lap on the bed, I scroll through Nathan's phone. Our history of text messages. Up and up, years appear. Plans to meet. Questions about assignments. Comments on a man I was dating. I was almost sweet before. Then photos from the Vatican, from Mongolia. Back in Santa Teresa. Drug dates and movie lists. Job searches. Bills and Phils and Chucks and fucks.

Flopsy's needle is still on my bedside table. I haven't called the police. I haven't told Jessica. One, I suspect, would be useless. The other, too useful. My hand is shaking; my aim is off. I haven't told them because of what I want to do. I tap the phone icon. Three missed calls from me, one week ago. He was dead by then. One call to me the Friday before. He was alive. Earlier calls to his sister, to me. An unknown number. I dial it. An automated message from a pizza place, telling me they're not open yet. I scroll down. Me. Jessica. Pizza. Two calls to his adviser. Me. Pizza. Me.

I open the search engine. His Gmail account. An email he received from the library on Friday afternoon. An overdue book. Like me, he forwards his university emails. I press the "back" button, and his inbox appears. Like me, he stays logged in. In bold, a list of unopened messages, including the notification of his death. I guess no one thought to remove the dead guy's address from the dead guy's condolence list.

I scroll down. The message from the bank alerting him that his account has been locked because of too many incorrect log-in attempts. I follow the link. The app opens. I click "forgot username." I return to his email. N@th@n0214. Valentine's Day. Our favorite holiday. We get baked and watch *Alien*. I return to the app. I click "forgot password." I open the email. NathanIsDead. Password not accepted. Not special enough. #1N@thanIsDe@d! Accepted.

I open the app. N@th@n0214, #1N@thanIsDe@d!. Two accounts. I open the first. Monthly deposits of $1,900 from UCST in green. His TA-ship salary. Expenditures in red to Chase. Credit card payments. I scroll down. UCST in green. Chase in red. The occasional overdraft. Nothing else.

I click on the other bank account. $25,000 in green. $25,000 in red. Every first of the month. Green from CB&P. Red to LMC LLC. I scroll down. $25,000 in red. $25,000 in green. I keep scrolling. This year. Last year. I click the right arrow. The year before. I click the right arrow. The year before. I pick up my phone and open the search engine. CB&P is an L.A.-based wealth management firm.

"Good afternoon, this is Suzanne. How may I direct your call?" She answers on the first ring.

"Hi there." I clear my throat. "I am looking to make some investments. Is that something you do?"

A brief silence. "Let me connect you with a member of our wealth management support team."

"No, thank you. I just want to know what services you offer."

"We offer comprehensive planning for estate management and growth." Another pause. "What sort of asset classes are you looking to discuss?"

"Big ones. Big trust assets." I cough.

"Ma'am, why don't I—"

"Thank you." I hang up.

CB&P in green. Possibly where Nathan keeps his money. Or whoever is giving Nathan his money. $25,000 a month. Holy shit.

LMC LLC in red. Google shows 7,400,000 results. I open the first one. A construction company. The second one—the same construction company, this time on LinkedIn. The third one—a subsidiary of the first, focused on bathroom renovations. The fourth one—another subsidiary, focused on development in the Sarasota area.

I call Jessica. She doesn't pick up.

"Hi, Jessica. It's Sarah." I tap Nathan's phone against my leg. "Was Nathan investing in building something? Maybe, construction?" I look down at the needle. "Thanks."

Dog looks up at me. I bend forward and kiss her nose. I can't imagine a secret Nathan would keep from me. We've known each other almost seven years. I've cried in his arms. He's cried in mine. We've been passed out and fucked up and bought more tequila than a Massachusetts resident in a New Hampshire liquor store. No wonder Jared assumes I was there that night. The sound of bottles and glasses and empty containers. That's what Nathan and I did. We consumed. We expelled. What one absorbed, the other secreted. There was nothing in his life that was not also in mine. Even Jessica. He visited her monthly. Told me when she was in rehab, told me when she relapsed. I knew her secrets as well as he did.

My phone rings.

"Was Nathan building a house?" I ask before Jessica says anything.

"What? Of course not."

"What is LMC LLC?"

"I have no idea."

"Does your family keep their assets in CB&P Wealth Management?" I wait. "Jessica?"

"Some, yes."

"Is that where Nathan's trust fund is kept?"

"Yes." A beat. "How did you know that?"

"I got into his bank account."

Silence.

"Why was he sending twenty-five thousand every month to LMC LLC?"

Silence.

"Look, I know it's none of my business—"

"That's quite the understatement."

"—but that's a lot of money, even for you people, and I can't help but wonder if there's some . . . connection."

"What kind of connection?"

"I don't know."

"You're not a very good detective."

"Well, I'm trying." I look at Flopsy's needle. "I broke into a house."

"You did?" A sound. Something small. Maybe a laugh.

"There's this guy in our department. He hates me, he hated Nathan. He's a fucking wack job, and if anyone killed your brother, it's probably him."

"Did you find anything?"

I stare at the needle. I think of cops and the procedures they follow, families like Jessica's, the procedures they ignore. I think of knives and guns and doing it myself. "No."

"You didn't vandalize anything, did you?"

I smirk.

She sighs. "CB&P is the firm handling the bulk of the trusts my parents set up. Not everything, obviously."

"Obviously."

"I don't know about LMC." Another sound. Tongue against teeth. The same sound Nathan made when he was thinking. "It could be a services payment. For asset management."

"Twenty-five thousand a month for asset management?"

"That's not a lot of money, Sarah."

This time I'm quiet.

"Wouldn't the payment go to CB&P if they're the management people?"

"CB&P is the firm holding the assets. They aren't the only team in charge of managing the assets. Don't you know anything about money?"

"I guess not."

"Nathan didn't spend his money, but I don't think he ever dissolved the trust. Assuming it's still in existence, he would need to pay his advisers. Paying on a monthly basis, an automated fixed percentage, is typical."

"A fixed percentage?"

"Yes."

"Twenty-five thousand a month is a fixed percentage?"

"Yes. Usually one-half or one-quarter a percent annually. I suppose the value of his trust has gone down. He never did have an interest in the market."

I nod, glad she can't see me.

"I was going to call you. Can you come down?"

"To L.A.?" I blink. "Is everything OK?"

"I've got someone I want you to meet."

"OK." It makes me nervous, the thought of meeting someone through Jessica. The last shared acquaintance we had is dead.

"Great. Is tomorrow night too soon? I'll text you the address."

"If there's traffic, I may be late." There's something very Californian about saying "if there's traffic," as if there isn't always traffic.

"That's fine. We can wait."

"And while you're waiting, ask about the LLC thing, would you?"

"Sure. I'll ask Gerhardt."

"Who's— Never mind."

I hang up. She sends me a link to an address. Google Maps says it's two hours south of Santa Teresa, so it's four hours away. She sends two more texts.

> sorry it's so last minute.

> Maybe you can bring a book for the drive?

I smile. Some people drive themselves, some people don't.

I scroll through Nathan's bank records again. $25,000 a month. A fixed percentage. One-half to one-quarter a percent annually.

Fuck me, Nathan. I guess you did have secrets.

SIT IN the TA office and wait for Raymond, the student who said he needed to speak with me. I scroll through my phone, looking at the photo I took of the tunnel, the names in black, Nathan's in pen, my shaky handwriting barely visible. A third-year is in the office with me, the militant vegan with the Animal Warfare T-shirts. He is eating cashew yogurt and staring at his laptop. He gets a new one every year. He's got an iPad, too, propped open on the desk. A stack of books to his right. Next to the wall, a glass jar. Not a mug or a thermos. He crosses his legs at the ankle. He doesn't wear socks, and his pants are short. His ankles blink at me from beneath the desk in the late-afternoon light. Thin and bony and covered in sandpaper hair. He is not a tall man. He slouches, eyes fixed on the laptop. It glows across his thick-rimmed glasses. A drop of fake yogurt, glossy and white, lingers at the corner of his mouth.

My own computer—old, dirty, a chip in one corner, and a crack across the screen—has another email from Colette. She wants me to edit her latest article. It is forty pages long. She asks me to double-check her sources and phonetic transcriptions of the Sanskrit, Tibetan, and Mongolian. No comments on the draft I sent her four months ago.

No more requests for contraband papers. ChatGPT is killing my side hustle.

I look at my phone. Raymond is thirty minutes late. I unplug my computer and put it in my bag. I wave to Vegan. He ignores me. I look at his laptop, iPad, iWatch. His shoes are crisp, sharp, and angled with long, pointed toes and contrast stitching. Inside, I bet his feet are smooth, softly pumiced by an organic stone kept in the corner of a solar shower. Maybe PETA is subsidizing his research. Maybe rich chicks dig dudes who drink oat milk.

I leave the office and walk down the department hallway. I look at the notice board next to the elevator. One guest lecture. Someone lost a bike. No job advertisements. This morning, I stole two more espressos from the Engineering Department, and three muffins from a basket with a handwritten "help yourself" in colorful, curling letters. Their board had four job fairs listed and a sign-up sheet for two department lectures: "How to Handle Competing Offers" and "Industry vs. Academia."

I stop inside the tunnel. T-shirt over my face, I lean forward and take another photo of the names. Nathan's, in black now, a thicker line drawn over my earlier pen, stares back at me.

Miss you. love you.

On the left, next to a name that was written over the summer, in small, crooked letters of pen, or maybe even pencil.

fuck you

———◆———

There is traffic, of course. The smoke mixes with gas and highway, and I shut my vents. I reach gridlock in Ventura and scroll through my messages with Nathan.

> Why do you put up with me?

One month after we returned from fieldwork, I woke up topless in his bed. He was sleeping, but dressed, curled like a pill bug in a quilt on the floor. I staggered to the bathroom, pulled on my shirt, and crept out the door.

The night before, between Quaaludes and Bridget Everett, I slipped my hand between his thighs, cupping his balls, and bent my head toward his waist.

Sarah, he said, and covered my hand in his, pulled it up and over his chest. My other hand replaced the first.

Hey, he said again, both of my hands in his now, balls out of reach.

I leaned forward, pressed my face to his. He pulled back. I pushed again, as aggressive as one can be on disco biscuits, and stripped off my shirt.

Sarah, no, he said, sprawled across the mattress as I crawled on top of him. He rolled me off, gentle despite my struggles, and moved to the floor, pulled a blanket with him, and went to sleep.

> Let's have coffee.

I'm surprised you wanted to see me, I muttered, eyes averted as we sat on a bench in downtown Santa Teresa.

It's all right, Sarah, he said. He held out an Americano, no milk, no sugar, because he knew me.

Is it? I asked, staring at the cup in his hand. My attempted rape?

It wasn't an attempted rape. He put the coffee on the ground when I refused to take it. Well, maybe it was. He blew across his own Americano, with milk, because I knew him, too. But I forgive you.

It's not forgivable.

I'll make an exception for you.

We sat and watched homeless people and rich bitches—who might be lovely women, but that doesn't have the same ring to it— walk by.

I have my vows, he said.

You know, you chose the worst ones. Poverty and celibacy are, like, the least fun vows you could pick.

He grinned.

What if you kept different vows?

Such as?

Well—I leaned back—we could get sober. You'd have that.

Sobriety isn't a vow in most Catholic traditions. He took a sip. Priests drink wine. Monks have made it for centuries.

We're pushing the boundaries on that, and you know it.

He laughed.

So—let's dry out, empty your trust fund, and move to Bali.

What are we going to do in Bali?

Fuck each other's brains out. I picked up the coffee. Live happily ever after.

He laughed again. He looked down at me, placed a kiss on my forehead. I can't do that.

Time slows when you step forward, when you leave something behind. The part of me that thought he would change his mind, that thought I could leave the Chads and Brads and just have Nathan. It felt like winter, this apple of hope I didn't know I had grown finally falling from the tree.

We sat for the rest of the afternoon, talked about lining up TA-ships to cover tuition, which departments would take us since our own didn't have enough positions. I gave him a ride to his apartment, something small and rickety behind a big house, in a different part of town. Minimal space but excellent internet.

I'm not coming in, I said, and I promise, from now on, my shirt will always stay on.

He climbed out of the truck. I put it in drive and turned the wheel, but he walked around the front and tapped on my window. I rolled it down.

Sarah. He looked at me, like Romeo, like Cyrano, any of those doomed romances where the guy's outside and the girl's inside and there's a balcony or a window or some other metaphor separating them, and one says one thing and the other says another thing, and then they make out and then they die.

I'm keeping the vows, Sarah. I'm keeping them my whole life.

I know. The sun began to set, no ash, no smoke in the air. Just streaks of orange and yellow and pink. I thought of Mrs. Sanghera, her soft fabrics and warm arms. Palm trees overhead. A bird called to its mate.

But if I wasn't going to . . . His knuckles turned white, the sprinkling of hair stark against his skin. If I wasn't . . .

I could have kissed him then. I could have kissed him, and followed him into his tiny house with no space and great WiFi and slid my body across his like ice on a hot stove. We both knew it. We all have that person, the one who can get you to do anything. Nathan was keeping his vows. I was keeping his vows. I didn't like to think about it then, and I don't like to think about it now, but sometimes the no we tell ourselves, the no we keep inside, means: Try harder, prove you want me enough to have me, convince me, because I'm not sure you're worth it. I'm not sure I'm worth it.

I leaned back. OK. We'll just keep blowing up that sobriety vow.

The crinkle and crackle of his voice. I told you, that's not a vow.

It should be, the way we do it. I pat his head.

Traffic picks up, and I crawl toward the city. Sun down, cars honk, limos and Teslas and long, low things that look like brightly colored cocks. Nathan told me once that money flies. Rich people hate traffic, he said. That's funny, I replied, because poor people love it.

It's almost nine by the time I reach the address. It's a bar. Or a restaurant. A gallery? One of those L.A. places where no one eats but there's plenty of food and you have to be on a list to get in. The outside is large and plain, with double doors two stories high. There is no sign.

Inside, a hostess/model/curator smiles like a politician and asks how she can help. I mention Jessica's name, and she leads me past an installation of lights inside a box hanging from the ceiling. Tables with translucent legs and thin couples with glittering strips of metal across their wrists, ankles, fingers, and collarbones. I notice, on closer inspection, the thinner and younger the people, the more disheveled the appearance. A teenager in torn jeans and a torn top walks past. A girl, who's drinking a martini but looks about fourteen, wears an oversized nightshirt and bunny slippers. Behind them, slightly older, slightly fatter patrons in expensive clothing, bedazzled by handbags and watches the size of golf balls. The shifting demarcations of wealth and age.

Jessica isn't here yet, and I end up in the back, against a floor-to-ceiling window that looks out onto a collection of other floating light boxes. I can't tell if they are in an outside garden or if the light boxes are boxed within a larger box and it's all supposed to mean something. The servers/models/museum assistants are slim and smooth, with sculpted cheeks and slender arms that only look odd from behind, when you notice how much bigger the elbow is to the humerus.

I sit on a chair with legs so clear it appears to hover in midair, and I realize that's the point. The chair is smaller than I am used to. The back is made of a single glass tube topped with a small rectangle, an invisible "T" designed to give the illusion of no support. I glance around and see that the illusions are effective—beautiful people in various states of undress hover, illuminated by invisible fixtures, seemingly straight-backed.

The table is also clear and thin, and through the top I see my stained jeans and faded shoes. As I look down, I realize that the floor is actually illuminated glass, hovering over water. Like those desk toys they used to sell in the mall to executives, or to the wives of executives who felt the need to decorate their husbands' offices. A narrow slip of liquid caught between two panes of glass, the colors and shapes moving as you flipped the piece from side to side.

I tap my fingers. I attempt confidence, spread my thighs and straighten my shoulders like a white guy, but the chair creaks and the table moves, and I shrink in on myself. I reach for my phone and open the photo of the names in the tunnel. I stare at Nathan's. Thick black lines against the white background. I zoom in. I recognize some of the names from the awkward emails. One girl died of meningitis. Another had a car accident back home in Chicago. I sing under my breath.

Un-der-grad-u-ates sitting in a tree,
D-Y-I-N-G

That doesn't work.

Un-der-grad-u-ates sitting—

"Sarah."

Jessica reaches for me and I lean toward her, letting her kiss me on both cheeks. I think she's actually happy to see me. I smile. She sits next to me at the translucent table; the glow of the light boxes illuminates her face. I'm tempted to ask if she designed this place. I'm tempted to ask her where the fuck we are. She is dressed in an oversized T-shirt, torn across the midriff, beneath a cropped, fitted jacket. I guess her age puts her in a transitional stage for fashion.

"How are you?" she asks.

"Good." I nod, the word interrupted by the arrival of a lowball of golden liquid, a single ice cube, salt on the rim.

Jessica, smooth and graceful and utterly in her element, gestures to the glass. "Nathan told me."

"How are you?" I glance over her shoulder. "Where's your guy?"

"I'm good." She smiles and waves a hand over her shoulder. "Frederick is around."

I lean forward, trying to be subtle but obviously staring at the long, slim glass of clear liquid placed in front of her.

She takes a sip. "This is water."

"I didn't mean—" A man pulls out a clear chair and sits at the table with us.

"This is Jeff." She lifts a hand, wrist toward the sky, and I glimpse silver slivers perpendicular to the soft swell of her palm.

Jeff used to be one of the beautiful people. Not anymore. He seems comfortable enough, jacket across the invisible "T" of his chair, one arm on the table. Beneath the glass, his legs spread wide.

"He's also working on Nathan's case." Jessica looks from one of us to the other, collarbone and eyes twinkling beneath the floating orbs of light.

"His case?" I ask, tequila in hand. I lift my tongue to the rim, that sweet burn of salt, and inhale my favorite scent. "I thought you said there was no case?"

Jeff grunts and snaps his fingers at a waiter. I'm beginning not to like Jeff.

"Well, you seemed so sure." She sips from her glass, as translucent as moonlight. One piece of ice, long and slim, spins below the water; light is reflected and refracted across her face, the table, every surface covered in pixelation and patterns of rainbows. What would it be like to be born into a life where even your beverages dance?

"OK." I turn to Jeff.

He looks at Jessica. She nods. He leans to one side and pulls a leather folder from under his arm and holds it out to me.

"You're here to compare notes," Jessica says. "These are his."

"Are you a cop?"

Jeff shakes his head. He waves the folder.

"PI?"

He nods. He waves the folder.

"If you're a professional, why do you want my notes?"

"I work for Jessica," he says, and gives up. He lets the folder drop in the middle of the table. The smack jostles my drink, gold liquid sloshing, and almost knocks Jessica's over. He leans back in his chair, thighs wide.

Fuck you, Jeff.

I press my lips together, a grain of salt between them, and pick up the folder.

He leans back farther, eyes on me. Jessica looks over my shoulder and gestures. Small plates of delicate things come to the table.

Jeff writes like an undergraduate in the Accounting Department. It's all Name, Date, Location. No descriptors, introduction, or analysis. Build a narrative, I want to write in the margins with a green pen. Position your data within a broader context, so your reader understands your argument.

Someone hovers to my left, and I notice something edible and ornate at shoulder level. I angle the folder against the edge of the table as more plates, no larger than my palm, are sprinkled between us, each of them transparent and lightly curved. Small portions nestle inside.

Jeff reaches forward, picks two of the plates, and begins to eat. Jessica shifts toward me and slides a plate in his direction. I read.

November 5, 08:00—Arrive at 322B Backer Avenue. Observed residence for twelve hours.

I look up. "You sat outside his house for twelve hours?"

"Surveillance," Jeff says around a mouthful.

"He's dead. What's there to surveil?"

Jessica clears her throat; slim arms and shoulders jerk beneath the long sleeves designed to cover her scars.

"Sorry." I reach a hand toward her. "I'm sorry."

Jeff coughs. "It's not uncommon for perpetrators to return to the scene of the crime."

November 6, 06:00—Began observation of Jared Holmes, resident at 322A Backer Avenue.

I flip the page. I flip the next page. "Why are you following Jared? For"—I flip the page—"six days?"

"He lives in closest proximity to the deceased."

"Is he a suspect?" I look toward Jessica. Her eyes are fixated on a floating bowl of something green in front of me. I pass it to her.

"I maintained surveillance on all of his associates."

"The entire department?" I close the folder. There are a few more pages, but this is not helpful. This is bad writing—a lack of rhetorical strategy and no discernible argument. What is your thesis? I would write at the bottom of the final page, above the C−. It deserves an F, but I wouldn't want to deal with the paperwork and the parents.

I hate Jeff's summary of Nathan's life, as if all he left behind are a studio apartment and a boring neighbor with a computer lab, a grocery store, and no responses to his dating profile. But at least Jared isn't totally alone. I take a sip of tequila. He has that naked cat and a caterpillar beneath his nose.

"Just his friends."

I put my drink on the table. "Nathan didn't have any friends."

Jeff looks up. He stops chewing. My fingers dig into the sides of the folder; tiny crescents press into the leather. He raises an eyebrow.

"You followed me?" The folder is against my chest, its edge pressed into my lap. "Where?"

"Wherever you went. Just for a few days."

"What the fuck, dude?" I almost shout, my voice and clothes disrupting the delicate dishes, the translucent table. Volume and profanity shatter this floating Gwyneth world.

"I told him he didn't need to," Jessica says to me. She has finished the small dish of green. "But he recommended we pursue all options."

"What option was I?" I clutch the file. "Jesus Christ, Jessica, you didn't even think someone killed him, and suddenly I'm a suspect?"

"You're not a suspect," Jeff says, eyes on mine. Jessica shakes her head.

"Then why—"

"It's not uncommon for perpetrators to maintain contact with connections to the victim."

Leaning forward, mouth open, eyes on him. *Fight or flight,* I lectured in Psychology 101, having learned the material twenty minutes before I taught it. *Freeze,* Therapist 1 and Therapist 2 explained in Fridays at Four. The most common response, but not sexy enough to make it into textbooks. That's why you didn't move. That's why you didn't fight back. You can always tell how sheltered someone is when they ask, "Why didn't you just run away?"

"What the fuck does that mean?"

"They may have been following you," Jessica says softly.

When you're home and you can't turn off the movie in your head. The swarm inside your brain. You want to call Clark or Mark just so you're not alone, but the edges of your vision collapse and the light around you expands and you can't breathe, because nothing makes sense and you're not sure if you'll ever breathe again, because you don't remember how, and, besides, after that thing, that terrible thing happened, what's the point in breathing anyway? No one survives that thing.

Jessica puts her hand on my arm. She nods over my shoulder, and a glass of water materializes to my left. I sip.

"I didn't tell you, because I didn't want to upset you," she says, watching me drink.

I breathe through my nose and exhale twice as slowly. Even if it was only Flopsy, the thought of being stalked instead of stalking is unsettling. Jeff reaches for another plate.

"Did you find out anything?" Jessica asks, when my breathing slows. Her eyes are softer than I've ever seen them. Sympathy for her brother's fucked-up friend. Like my high-school teachers after Dad died. Or Mrs. Sanghera when she saw me packing the truck and offered to look after the little black dog while I was at college and I said there was no little black dog. Not anymore. The buzzing fades, the edges recede, the lights retreat to their normal vibrancy. I see my reflection in Jessica's face and I remember how quickly I lose my footing, how close I am to the edge.

I finish the water. I didn't bring Flopsy's needle. I don't want Jessica to know about it. I don't want anyone but me to know about it. I shake my head.

"Anything." Jeff keeps his eyes on mine. He observes my movements. He sees my hands shake.

"What would you like to know?" I clear my throat and smile, as bright and vacant as a magazine cover. I put the folder in the center of the table. "What detail of my private life have you not uncovered?"

The side of his lip lifts.

Prick.

Jessica looks between the two of us. No doubt this note comparison isn't going as planned. "You never know what might be helpful." She smiles. Dad smiled like that, near the end. We'll go in the woods soon, he said from the bed. Tubes and wires running through him, so pale he blended in with the sheets. I'll be out of here, don't worry. And I gave him the same smile. Neither of us knowing if we were lying for ourselves or for each other, but both of us knowing we were lying.

"Even some detail? Something you noticed around campus?" Her voice wavers, almost cracks. A lifetime of performance that only an addict can master. "You said you broke into a house."

Jeff doesn't blink. I cough, even though the air is clear here. Filtered and smooth, and I would forget that the real world is burning if it weren't for my clothes, my skin, my hair. Some of us can never escape reality. "I thought I had someone, but I don't think so."

Her eyes get brighter. Her lips press together. "Well, thank you for coming down."

"We could reconvene in a week if you find something." Jeff speaks with his mouth full. "How's next Friday?"

"I'm busy on Fridays."

"Too busy to figure out who killed your buddy?"

Jeff, you absolute thunder cunt.

"Fridays are rape-therapy days." I pull a tray of something cubic in front of me and pierce it with my fork. "But most other days should be fine."

Jeff stops chewing. Jessica stares at her water glass. The slim curve of ice. "Why do you go to rape therapy?" he asks.

"Free toaster oven." I pop the square into my mouth. Guess he didn't follow me there.

Jeff taps a finger against the table. Jessica looks at him. She shakes her head.

"What?" I ask.

He opens the folder. Jessica shifts in her chair.

"I'm surprised, that's all."

I jab something pink and soft with my fork. "Guess I don't look the part." I stick the pink thing in my mouth, and close my eyes as I chew. Delicious. No idea what it is.

"How long have you been going?"

"Shouldn't you know that?" I finish my tequila. My eyes are heavy, and my stomach is warm. Maybe I'll sleep in tomorrow. Take

Dog to the beach. Tonight, I will dream about breaking into the house. Carving out Flopsy's throat. Carving something else out of his friend.

Jeff flips to the last page in the folder.

Jessica's eyes are wet, that soft shimmer Hollywood is so good at. Her head tilts to one side, the sympathy angle.

The cold burn of the expensive drink is hot now, rising from my stomach. The pink thing climbs back up. Her head is pulled back, her chin dipped. A defensive pose, to protect the throat. "Why are we talking about this?"

Jeff mutters to himself. Between us, hovering like bumblebees, the conversations of the other tables. References to a beach house, a screenplay, the new Dior collection. Whispers of unrelatable lives, incomprehensible in subject and volume.

"Sarah," Jessica whispers, her fingers almost touching mine.

Jeff hands me the folder, open to the last page. "I assume you know. You were his friend."

I take the folder, my eyes on cheekbones sculpted by genetics and heroin. A single tear down a perfect cheek.

I look at the last page of Jeff's stilted writing.

History cont'd:
- *Trust fund—$10 million in assets*

"Sarah." Jessica's voice reaches me. Her hand on mine, gentle as a bird.

- *Multiple instances of drug consumption—removed from record*
- *Multiple instances of aggression and resisting arrest—removed from record*

I move my hand away from hers.

- *SATs and transcripts adjusted in grades 11–12*
- *Multiple instances of plagiarism and delinquency—*
removed from record

"Sarah." This time a whisper, a plea. I reach the bottom of the page.

I look up. Two tears on her cheek. I look at Jeff. The smirk falls.

I can't understand the words, even as they are printed in front of me. I can't breathe, and I can't read, and what's the point? No one survives that thing.

- *Accusation of rape, age 17, by L. Martin, age 16, settled out of court—removed from record*

———

I don't know how I leave. Walking, I guess. Jessica tries to hold my hand like a boyfriend in a Korean drama. Jeff opens and closes his mouth. Maybe I run. The floating people in the expensive place, their fantasy lives and plastic faces fading behind me as I topple my chair, throw the folder to the ground, and sprint to my shitty truck, parked three streets down, in the cheapest lot I found.

Smoke streams through my vents, because even when I shut them they still let all this shit in. It swirls across my cheeks and down my throat. I guess I'm crying, because it stays there, coating the inside of me, the outside of me. The flames dance along the mountains to my right, past Thousand Oaks, Ventura, Carpinteria. I tear up 101, passing hybrids and Bentleys, someone texting, someone smoking. The outlets. The surf spots. The bridge that gets washed out every year. The winding road between flames and sea. The ocean black on my left, sometimes thirty feet down, sometimes hundreds of feet down.

If I had known, all those times we drove together, all those trips we took, if I had known, would I have driven us to the left or to the right? Off a cliff or into a mountain?

Asshole.

The smoke is thicker now. If I had known, would I have gotten into the car with him at all?

Cocksucker.

If I had known, would I have.

And there is no end to that sentence, because there is no end to all the things I would not have done.

I speed past a Lexus, swing into the oncoming lane, and swerve right as the blare of a horn rings past. My tires are smoking, or maybe that's just the air. My hands grip the wheel, slick and wet beneath my palms. The gun rack bangs against the rear windshield, loose and crooked and not designed for this place. The nights I spent in his room, blacked out on bottom-shelf tequila and a boxed-wine chaser, blitzed on E in his boxers and T-shirt, seated next to him, the door shut, the windows closed, no one around to intervene if he wanted to.

And there is no end to that sentence, because there is no end to all the things they get away with.

I'm north, past the traffic, more honking and swerving and a middle finger from a fourteen-wheeler as I overtake it on the shoulder, and I am on campus. I pull into the overlook, the bluffs beside the formal entrance with the big sign and the great view and the Engineering building behind it, the padded seats and espresso machines and job opportunities. I see overhead lights in distant rooms and shadows moving between buildings in my rearview mirror. I cut the engine and push open the door. I brace myself against the frame and lean out. The expensive dishes and fancy booze and sparkling water imported from Iceland splatter against the sand beneath me, and I wonder why rich people eat fancy things when it all turns to shit in the end.

I leave the door open and bash the overhead light off. Below, I hear voices, young and happy and probably stoned. Giggles waft upward, and I picture the freshmen and the sophomores, streaking perhaps, or skinny-dipping. Maybe equipped with professional, late-night dive gear, because there is a dive club at this university. You have to have your own equipment and be pre-certified to join. If you aren't, they recommend the sailing club. Students bring their own boats. The laughter from below. They sound happy.

I swallow. Razors in my throat. The smoke is less here, close to the water, or perhaps the sounds of waves and youth distract me enough so I don't think about how hard it is to breathe. Nathan, naked and still and a needle in his arm. The nausea surges again, and I lean my head back. Count like I'm supposed to, fingers in a chapel like I'm supposed to. Remember to breathe like I'm supposed to.

I picture the other him, who rings panic like a bell through my blood. Whose scent I know. A deer recognizes a man in orange. The crack of underbrush beneath his feet. The man on my back. And there is no difference between these two. One did to me what the other did to another. Maybe it was less painful for her. Maybe more so. Maybe people believed her. Maybe they didn't. Maybe she still dates, still loves. But the men are the same.

I'm always there, even as I am here, falling out of my truck in the dark, listening to the world's richest children splash in the oil-slicked sea. I'm always there, in that morning, standing in that bathroom. The blood and the shit and the pain and the fear and, above it all, the confusion. The party is over, the guests are gone. My body is broken, and he is replacing the coffee filter.

I hold my hand to my mouth to hold my insides in, so my body doesn't fall outside of my body, not again. I wipe tears from my face and wonder why there are still tears on my face. Shouldn't I be over it?

Before the bathroom, before the night that led to the bathroom, I saw him in the department. He was tall and slim and quiet. He slipped through the poorly funded hallways, head down, shy. His nice shoes and soft voice. He audited a class given by his adviser. He sat next to me. He was slouched and nervous, tapping one thin leg against another while the alphas pounded their chests. I remember my sympathy for him, for his discomfort and absence of place. The few times I saw him, his awkwardness and uncertainty elicited a protective response in me. Maternal, perhaps, the tingling in my breasts.

He's changed now. Stands straighter, walks faster. Eye contact. The years wear on and he grew up, found his place, got away with it. But before all that, I recognized impostor syndrome and disbelief, equal parts intimidation and exasperation at colleagues who showed no self-consciousness, who covered anxiety with noise. No room for criticism, no room for anyone. This is their defense. They shoved us down, pushed us out, louder and louder, so they never had to hear their mistakes. Feminist Carl. Ann with no "e." This is their protection. But those early years, Rapist and I sat quietly. Unobtrusiveness our shield. Shyness our armor. Silence and fear like the leaves on the trees beneath which we stood.

I wonder sometimes, late at night in the box, when the world sleeps and the flashbacks start, if he knew this about me. If he saw that I saw him, his weakened state. I never met him at parties, where, I am told, he is loud and drunk and aggressive, staring at women, standing too close. I did not know him in his home, friends with Flopsy, reading Schopenhauer's *On Women*. I see him now. He is those things. But back then, before he knew what he could get away with, before he knew how easy it was, he seemed so faint and flimsy in the hallways, hiding his height and stepping aside as the loud men pushed past. Back then, perhaps he noticed me watching. I saw his underbelly, so he decided to rip out mine.

I text the number that never texts back.

Was it funny? Knowing I didn't know?

Most nights, I lie in bed, ash in the air, Dog in the doorway. It is a pleasant story to help me sleep, this narrative of a misunderstood man. This past self of his, confused and delicate, made hard and cruel, made ugly. The villain's origin story.

I sit upright and wipe my cheeks. I remove my hand from my mouth and press it against the steering wheel. The bedtime story is pleasant, but the truth is not. I did not know him then. I do not know him now. Maybe he was quiet and shy and submissive. Maybe I did see his underbelly. Or maybe I walked into the trap he set, the light above his jaws.

> fuck you nathan

> fuck you

> fuck you

I stare at the dark that is the ocean. The sounds of the students beneath me, laughter and waves and a starless sky on America's most expensive coast. Even the ash is beautiful here, dancing across head-lights and flashlights and the bright white teeth of the eighteen-year-olds with their diving certifications and their sailboats. The fires seem far away, burning somewhere else, someone else.

The truth is, whether he saw me or not, whether he noticed or not, I didn't matter. I don't matter. I was within arm's reach. If he has an origin story, it was written long before me.

But in the night, when I cannot sleep and I cannot breathe and the flashes come, and the pills and the booze and even Nathan, curled behind my back, tears wet against my shirt, do not help, I tell myself the other version. The poignant one, in which we are both victims. The narrative is rich with complexity and compassion. The complicated antagonist. The sympathetic survivor.

It is a nicer story.

SABELLA FLEX, PROFESSOR of South Asian Studies, walks into Trader Joe's. She is shaking off her shawl and wheeling a small carry-on. Professor Flex does not carry things. Flakes of gray swirl around her skirt and sandals. She removes the shawl from her face. Professor Flex shops at the one store downtown that fits women larger than a size eight. She wrote a book twenty-three years ago.

I stand in the checkout line and avoid her gaze. My first year, I made an effort to say hello, introduce myself. Now I hide in a sea of yoga pants, shorts, young men with beer, and old men with wine. One row over, a fat baby stares at me. His mother is looking at her phone.

I reach for my wallet, spring in my step and space in my bowels. I pass the flower display outside the grocery store. Next to it, a hand-painted sign tells patrons that this grocery store does not allow homeless people near the entrance. Farther down the sidewalk, three homeless men sit.

My bag hangs on my shoulder. Next to Flopsy's evidence is one small envelope of K. I thought of taking some and calling Dan or Stan for a bounce. I thought of rubbing it across my gums and sitting behind the avocado tree, waiting for Rapist to come home, to make dinner, to climb into bed. Or letting it dissolve beneath my tongue on the lawn next to Elaine, Flopsy's needle in my box, thinking about what I want to do to him, to both of them. Maybe Elaine would tell me what she sees when she stares into the dark and her wife yells from her tower. Maybe I would see it, too.

Or maybe I'll save it for campus—snort a line and write "fuck you" across a certain name in the tunnel, watch the other names float in front of me.

I push the cart across the parking lot. My truck is bigger than the collection of electric vehicles, the white lines of the parking spaces wide on either side of them. The gun rack stares at me through my window. Jessica's drawing crosses my mind.

I open the passenger door and realize the Tesla next to me is too close.

"Dick," I mutter as I reach over the cart, push the door closed, and pull back.

"Hey."

I look up. Blond. Slim. Shorts, of course. Nice legs, but God forbid a Californian dress like an adult.

"Hey." I nod toward the Tesla. "This yours?"

He shakes his head. "No, I just wanted to see how you were doing."

I roll my eyes and continue backing up the cart. The older I get, the less pickup lines make sense.

He steps forward. "I'm Eric Hollis."

"Hi, Eric Hollis." I angle the cart and push it behind my truck. I round the other side, planning to load my groceries through the driver's side. A Prius is wedged next to the door. Where do these fuckers learn to park?

And he's there. On this side now.

I don't like when they do this, when they follow me or surprise me. That's why I use the apps. They don't know where I live, they don't know where to find me, but men are like buses, and when I want to hop on one, I know where to go. I glance around me. The sky clings to daylight. I pivot my body so the length of the grocery cart is between us.

"We met last week."

I shake my head. "No, we didn't."

"I came to your friend's house. When you called the police."

I lean closer. A classic eighties pop song dances through my head.

"The cop?"

He nods.

"You're in shorts."

He looks down at his legs, then back up at me. "I'm off duty."

The Tesla leaves. I push the cart to the front of the truck, past Rick Astley's doppelgänger, and pull out a paper bag. I carry it to the passenger side and fish out my keys.

He's behind me. My other grocery bag in his arms.

"What are you doing?"

"Helping."

"Why?"

He blinks.

I place my bag on the floor and step back. He moves forward and places his bag inside with care. "These are the eggs."

"OK."

He brings both his hands to his sides. We look at each other.

"Did you need something?" I already gave my follow-up report. A brisk woman with a lisp called me, and I answered her questions.

He shakes his head. "No, but I saw you coming out of the store." He pauses. "I just wanted to see how you're doing."

I look back at him, this strange, kind creature in—I glance down—Crocs with socks. Jesus Christ, Eric, you're worse than I am.

"Nathan is still dead," I say, eyes on his feet. "And you don't know what happened, right?" I smile. I know what happened.

"Well..." That pause, the drawn-out vowel, taking up time so he doesn't have to say the thing I don't want to hear.

"He didn't do heroin." I shut the passenger door. He jumps slightly. "Someone stuck that needle in his arm." It sounds ridiculous. A desperate woman defending a desperate man. I have a flash of empathy for Flopsy's mother, the hoops she must jump through to keep her son out of prison, to believe him when he says, again, he didn't do it. And besides, what do I care about Nathan anyway? Flopsy may have done it for the wrong reason, but that doesn't mean he didn't deserve it. Coincidences, the New Age Buddhists like to tell me, are the universe making things right. I can't believe I'm saying this but, in this instance, those morons might be right.

"We're still working on the report."

I walk around the front of the truck and retrieve the cart. He meets me there and holds his hands up. Maybe he's worried I'm going to run him over.

"I just wanted to see how you're doing," he repeats.

"You said that."

He takes a deep breath. "I read your report."

"Aren't you writing the report?"

"Your other report."

Maybe I will run him over. My voice is low and hoarse, but it has nothing to do with the ash in the air. I clutch the round bar of the shopping cart. "What?"

"I'm on your case," he says, voice soft.

"That's not part of this case."

"It's important we know who our witnesses are." Those eyes. Eighties pop-star realness.

"I'm not a witness. I didn't see anything."

"As the first person at the scene, you're part of the investigation, so—"

"What the fuck does that have to do with—" I can't bring myself to say it. Not because it isn't relevant. It's a crime, and he's a cop. Not because I'm worried I'll lose my audience when I say the word. Not because I've internalized the messaging that it was my fault, and it wasn't a big deal—boys will be boys. But because raped women don't always want to talk about rape. We don't always want to think about rape. We don't care that you've read an article or learned a statistic or it happened to your sister and you're deep into your feelings. Sometimes, we just want to buy groceries, walk the dog, read bell hooks, and feel really good about taking a dump in a douchebag's bed.

He holds his palms out by his sides. Soothing and docile. Burritos thaw on the hot floor of my old truck, and something shimmers between us. I am a nervous animal, and he is letting me know his presence. He knows, so I don't have to tell him. He read the report, so I don't have to say anything.

I glance at the sky. The sun slides behind gray toward the coast. "I have to go." He nods. "I don't like being out after dark," I say. Even the parking lot of a grocery store, with the red carts and the potted plants, frightens me. I want to drag the display inside and protect the flowers from things that go creep in the night. That's another reason I hop on the Bills and Phils. As long as I'm on top, clear view to the door, it's better than being alone. "It was nice seeing you again, Officer Hollis."

"Eric. Detective Hollis, but just Eric."

He does look like Rick Astley, a face so sweet that singing alone in a trench coat beneath a bridge at night isn't terrifying. "Do you have a card, Eric?"

He looks surprised, but reaches into his back pocket and pulls out a wallet. "Sure." He hands it to me. "If you need anything . . ." He smiles, shy and earnest. "Or if you just . . ."

I look to the sky again. I was out after dark after the Welcome Reception, Flopsy dripping down my neck. The week before, too, dropping off—

No. Enough. I'm not thinking about him anymore.

I open my mouth, but the gentle man with the childish clothes speaks, softer than before. "I'm sorry, by the way."

I blink.

"About what happened to you." There is a slight head tilt, a hint of sympathy, but it doesn't bother me. It feels less a preprogrammed response to a socially uncomfortable situation and more a natural reaction. The sound we make when we pick up a fussing baby. The sound I made when Jessica cried. He takes a step back, hands on my empty cart, and rolls it away, across the lot and into the square marked for returns. He waves, then pauses to let a woman go past. He continues to the end of the concrete, where it dips and becomes parking for a gluten-free, vegan pet-food store, to his own car, simple and small and blue. He drives off.

And all the while, I am standing. Burritos in the truck. Eric's words in my ears. The words I wanted to hear for three years. Not the right man, not the guilty man, but a man nonetheless. It makes no sense that they matter, coming from him, that they mean anything. I look at his card. Detective Eric Hollis. Santa Teresa Police Department. I tuck it into my bag, next to the baggie and the journal. It feels heavier now, three men on my shoulder.

I start the engine and head back to the box. Smoke intensifies as I reach the highway. I squint against the orange, the gray, the red. The eggs fall when an Aston Martin blows past and I slam on the brakes. I rearrange the bag, one hand on the wheel.

I open the garage. Dog cries. The scent of hunger and urine and an old, neglected body. A note from Empress, taped to the inside of my door. I need to start parking at the bottom of the driveway. The sound of my engine disrupts her sleep. Elaine will come by tomorrow morning. She will linger near my truck and wait for me to appear. She will remind me to park down below, remind me to protect her sleeping wife.

I let Dog out. I fill her water, fill her food. I stack my burritos, my eggs, my milk inside the minibar fridge. The sun is setting, and the box gets darker. I step outside and sit on the bench next to the garage. The moon, the stars, the view. All the things I cannot see. I open a beer. Dog sits at my feet.

In my ears ring his perfect words.

———

I pull into a professor's parking spot behind the Humanities building. I sit in my truck. Friday. Three-thirty in the afternoon. A short, fat man from my department hurries across the parking lot. Fourth-year by the looks of it: he has the haunted expression of someone approaching his qualifying exams. I open my laptop and review my bibliography. I think of the needle. Colette has the entire draft, but I cannot send it to the rest of my committee until I have her feedback. I email Colette. I tell her she will have the edits for her own paper by the end of the weekend.

Fourth Year opens the doors to the Humanities building. Eyes frantic. A pile of notecards, four inches thick, gripped in his chubby fist. Don't worry, I want to say. No one cares about your qualifying exams. They don't qualify you for anything anyway.

I close my bibliography and prepare a cover letter for another job application. I am in the triple digits now. All I can muster is a search-and-replace on names, addresses, and course titles. My pile of statements has been "saved as" so many times I need to upgrade my Dropbox subscription.

I check my campus email. I look for a message from Raymond. An excuse for why he didn't show up the other day. I scroll down and see an old email from Na—

No.

It's quarter to four. I put my computer into my bag, silently wish Fourth Year good luck, and climb down from my truck. I walk across the parking lot, down the sloping bike path, and into the tunnel. More a cappella. Vegan Thanksgiving protest. Slut March. I pass the names. I don't count them. I don't read them. I know where his—

No.

I walk to the Women's Center.

We take our seats. We shuffle our bags. We silence our phones.

Breathing exercises. Updates. The awkward silence as Therapist 1 and Therapist 2 wait for someone to start.

"My rapist is dead," Junior says. We turn to her. I glance at Chemistry, who looks at Lanky, who chews her gum.

"I mean"—she shakes her head—"the guy who attacked me. He's dead. I found out this morning."

Therapist 2 looks at Therapist 1.

"How are you feeling?" Therapist 1 asks. Chemistry slides the box of tissues across the low table in the middle of our circle.

Junior opens her mouth. Closes it. The circle is silent. We don't usually speak about death.

"I feel like I'm to blame," she says. She grips one hand with the other, presses them against her knees.

My eyebrows crawl toward my hairline. Junior is small and quiet. Her top sparkles. An excellent anglerfish.

One of the sophomores leans forward. "Girl, what did you do?"

Therapist 2's pen begins to shake. Therapist 1 takes a long, slow breath.

Junior shakes her head. "Nothing." Her chin quivers. "But I wanted to."

Everyone in the room nods.

Therapist 2 looks at Therapist 1 again. I glance away when she catches my eye. She's in training. My life revolves around textual analysis and semantic derivation. I can't imagine a career like hers. Doing work that actually matters. An article no one will read doesn't get written? A class no one is paying attention to is more boring than usual? Fine. Coming to work and hearing a raped woman tell you she wants to kill a man? That's, like, a real job.

"Or maybe I didn't want to kill him, but I wanted him . . ."

"To go away," Freshman says, "and never come back."

Junior nods, eyes bright. "To remove him from the world."

"I want to kill mine." Lanky pops her gum. "Every time I see those fuckers walking around, I think, 'You don't deserve to be walking around. You don't have the right.'" She shrugs. "I'd kill them both if I could get away with it."

"It's natural to feel anger," Therapist 1 says.

"Yeah." Lanky adjusts her position, draping long limbs down the sides of her chair. "But I'd also like to kill them, so they can't do it again, but also to know that I did it." She pauses and tilts her head. "I think it would feel fair. Like, you got yours, now I get mine."

Therapist 2 clears her throat. Her foot bounces. School didn't prepare me for this, she's probably thinking. Oh, child. School doesn't prepare you for anything.

"My friend is dead," I say. Fuck. Of course I bring him up.

"Your rapist?" Chemistry asks. Her rapist is dead. Junior's rapist is dead. I guess it's natural she'd think there was a theme.

I shake my head. "I wasn't friends with my rapist."

"Lucky," someone mutters.

"Did you kill him?" Freshman asks. She smiles.

"No, but . . ." I shrug. "Police are investigating." Maybe. Maybe I wish someone killed him. Maybe someone did and it doesn't matter. Maybe he deserved it. I choke on a laugh. Maybe I owe Flopsy a thank-you.

Therapist 2 shifts in her seat, her movements tight. Wow. Rape, death, and now murder? You sure are earning your class credits today.

"How do you feel?" someone across the circle asks me.

"I'm sad." The tears almost spill. I clear my throat. "How do you feel?" I ask Junior.

"I don't know. Like, I'm glad he's gone, but I'm . . ." She looks down at her hands, then up at all of us. "I hadn't even processed the rape, you know, and now I've got to process this? And my friends are saying to me, 'Oh, isn't this great? Karma's a bitch.' And I don't know. Is this how karma works? Do rapists deserve to die?"

No, the Buddhologist in me wants to say. No, this is not how karma works. As for the second question . . .

"When I found out mine was dead, it didn't affect me." Chemistry pauses. "Well, it didn't help me. My friends thought I would feel better. His friends thought I should forgive him." She shrugs.

Blue raises her hand.

"Did you have something to say?" Therapist 1 asks.

"What?" Blue puts her hand down. "No, I was just adding my name to the Rapists Deserve to Die list."

"I'd add my name to that list." Quiet Freshman speaks.

"I wouldn't," one of the sophomores says. She looks shocked. "How would that make anything better?"

"Studies show most rapists are repeat offenders," Lanky says. "Can you think of another way to stop them?"

Sophomore closes her mouth.

I press my lips together. Two days after the rape, when my course grade depended on my presentation of Foucault and an analysis of his panopticon, I took six Advils and lined my underwear with extra-long, overnight pads. I ignored the bleeding and the prolapse and spoke around the razors. Flopsy was in that room. Feminist Carl was in that room. I wasn't nervous. I stood and I spoke and interrupted the loud men who interrupted me. I stood outside myself and did what I was trained to do. It's amazing, really, when you know how to be still in the cold and the wet and the dark, when the rain falls and the wind blows and the centipedes crawl over your boots and up your pant leg, that you can be still in a different sort of storm, with a different sort of insect. Around me, the women debate the ethics of killing rapists, their own or the demographic as a whole. I am still in the rain and the wind. My brain active. My body silent.

Another way to examine the question, I would interject if this were a class, is through agency. Do Rapists Deserve to Die? Or: Do Rapists Deserve to Be Killed? The former is noncausative. Rapists are mortal beings. Mortal beings die. Ergo, all rapists die. Whether mortal beings and, by definition, rapists, are deserving of death is a question of mortality, not morality.

The latter question is causative. To kill means to make something dead. The use of the passive voice anonymizes the killer. If rapists deserve to be killed, someone or something is required to do the killing. Thus, the question actually has two parts: (a) Do rapists deserve to be killed? and (b) Who deserves to kill them?

But this is not a classroom, and I do not interject.

"The Title IX office told me it was too late for me to read my report," Junior continues.

Chemistry nods. "That happened to me. Something about privacy laws and protecting the people involved."

"But I was the person involved," Junior says, "so who are they protecting?"

"Who do you think?" Blue asks.

No one knows how Title IX works. You get raped, you go there. It doesn't do anything, and it doesn't make you feel better, but the administrators, the RAs, the department chairs, they all want you to go there so they can check the due-diligence form on their conscience. Title IX has their own words. Respondent. Complainant.

Responsible. A preponderance of evidence. Fifty percent plus a feather.

Except it doesn't work that way. There isn't enough evidence. Everyone was at the party, but only two were in the room. Even in public. Even on videotape. The respondent says the complainant wanted it. She says she didn't. Where is the feather? I think of holding the lower inch of my intestine inside my body. The feather, one assumes, is the blood and the shit and the insides hanging outside. Some people love pain, and accidents happen. Technically, how can I prove I didn't want it?

I am still, but my brain is moving. L. Martin. I wonder if L. Martin knew—

No.

"One report isn't enough. They want a pattern of behavior." Blue shrugs. "You gotta go full Cosby to get anywhere."

"My trial"—Chemistry uses two hands to mimic quotation marks—"was through the school. The student discipline committee or something."

We nod.

"And on that committee were a bunch of freshmen, and they're, like, seventeen and just trying to get a better résumé for law school or something, and I'm sitting there, listening to the testimony of the rapist, and it's . . ."

"A joke?" Lanky asks.

Chemistry nods and looks at Junior. "But at least he's dead, so he can't do it again. If that helps?"

"My rapist is a member of the Student Safety Squad," one of the sophomores says. "Those volunteers you call if you want someone to walk you home from the library at night, you know, so you don't get raped? He's on that."

"Dude."

"Well, I just want to read my report," Junior says. "I think I should have that right."

"Break in. KKKathy keeps her passwords underneath her phone." Blue pops her gum.

Quiet Freshman says, "My cousin works as a janitor. They have master keys to every room on campus."

Therapist 2 looks at Therapist 1, who says, "Well, now, let's not—"

"He said the keys with the yellow base open all the outside doors—"

Therapist 1 puts down her pen. "I don't think—"

"—and the blue ones open the office doors."

"I don't want to get a janitor in trouble," Junior says.

Therapist 2's eyes widen. Looks like breaking and entering is another subject not covered by her training.

"Just borrow them. Bring them back after you—"

"OK!" Therapist 1 drops her notepad on the central table from a higher-than-usual position. The slap echoes in the small room.

"When did you find out about your friend?" Sophomore turns to me.

"Two weeks." The storm rages. "I think."

"And you?" Chemistry looks to Junior.

"This morning," she says. "I got an email from the RA. They found him after a party." She looks at us. "You'll all get that email, you know, later today."

We know.

"Was your friend Nathan?" Sophomore asks. "From the last email?"

I nod.

"He was my TA for Writing." She smiles. "He was really nice."

Therapist 1 clears her throat. We pack up and rearrange chairs, shuffle out and shut doors. Chemistry puts her hand on Junior's shoulder and whispers something in her ear. Junior nods. Chemistry turns to me and tilts her head. I follow. We walk into the tunnel.

We stand in front of the names. Chemistry opens her bag and

takes out a red Sharpie. She traces the "fuck you" next to a name on last year's list. She hands the pen to Junior. She leans close to the wall, writes a name below Nathan's. She drops her arm, then leans forward again, and across the name, she writes "rapist" in bold, stiff lines. She stands back. She gives the pen to Chemistry.

"Raymond Philips?" I ask. "Tall guy? Brown hair?"

Junior nods.

"He was supposed to come to my office hours."

"Glad he didn't."

"Do you want to write your friend's name down?" Chemistry holds out the pen.

"It's already on there."

"Do you want to write anything else?"

miss you

love you

fuck you

rapist

I shake my head.

She puts her hand on Junior's shoulder, and they walk out, past the names, the a cappella, into the gray.

I remain in the tunnel. Still in the storm.

———◆———

I pull my shirt over my mouth and lean against my truck. Five-fifteen. No one teaches after six, so the hallways will be empty soon. Flopsy is probably gone, back to his boring room and brand-new clothes. Rapist might be in the building if he's avoiding his bed-room. Less than an hour of daylight left. I could call Eric and report the needle, come up with a reason for why I was in the house (Girl Scout cookies?). I could call Jessica, and she could call Frederick. I tap my phone against the driver's-side window. I could snort five lines of the white powder inside the baggie inside Nathan's journal. Across the quad, KKKathy walks toward me, the hair and the march unmistakable. I think about what Freshman said, about the keys.

I have never read Rapist's report. I tried, but KKKathy told me the report was closed. I was too late. The first time I went into her office, I handed her a printed page, outlining details of what I could remember. Descriptions of the postcards. Everything except his name. KKKathy told me that, without a name, there was nothing they could do. She huffed when she said this, as if I were wasting her time.

I told KKKathy my department had eight graduate students a year. If I reported a rape with names attached, everyone would know. KKKathy shrugged. We'll keep this on record, but there's nothing we can do. She emphasized the "can" rather than the "nothing." It was my fault, after all.

I thought it happened between strangers or creepers or men you had a feeling about. Not the quiet nerdy ones, all skinny legs and shy eyes with nice shoes from South America. Not the ones in my own department, the ones who held the door open. It didn't make sense. I went to Title IX because, the third time I burst into tears in Colette's office, she told me I needed to make sure he didn't do this again. I was trying to have it both ways. Stop him from doing it again. Deny he had ever done it.

When I told her the name, KKKathy read the report in front of me. She wanted to make sure the details were correct. She pressed a tissue to her chest as she read. It was hard not to stare. I thought it was odd, a plunging V-neck in an office that exists to penalize people who notice plunging V-necks. Perhaps I was committing a Title IX offense. Perhaps I was looking for a distraction while she read aloud "prolapse."

We look for patterns, she said.

But what if I'm the first? I asked.

Then we can keep his name on file. When another person comes forward, we can compare her story to yours. That's how we find the pattern.

In science, two events can be considered a pattern, but no self-respecting researcher would rely on two. Depending on context, you would observe until you had several, a dozen, perhaps hundreds. The full Cosby. But that's research. KKKathy never specified how it worked in Title IX.

It was silly, really, thinking I could have it both ways. My father taught me better than that. Mrs. Sanghera taught me better than that. There were interviews. Rapist found out that I knew. Flopsy found out that I knew. Hallway whispers grew, rooms silenced when I entered. There was no point, of course. It just made everything worse. But I did my due diligence when I came back from fieldwork. I thought there would be a pattern by the time I came back, but there were only rumors. Another woman, over in Anthropology, who quit before her qualifying exams, but scientists can't rely on rumors.

I tap my phone against my truck. I have thirty minutes of daylight to take Freshman's knowledge about janitor keys and further my reputation as a troubled young woman. I'm not interested in Rapist's report. When you're involved in the crash, you don't listen to the broadcast. But I found Flopsy's needle. I read Nathan's diary. Title IX is where women go to record men like Flopsy. My hands shake. If I want to do the thing I want to do, maybe I should read the records of his violence, listen to the survivors of his crashes, make sure my aim is steady.

"I need to leave here." I speak the words to a man who is no longer alive, who I would not speak to if he were. KKKathy walks past. She does not look at me. It is my seventh year with these people. Dad told me to stay in school. The Vice Principal told me to stay in school. Education is the key, she said. You can do anything, he said.

The panic attacks, the routine in the box. I used to think my brain was warning me. Rapist and Flopsy and Colette, Feminist Carl and KKKathy and Ann with no "e." I used to think my brain wanted to keep me downwind. Now I wonder if my brain isn't keeping me from them but, rather, them from me. They do not recognize my scent, because they do not understand what I am, what I am good at. Buffered from the cruelty of the world, they do not pause before walking into the clearing. They do not know what a sightline is. They do not know they are standing in mine.

OPTION A

- your friends know
- your family knows
- your colleagues know
- the police don't do anything or
- the police do something and it doesn't matter
- the law doesn't work
- neither consent, nor lack of consent, can be proved, but the arc of legality assumes you wanted it
- he says you wanted it
- you can't prove you didn't want it
- even if you die, "sex games gone wrong" is a common homicidal defense
- he's done it before
- he'll do it again
- one rape isn't enough
- two rapes isn't enough
- patterns of rapes must be found
- but he'll avoid jail, produce movies, become president
- if he only rapes a few women, that's not really rape
- at least, not rape that counts
- it's your fault
- you deserved it
- boys will be boys
- his friends protect him
- his family protects him
- colleagues and professors and legislation protect him
- this is what they do
- you are not safe
- you never were

OPTION B

- sometimes women lie

DID YOU GUYS TAKE HIS COMPUTER?"

Eric stops, one hand on the back of the chair across from mine. He's not in his police uniform. Or his children's clothes. He is wearing a clean button-down. I wonder if he uses fabric softener. He looks like someone who uses fabric softener.

"I thought you said you didn't want to talk about the case."

I shrug.

His eye contact. Calm. Steady. Reminds me of an old horse. "I can't talk to you about any of that." He pauses. "Or any evidence associated with it."

I bet he smells like lavender. His shirt, at least.

"And I'm not the lead, so if you have questions, you'd be better off talking to—"

"I didn't call you to talk about the case." I nudge his chair with my foot, Flopsy's needle in my bag. "Forget I mentioned it."

He remains standing. "Can I get you a drink?"

I'm tempted to tell him no, because I know what happens when men buy women drinks, but my net worth is negative six figures, and if beggars can't be choosers, then people in my situation can't do shit. "Tequila over ice, extra lime, salted rim. Please."

He walks to the bar. He stands behind two young men. Philosophy majors probably, just turned twenty-one. Think they've really gone off the grid by discovering this place. They probably have a pact not to mention it to anyone else, in case it gets ruined by people just like them. Deep down, everyone is a colonizer.

Eric returns, with a double for me, thank God, and a beer for him. He balances a tray of chips and salsa on both glasses. I imagine him as a teenager, waiting tables to save for college, coming home late, and letting the dog out before he goes to bed, careful not to wake his parents. I wonder if he's had eighties icon hair all his life.

"How are you doing?" He asks it just like Nathan used to. Serious. Waiting. It comforts me, and I hate that.

"Fine."

The world does not teach us how to handle sensitive men. Those eyes. You can't help but be honest.

"I am sorry his death causes you so much pain."

"Well . . ." I shift in my seat. "Maybe it shouldn't." Christ, now I'm asking for it. "Where did you grow up, Eric?"

He puts the tray on the edge of the table, lifts my drink, and places it on a small white napkin in front of me. "Albuquerque."

I slide a napkin to his side of the table. "Parents?"

"Single mom." He smiles. "The bartender was convinced you wanted a margarita."

"I would never order a margarita."

He laughs like I'm funny. He puts the chips in the middle, places three containers of salsa around them. "You?"

"Me what?"

"Parents?"

"Not anymore."

"Oh, I'm sorry." He reaches across the table. He lays a hand, palm up, next to my glass. I stare, just for a second. It looks like a trap, or the hand of a dead man, stretched toward me. Holding hands isn't something I usually do. I put my hand on his, my fingers over his wrist, the soft beat of his blood. Behind him, the Philosophy children get louder.

"There's another bar down the road," he says, when I look over his shoulder and scowl at the undergraduates. "I've heard they do good drinks."

I shake my head.

He squeezes my hand and lets go. "You don't like that bar?"

I swallow a mouthful of chips, partially chewed and painful as they go down. "I've been there before." My fingers tingle from where he touched me, from where I touched him.

He waits.

He does remind me of Nathan. And Dad. And Rick Astley. Three men no longer, or ever, in my life. But I didn't call him because of Nathan, to ask questions about Flopsy and murder and what evidence counts in court. I didn't call him because of daddy issues or a celebrity fantasy.

Maybe I called him because I wanted a distraction. Because I am heartbroken. Because I am lonely and too sad to hook up. Because I spent all weekend thinking about the tunnel and editing Colette's paper and wondering will I ever be done, will I ever be free, and what would that even mean? Western philosophy debates the nature of freedom—can a person be free, or are we only ever free from something? Is freedom a blank slate or a forward focus? I used to think that was just semantics, but now I'm not so sure.

Or, maybe, a man gave a woman his number. She called him. Normal people on a normal night. Dating, it would seem. Another thing I haven't done in a long time.

"That bar"—I wipe my hands on my jeans—"is popular with my department."

"And you like your privacy?"

"That's where Flopsy attacked Arjun."

His eyebrows go up. "Who's Flopsy?"

"A guy in the department. Flopsy strangled him, right in the middle of the bar." I push the chips toward him. "It's also where a bunch of colleagues told me Flopsy raped his girlfriend when they started dating, and again when they stopped."

His hand, reaching for the basket, hovers. "Your colleagues talk about that?"

"Oh, yeah."

His nostrils flare. "Is he in jail?"

I choke on a chip. I grin.

He waits.

"Flopsy is not in jail." I sip my tequila, cold and crisp and perfect. "He's finishing this year. Looking at jobs. His mom got him an interview." I put the glass back on the napkin. My hand shakes. "She's a bigwig at Google."

Eric blinks. I guess this is a lot. Or not. My department has stripped me of my perspective on appropriate human behavior.

"How's the girlfriend?" He pauses. "How are you?"

"She quit. Works in a nonprofit, I heard, somewhere in Boston." I tap my glass. "I'm fine."

"I'm sorry," he says again, like he means it, like he wishes he could make it better or make it all go away. Dad, seated next to me in the kitchen, algebra and Shakespeare from the private school spread across the table, gas lamps glowing. I needed help and he couldn't help me. He was sorry, too.

I smile. It doesn't reach my eyes, but it reaches another part of me. The part that learned Dad didn't read well, didn't understand numbers well, but sat with me, night after night. The part that appreciates the effort. Motivation is more important than outcome, Buddhist sutras say. I eat another chip.

"Well." Eric sips his beer. "I guess you don't go to that bar anymore."

"I guess not." I shake crumbs from my shirt. One drop of beer hovers on his lower lip, glistens in the bar light. A tongue, firm and slow and surprisingly pink, sneaks out. I let out a slow breath. I shouldn't have brought up Flopsy. I don't want him or his friend in this room. I don't want them anywhere. "What's it like being a cop?"

"I like it."

I lick the rim and take another sip, the cold burn of top-shelf liquor. The drink hits me, warm and thick through my belly. He smiles, and my breath catches. It has nothing to do with Flopsy. All the men on all the apps, and my breath never catches. Even my orgasms are perfunctory.

I want to laugh. Tell a joke. Something crackles between us, and I want to kill it. If Nathan were here, we'd make eye contact and head for the door. He'd describe Eric as a character out of an after-school special. I'd call him a Boy Scout. We'd pass out on his floor while Blanche, Dorothy, Rose, and Sophia made sex jokes over cheesecake.

If Nathan were here, I wouldn't do any of those things. Not anymore.

I tell Eric about Maine. He tells me about New Mexico. It snows there, which surprises me. Maine has sand dunes, which surprises him. Our words are casual and calm. I realize I am leaning closer. His fingers caress my knuckles.

"Do you want another?" He points to my glass, and of course I've finished it.

I shake my head. I feel like I've witnessed a magic trick and want to know how he did it. "You're very flirty, Eric."

"You called me." Eyes on mine in that calm, steady way. Darker now, after the beer, from brown to black. "And I'm the one who could get in trouble."

"Sorry about that."

"Sometimes it's worth getting in trouble."

People laugh around us. Swig drinks. Crunch chips. A bachelorette party staggers in. That's rare. In a town defined by wineries, dive bars attract a different crowd.

He is quiet, his hand on the curve of the bottle. I should tell him. The needle, the journal, the phone. I should tell him how much I steal. And the clues: $25,000 a month coming in and going out. LMC LLC. He doesn't need to know about Nathan, but he can know Flopsy is a suspect. He can do his cop thing. Or Jessica can do her family thing. I can't tell both. Eric's earnest, law-abiding eyes, and Jessica's, dark and desperate, with hot Frederick behind her. These worlds can never cross.

Eric is smiling. His shirt is open, just one button. Enough for me to see the tiny indent at the base of his throat. A dimple, I used to call it, when I was younger and men's bodies were mysterious. It's been a long time since I noticed someone's dimple.

There is another option. The option of not doing either. The option of running my tongue along the base of his throat, discovering his scent, his taste. The option of letting it all go, Nathan, Rapist. Leave Flopsy to his mother and Jessica to her drawings.

"How long have you been here?" Eric smooths the corners of the napkin beneath his bottle.

"Seven years."

"Why?"

"Ph.D.'s take a long time."

"No, I mean"—he concentrates on the napkin—"why stay?"

Because education is the key. Because the cycle of poverty can be broken. Because Dad wanted me to have everything, but, near the end, knew I would have only myself.

His fingers still. He looks up.

I open my mouth, I start to make a joke, but his eyes are clear. He's not waiting to speak. He's actually listening. I cough and angle my glass, roll the edge along the tabletop. Now my fingers are busy and my eyes are down. "We don't all have the same options in life." Ann with no "e." Vegan and his iPads. The students with the latest phones and apartments off campus. The years of applying for scholarships, tending bar and waiting tables, writing illegal papers and cleaning houses, while others have family vacations and unpaid internships. Not that this is unique to academia, but academia is where I live. "This was the best of what was available to me."

He lifts his beer and clinks it softly against my glass. "Here's to doing our best."

His dimple moves inside the soft hollow at the opening of his shirt. I cross my legs and pull my phone out of my bag. I ignore the needle, the journal, the other phone. Everything I should show him. Everything I won't show him. The sun is down. "Well, thanks for the drink." I shift my weight in my seat. "It was nice to chat."

"Thanks for the company." He smiles again. Always smiling, this one. "I'm glad you called."

"I'm going to head out." I shift farther forward.

"Can I walk you to your car?"

"OK." We stand. He puts five dollars on the table. His beer, only half drunk, remains. "Do you want to finish that?" I ask, the way poor people do.

He shakes his head and walks to the door, holds it open. We step into the evening, warm and gray and dark.

Over his shoulder, I catch the eye of one of the Philosophy majors. The kid is young, probably not even allowed in here. He smiles at me. He thinks this is a date. Maybe it is. I look back at Eric and realize how close he is, how much taller he is than me. This man was born in the desert, but now lives near the beach. He seems happy. Maybe he loves it. I could never have loved it, no matter how hard the Beach Boys and Katy Perry tried to convince me. I am a woodland creature, born in the deep and the green.

I could never have loved it, but I wonder if I could have liked it, if I could have built something, even for a short while. My students, so often brilliant and hilarious. The reading, the writing. Even the discussions, when I can get a word in, when bravado fades and neurosis calms and we actually engage with the material. There was a time when I was doing what I wanted to do, when I thought what I was doing would lead me somewhere safe and Dad would have been happy. But that was before the razors and the debt and the realization you can work on something for close to a decade and come away with nothing, less than nothing. Time, money, age. Throw in everything you have, but some holes never fill.

The light turns, the little green man appears. I let Eric take my hand and we walk across the street, the beach to our right. It's been years since I walked along the beach. Maybe I would hate this town less if I did more hand-holding and beach strolling. Or maybe that's another bedtime story, one about self-actualization and the power of positive thinking.

We reach the other side, and he looks into my eyes. Again the smile. It makes me want to cry. I want to pull my sixteen-year-old self aside and say to her: This is who you should spend time with. Not the fancy kids inside the school your dad can't afford, or the angry kids whose fathers can afford even less. Just find someone nice.

The air is clearer near the water. The wind is stronger, and the palm trees swish in the night. Twenty-two percent contained. We pass a couple walking in the other direction. Hand in hand.

"This is me."

I slide the bag down my shoulder and reach for my keys. Ignore the needle. His fingers find my cheek, tuck a strand of hair behind my ear. He leans forward. His lips, as light as butterflies, press against mine.

"Would you like to see me again?"

I nod. Silent. Terrified of the thing awakening inside of me, the thing that is so much more than sex. Life is easier when it stays asleep.

"Great." The tips of his ears turn pink. "What are you doing this weekend?"

"Cross-referencing my appendices."

He finds that funny. "Want to take a break sometime?"

I nod. He nods. We stand there nodding. If this were a movie, someone in the audience would scream at us to make out already. He pulls me to him, no kissing, just a warm body against my own, then lets go and crosses the street. He waves before the little man turns red, and walks into the night.

I open my truck door and climb inside. I pull out my phone and text the number I promised myself I'd never text again.

> I just had a date

> A real one

> I want to tell you all about it

> I hate you

> I wish you weren't dead

———◆———

Jessica has left five voice messages. Ann with no "e" texts. She wants to practice her interview questions, and since we're applying for the same job, it could be fun. I look through Nathan's phone. The goat farm on his Instagram makes little videos set to music. I send out three more job applications, to schools I've never heard of, in places I don't want to go. I leave Colette a voicemail.

Eric meets me downtown on Monday, we go for a walk on the beach, the way I read about when I was a teenager. At some point, he reaches over, the hand on the cheek, the lips on the cheek, and I turn and the lips are on the lips and the hands are on the body and we're doing things that people sing about and make movies about, things I've done so often, but it's different this time. The warmth, the breath, the smooth, soft movements.

We repeat this. On the beach on Tuesday, next to my truck on Thursday, even up in the fields owned by the billionaire on Saturday. I give him my address and the code to get in the main gate, the code to get in the house gate, and he drives up the mountain, waves at Empress on her perch. We trek with Dog through the fields and the cows and watch two coyotes in the distance, trotting away, in step one with the other. He says we should go see a movie on Friday, and I say I'd rather stay in. He says we can watch something at his house, and I say I'll have to stay over. Longer than any Tinder chat, but the endgame is the same.

"Aren't you going to roll up your windows?" Eric asks as I walk toward him. I stuff my keys in my pocket. He reaches for me, and I kiss him softly on the lips.

"No."

He laughs and loops my hand in his.

I glance at my phone. Jessica is still apologizing. Ann with no "e" still wants my help. I follow Eric inside.

The apartment is small and tidy, with decorative touches that make me wonder if his mother visits and brings him knickknacks, the way I've heard mothers do. I peer around the corner, catch a glimpse of the bathroom. Folded towels, different sizes and matching colors. The kitchen, the back wall of the main room, is sparse. A bag of apples. A box of bullets.

I walk to the center of the room. "You're very tidy." It smells like lemon. He ducks his head and says something about natural products, avoiding chemicals, the rain forest. I suspect he shops at Whole Foods.

"I downloaded some movies." He walks to the kitchen and pulls out a bowl of fruit from the fridge. "All the ones you said you liked."

He fiddles with the remote and turns on *Aliens*. He has an actual TV. It's mounted to the wall and everything. He also has a couch. There are two glasses and a bottle of wine on the coffee table. A throw across one arm. I sit, and he brings the fruit bowl, pours me a drink, drapes soft fabric across our laps. He cups one of my hands in his.

Machine guns blare, and Eric makes a joke about a man directing the quintessential feminist action film. I remind him that Ridley Scott did *Thelma & Louise*. Bill Cosby was America's dad, and Harvey Weinstein worked at Disney. He asks my thoughts on cancel culture. I paraphrase the discourse on removing the artist from the art.

He refills my wineglass before he refills his own. Nathan did that, but I don't want to think about him. I tell Eric that the first movie only stars Sigourney Weaver because the seventies were full of alien films, the creators wanted to stand out, so they made the hero a chick. He feeds me blueberries. I explain the inverted heteronormativity, how Sigourney rescues the love interest and saves the world.

"She's the archetypal mother figure, which makes sense, as the movie begins with her having lost a child, so by the end she saves one. It's pretty reductive, really."

He feeds me another blueberry. "Yeah, but she's such an ass-kicker."

After the other mother is sucked into space and Sigourney rescues humanity from a species that survives through forced insemination, we lie together on the sofa, me on top of him, legs tangled. "I'm surprised that's your favorite movie," he says.

I lift my head and peer down at him in the dark. "It should be everyone's favorite movie."

"When you said you loved action films, I thought you meant *Death Wish* or *I Spit On Your Grave*."

"The rape revenge thing?"

He nods.

I wiggle upward. "Those movies don't work."

"How so?"

"Action movies are man movies. Rape isn't something men understand."

He shifts so he is on his elbows. "Some of us try."

I laugh.

"Wait." He lifts a hand. "Help me understand this. Please."

I rest both hands on his knees. I tap two fingers. "I think men think rape is unwanted sex. And sex is great. So how bad can unwanted sex be?" I try again. "You think it's like being force-fed a cookie. You didn't want the cookie, maybe it's not your favorite type or you're not in the mood, but it's just a cookie. And you eat cookies all the time. So—what's the big deal? There may be too many cookies, or cookies you don't like, but the world's worst cookie has still got to be pretty good, right? People love cookies. And you think, even if it's the worst fucking cookie in the world, big deal. It's just a cookie."

He stands, his eyes on mine. If I were a different sort of woman, in a different sort of life, I would see moonlight reflected in them. "Thank you."

I don't usually try to explain this, not to Dan or Stan. That's not what they asked for when they swiped right. "You're welcome."

He comes closer, his lips against my forehead, and reaches for my hand. He walks past me, flicks the light on the wall. I look down at the table next to the couch. He's reading Isabel Wilkerson. Maybe, behind the door I think is a closet, is a stable for his white horse.

"I got you a toothbrush. And I have some clean shirts, if you want to change." He holds his hand out. "Or we can say good night."

I look at the toothbrush. Thin and blue and wrapped in plastic. Cartoon gums on the front. "I want to stay."

"OK." He smiles and looks toward the sofa. "Well, I can—"

"With you. In bed."

He ducks his head. He blushes. "Great."

If I were a different sort of woman, in a different life, I would love this. The sweetness, the eagerness, the effort. I wonder, from a place I stopped listening to long ago, if I can be that woman.

"No more talk about movies." I take the toothbrush and shake it at him. "Or rape."

His bathroom is tidy. He uses Sensodyne and Clinique for Men. Two types of body wash. I pee and shower and help myself to all of it. He buys expensive toilet paper, the kind that feels like flannel and never leaves pieces in your butt. His towels are soft and his T-shirt hangs to my thighs. I switch my underwear for his boxers.

I go into the bedroom. He has a pillow tucked under his chin, face concentrating as he wriggles it inside a fresh case. He tosses it onto the bed and looks up at me.

"All set?"

I nod.

He smiles and walks past, a light hand on my waist. He closes the bathroom door. The toilet flushes, water runs; he blows his nose. We are in the bed. Soft cotton, lavender pillows. Lights off.

"No movie talk," he whispers against my head.

I slide my leg over his body. My hips follow. I breathe in his cedar and lemongrass and decide I don't mind if he shops at Whole Foods.

The rise of his chest. He murmurs something, a rumble beneath my ear. My thighs sink to either side of him. The boxers bunch at the crease of my legs and my mouth is on his, his tongue is on mine, and I hear a sound, low and deep, and it is my own. We roll and he slides me over, thighs open, boxers off, his breath on my face, my stomach, my legs, and when I come the moon is bright.

We lie together. He thwarts my attempts to touch him, presses my hands against his chest, pale in the night. His breath slows. My pulse calms. It begins to rain.

———

It's been more than two weeks since I found the needle. Since I found out about Nathan. My hands are steady. My aim would be accurate. Flopsy is an animal, but not one I can take down and dump in the back of my truck. Jessica and Frederick could take care of him. I think of Nathan, and wonder how much digging up, covering up his family did for him. Enough, it seems. Or maybe none, because no one cares about that sort of thing.

I remind the students I'll be away Friday through Monday and their papers are due when I return. I lie and say there are apps instructors use to detect ChatGPT. We pack up and walk out, past another adjunct waiting to come in. I recognize him from my department. He finished years ago.

I pull my shirt over my face and walk into the tunnel. The smoke is thick enough that the university has left the overhead lights on; a string of dull off-white, like the aisle of an airplane, illuminates the posters and graffiti.

I look at the dead kids. Whoever is in charge of whitewashing the tunnel hasn't done it recently. The names are stacking up. Nathan looks at me. Thick black lines. There was another email this morning. Community, concern, care. Counseling Center. All the "c" words except the good one. No one has written the new kid's name down. Martin Johnson. I pull out a pen and bend forward. I write his name below Raymond Philips.

I step back. I stare at Martin. His name scratches behind my eyes. I grip the pen with my teeth and pull my phone out of my bag. I take another photo of the tunnel wall. Ann with no "e" texts me again, asks which flight I'm on, asks if we can meet before I leave. She wants me to explain the background of my field, so she can discuss the background of my field in her interviews for jobs in my field. I don't respond.

I am grateful my paper was submitted four months ago. Nathan's was, too. I put a $99 polyester blazer on my credit card, fingers crossed as the teenager who makes more than me swiped it, and pack my shoes with no holes. I tuck Flopsy's baggie under my mattress. I tuck Nathan's journal next to it. I hold Nathan's phone in my hand, then put it, too, beneath the mattress, next to the words and the weapon. Empress will go through the box while I'm away, but at least she won't find this.

I have another job application, this one a manila envelope of printed materials for the College of the Honest Heart. It is a one-year position, 4/4 teaching load, in a fundamentalist school in Iowa, $32,000 a year. They do not accept electronic applications. They do not cover birth control. The required Faith Statement (I'm pretending to be born again) and the other statements (Diversity, Teaching, Research) with my transcripts and cover letter are in the envelope. Colette and Lurkstenstein left me reference letters, signed, sealed, and signed again across the seal, in my department mailbox. Black told me to collect his letter at the conference. I put the manila envelope in my carry-on, alongside my ziplock of toiletries, and two days of Please Hire Me clothing.

Eric drives up to say goodbye. "Have fun," he says. "Come back safely." He leans forward, lifting my hands in his, arms wide, and pulls me into a hug. I lean into him, as Dog sits at our feet and Empress glares from her tower. Jessica texts, asks if I want to talk. I cut open a bag of dog food and leave it against Dog's crate.

The airport is tiny, lined in custom mosaics and floor-to-ceiling windows behind a row of voluptuous succulents. Santa Teresa is a town you fly into when your jet is on the fritz, or your driver can't make it to L.A. Nathan and I came here late one night, pulled up to the parking lot, and watched the private jets come in. Helicopters land on the estates, he explained, so no one here is really loaded.

Then who are these people, I asked. Our backs flat in the bed of my truck. I pointed to the jet strip near us, where a black limousine waited. Overhead, something loud and low.

You know, he shouted over the noise, not really rich, but you know.

I laughed and choked on the smoke. I didn't know. I had no idea, but he always forgot that.

We walk across the tarmac. I remove the manila envelope for the no-birth-control school and hold it with my phone. Retirees with small dogs shuffle sideways ahead of me, single seats on one side, pairs on the other. Giant purses overhead. Tiny dogs underneath.

I sit in the back. My phone rings, and a woman with a marquise diamond the size of an almond glares at me across the aisle.

"Oh, hey." Jessica's voice is soft, surprised I picked up.

I can see her. The nervous movements. Protruding clavicle. Another perfect Hollywood tear. "I'm on an airplane."

"That's fine." She takes a deep breath. Probably closes her eyes. "I've only got a few minutes. They limit our phone usage."

"Where are you?"

"I'm at the facility."

"What—"

"I told you. I never make it a year."

"Oh God, Jessica. Are you all right?"

"Yeah, but I can only call or text once a day." A pause. "Or email, if you were wondering."

"OK."

"You're going to a conference?" I hear her effort over the phone. "That sounds fun."

"Yeah, it should be good." I force a smile into my voice. "Why did you call?" Now my voice is soft. There's only one reason she would call, because there's only one thing we have in common.

"I want to apologize."

"Step Nine, right?"

"I didn't know if you knew about Nathan, and if you didn't, I didn't know what the point would be." The words come out in a rush. "Sometimes the people we love do terrible things. But that doesn't mean we stop loving them."

No, it doesn't. Things would be easier if it did.

"I was thinking of what it was like once I understood what Nathan had done." Her voice hitches. "I know how hard it is, loving someone you hate."

She's right, of course. Hatred doesn't replace love, no matter how hard we try, no matter how much they deserve it. "When you're back, maybe we can talk."

"OK. Be careful, Jessica." I don't know what to say to someone in L.A. rehab. I don't know how to help rich women with rich problems.

"Thanks." She laughs. Soft, but real. "We have a lot of art therapy in here, so it's pretty good."

Something Dad used to say. He was used to pain, but not to weakness. Poverty, but not pity. The food. The nurses. The TV stations. It's pretty good, he said. He can't hold down liquids, the nurses told me. We're putting in a tube.

A flight attendant walks down the aisle. She points to my phone.

"You'll be OK." The last thing Dad said to me. The last thing I said to him. I hang up. I tuck the phone and the manila envelope into the pocket in front of me, next to the barf bag and the safety instructions. I heard Colette is taking a later flight. Ann with no "e" left this morning. Jessica is in rehab. Nathan is dead. I close my eyes.

When I open them, Rapist is walking down the aisle. Of course he would be on this flight. He turns to the limp, bleached hair behind him. Flopsy's signature bob. They pivot and sit three rows ahead of me. Flopsy turns on the lights above his head. He looks around.

Always look for the stillness, Dad said, his hand on mine, the gun pressed against my shoulder. That's when they know you're there. We all know when we're being watched.

Flopsy sees me. A lock of hair falls forward. He makes eye contact, but I do not freeze. I know what Flopsy has done, but I know what I have done, too.

I am not afraid of Flopsy, but I am afraid of Rapist. The part of me that saved my ancestors from bears knows what he is. The part of me that kills bears knows what he is. I smell my blood on him, just as other creatures have smelled their blood on me. But Rapist and I are not the same. I needed to. He wanted to. That difference is why I am afraid.

Rapist is looking forward. The flight attendant, slim-hipped and soft-eyed, leans above him, closes the overhead compartment. His teeth are level with her belly.

Flopsy stares at me. He lifts one hand. He points it toward me, forefinger and thumb in the shape of a gun. He fake-shoots me twice. I smile. His hand is high and unsteady. Bullets going in every direction. Don't get so excited.

He turns away, whispers something to Rapist. Rapist's spine goes straight, his shoulders drop. I'm surprised Rapist stills. My scent is in the recirculated air, but I didn't think he worried about me. Maybe he knows about Flopsy's needle. Maybe he recognized my smell tucked beneath his sheets.

It's hard to get rid of rats, Mrs. Sanghera taught me when I was in her barn, helping with hay bales and water buckets. They're social animals. They live in groups. A rat will stay in its nest even if another rat eats there, fucks there, pisses and shits there. I watch the cat she brought into the barn, a clawing, shrieking tomboy. You have to introduce a predator, she said, and let out the cat. If something else finds the nest, if the rat knows something bigger and meaner has been in his home, only then will he leave.

———◆———

The air is clear in Denver. Close to midnight, Mountain Time. A young woman in Uggs, swaddled in shawls, struggles with a bag above her head. I bring it down in front of her while a man checks his phone behind us. I don't have friends in the area, so I'm out the front and in an Uber. Directions to the hotel are on my phone, downloaded from a Facebook group of graduate students looking to save money by rooming together.

I check in, get a key and a funny look from Reception. "We've given out four keys to this room so far," the young man says, double-clicking his computer.

"Oh, gosh." I widen my eyes. "I'm so sorry to hear that. My friend is sooo forgetful."

Elevator to the eighth floor, down two hallways. I insert my plastic card into the black box. The light goes from red to green, and three young women wave at me. A lump in the corner, body curled around itself inside a sleeping bag, drawstring tight over the face so only a nose peeks out, lies halfway beneath the desk.

"Hi," one of them whispers. "You must be Sarah."

"Yes," I whisper back.

One gestures me in. They pass two bottles of wine between them.

"Want some?"

"Sure." I step over a carry-on, under a makeshift clothesline where a dress is hanging, and wind my way to the bed with one woman on it.

"You're sharing with me, right?" she asks.

"Yeah, if that's OK."

"I'm Amy." She hands me a bottle.

"Thanks." It's that cheap shit with the footprint on the label. Nathan called it hippie piss. No, I told Nathan. Hippies would never drink this. This is working-class piss. Nathan was intrigued. What's the difference?

"Did you find the hotel OK?" the first one asks. "I'm Sumi, by the way."

I nod. "Yeah. Thanks. That map you sent was great."

"Are you presenting?" The third, dark skin and dark hair. She passes a packet of peanut-butter crackers to me. "I'm Mary."

"Yes." I swig. "And I have an interview." I hand Amy the bottle. She shakes her head. I sit on the bed, with the wine, the carry-on, the layers of clothes I wore on the flight because so few would fit in my bag. I know what I look like.

"Wow." Three sets of eyes go wide.

"Are you nervous?"

"That's amazing!"

"I can't wait to present at a conference."

I look around. "What year are you guys?"

"We're first-years."

"What?" I say, too loudly. Lump shifts.

"But he's not." Sumi points to the sleeping bag. "He's finishing. Has two interviews tomorrow."

I lower my voice. "We should be quiet."

"He's kind of a grump," Mary says.

"All the fifth-years in my program got a room by themselves." Amy takes the bottle from me. "No one wanted to share."

"So rude!" Sumi whispers.

"I know it's stressful." Amy swigs and looks at me. She burps, not quietly. "But this is our first conference! It's so much fun!"

Sumi and Mary giggle.

"Is your interview tomorrow, too?" Sumi asks.

I shake my head.

"Then stay up with us!" they chorus, not whispering at all now. So young and bright, these sweet, brilliant women. So excited with their itineraries, complimentary (if you ignore the $850 attendance fee) book bags, and early-hour entrance to the book-selling area, where, they tell each other, one day they will see their own books, they will buy each other's books.

"I'm going to take a shower," I whisper. I stand and lift my carry-on, bypass Lump, and wind my way toward the bathroom with its department-store light and sandpaper towels. The countertop looks like a Sephora after a terrorist attack. Cosmetics and skin care and three separate curling irons. Piles of clothing. Nothing on hangers.

I strip, wash, and dry myself with a damp towel left on the floor. I brush my teeth and use my meager drugstore bottles in my ziplock bag. I put on a T-shirt and boxers stolen from a dead man.

"Do you want us to turn off the light?" Sumi asks, a fresh bottle of wine open, her hand on the cork.

I double-check my bag, the manila envelope, my phone, and tuck the whole thing against the wall next to a suitcase. They paid for luggage. I look at Lump. He does look like a grump.

"Have you decided which panels you're going to tomorrow?" I ask. They beam like angels. Amy makes room. I sit on the bed.

◆

The American Association of Religion is the foremost academic society dedicated to the study of religion. The annual conference brings in over ten thousand attendees, mostly from North America. Some Europeans fly in: Oxbridge and Sorbonne. A stray German or Korean, well groomed and punctual.

We attend in stages. First as graduate students. We send out pitches for papers we want to write and present. We are rejected. It's not about the paper. It's about finding the panel where you know someone who can guarantee you a spot. You don't know anyone, so you create a panel and invite other graduate students. Their research doesn't fit yours and the panel makes no sense, but it's a line on your CV. The goal is to have as many lines as possible, and you're not in one of those three-year Ph.D. programs where you and your buddies put your names on each other's papers and get dozens of lines a year. Any panel, no matter how nonsensical, is a line.

After enough lines, someone invites you to a panel. No organizing. Just write and read. Another line.

Next, you're a respondent to a panel. No organizing. No writing. Just read and comment on what other people wrote. Maybe add a joke or two. Question, rather than criticize. Remember, they're doing you a favor. Line.

When you have enough lines on your CV that people count pages, or when you have a book and the publisher is contractually obligated to subsidize the conference, someone creates a panel around you. No organizing. No writing. No reading. Just listen. They skimmed your introduction and conclusion. Mostly, they read the bibliography. If they saw their own name, they'll say nice things. If they didn't, they won't join the panel (unless they need the line). At the end, you make a few self-deprecating remarks. You compliment the people who complimented you. You get a mediocre dinner at a step above Chili's where you deflect questions about your department's hiring plans. You bemoan the state of Higher Ed, but imply there are always opportunities for the hardworking and the talented. Line.

My interview is tomorrow. Room 6127, sixth floor of the Denver Marriott Tech Center. The schedule tells you everything. If my interview were at three o'clock, they would keep me for forty minutes, the search committee cycling through eight to twelve candidates. Top-tier job search. If it were at three-thirty, they'd keep me for twenty minutes, one of twenty candidates. Midlevel job search. My interview is at three-fifteen. I'll have ten minutes. That's assuming the person in front of me doesn't talk longer than they know they should, in which case I'll have seven. I am one of dozens of candidates. Low-level job search.

The committee will ask me the same number of questions they would ask me if I had forty minutes, because they don't want to think of themselves as a low-level opportunity. At the end, they will ask me if I have any questions. I will ask a question that is not a question but, rather, proof, phrased as a question, that I am perfect for this job. They will give a noncommittal response. I will make a charming and memorable comment. I will leave the room and drop my pre-written thank-you cards into the hotel's mailbox. I will not hear back.

Today, I swim from one panel to another: mine; Nathan's, where he isn't; Flopsy's, where he is. Rapist lurks behind me. I feel his eyes when we're at opposite ends of a hallway. I do not freeze. I eat lunch alone. Colette and I meet for three minutes. She has two round-tables and a paper. She has a workshop as well, where she is meeting with master's students to talk about our department. She will not discuss our rate of completion (25 percent), the number of job placements (two in the past three years), or availability of funding (less than 30 percent for fewer than four years in a program that takes eight on average), but she will list her colleagues' prestigious awards and describe the beauty of the campus. I tell her I'm looking forward to her paper tomorrow, but will have to leave early for my interview. She didn't attend my paper today. She doesn't ask how it went. She says not to worry about attending hers. I ask about my dissertation. She says she'll get to it, don't send it to the committee.

Don't worry, she says, next year you'll have more interviews. Just stay another year. She leaves, trailed by someone who wants to work with her, someone who wants to be me.

In the evening, I go to the department reception. Finished Ph.D.'s, lapsed Ph.D.'s, transferred Ph.D.'s all join current Ph.D.'s for two drink tickets and a chance to remind their letter writers that they exist. They're still trying. The cheese is warm and the wine is boxed, but at least the room has chairs. I stand by the door and text Eric.

> What are you doing tonight?

> Upholding the law 😊 How's the conference?

I send him a GIF of Michael Scott rolling his eyes. He responds with Jim kissing Pam.

I scroll through my other messages. Nothing from Jessica. She doesn't have access to her phone. I find the last message I sent to the number that does not respond. I text.

> I miss you.

Ann with no "e" is in a group hovering over a postdoc I recognize from a guest lecture last year. I look down at my phone. My words stare back at me. It's been three weeks and I still expect to see three little dots.

> Do you miss me?

I stare at the space where the dots should be. I join the group. Someone hands me my drink tickets.

"I had two interviews today." Ann with no "e" beams. "I think they went really well. Although tomorrow's will be trickier."

"You have another interview tomorrow?" Postdoc asks.

Ann with no "e" nods. "Two. One for a Religious Theory position."

"Do you," asks someone I vaguely recognize, "have a background in Religious Theory?"

"Aren't you a historian?"

"Oh, sure." Ann with no "e" smiles. "But I know a lot about religion."

"How can you—"

"I'm sure it will go well," Postdoc cuts him off, "and even if it doesn't, you'll do more anyway. It never ends."

"You got a job, though," Ann with no "e" says, sizing her up.

"For one year."

"But you've finished your dissertation, and you're employed," a sixth-year joins in. "Doesn't that help?"

Postdoc shrugs. "The fact that I'm bouncing around postdocs says I'm a second-tier candidate. If I were any good, I would have gotten tenure track straightaway." She swirls her boxed wine. "Plus, I only got this one because I promised to be on their diversity panel, and changed my research to match. Don't tell the well-intentioned whities who hired me, but I don't actually think my skin color is the most interesting thing about me." She swigs. "Or anyone."

"My research doesn't touch on race at all," Aysel, the only other nonwhitie in our group, in the room, murmurs.

"It does if you want a job."

"I had a meeting with a professor at UCLA today, someone I thought could help me on my third chapter." A man a year ahead of me stares into his cup. "Turns out, he's applying for the same jobs as me. He wants to be back on the East Coast."

"You're competing against tenured faculty?"

"It's hardly a competition." He drinks.

"I'm lecturing at Dartmouth." Chubby blonde. "They opened

a tenure-track position in my field. I figured I'd be the inside candidate."

"I interviewed for that today," Ann with no "e" says, her voice unusually small. "You're the inside candidate?"

"I didn't get an interview."

"But you're already working there. You're teaching and writing and . . ."

"Oh, they'll fuck me," Blonde says, smiling. "They just won't marry me."

They continue to talk. Outside hires. Inside hires. Fake searches. Nepotistic chairs. Flopsy slouches toward the bar. He's burned through his drink tickets and has his credit card out. He turns, two glasses of red plastic in hand. "Fuck you," he mouths, slow and clear across the room. I bare my teeth.

Behind a group of professors, one in his eighties talking with six postdocs desperate for his job, stands Rapist. He's leaning forward, wine in one hand, the other under his chin. He pretends to listen to a pretty young student. She's new this year. She smiles and laughs and tosses her hair. He leans closer. Behind them, Feminist Carl takes the thirteenth step.

Drink tickets flow. Finances don't come up. We couldn't talk if they did. The wife of the ophthalmologist can't complain about her student loans. The boyfriend of the lawyer doesn't know about rent increases. The ones who live at home, who live off of others, mention student debt as a philosophical crisis and an existential dilemma. The failures of late-stage capitalism meet the reality of neoliberalism. The rest of us are without families or spouses or other secret financial pockets. If we want to talk to each other, we have to ignore all that. We focus on what we have in common. The work. The hunt. The depression. I think of my students, the ones with three jobs, the ones with three houses. I wonder if they follow the same social script.

I text Eric. I ask him if he wants to get tacos when I'm back. I text Nathan that I attended his panel. They mentioned his name, a quick nod followed by an enthusiastic eighth-year, thrilled to get a last-minute line.

It is late and I am sober. Different people. Same discussion. There is no money. There are no jobs. No one has retired. No one has been hired. Try again next year. I sneak out before Ann with no "e" can ask me to summarize twelve centuries of Eastern philosophy. The right names in the right places, she likes to say. That's all she needs.

Denver is cold in November, but the air is clear. It feels like Maine. I walk out and left to the hotel, to the room with the three graces and Lump. I hope they are having fun tonight, laughing and chatting and listening and learning. I hope Lump had good interviews. I hope he feels hopeful. Happiness isn't about getting what you want, the New Age white Buddhists like to tell me, it's about anticipating getting what you want. The worm, not the hook, they say, in their designer clothes.

My phone buzzes, but I don't look at it. More emails. Probably another name. Students drinking and driving and crashing and burning. I think of the tunnel. Soon, there won't be any space for a-cappella posters.

People walk around me. It's only nine o'clock. Men and women. Children and teenagers. Denver is active, and I wonder what it would be like to live here. To move to a town where I have a job that pays my bills, where I don't see Rapist or Flopsy every day. I'll see rapists every day—statistically, that's inevitable—but I won't know them. I won't smell myself on them. To me, they will be strangers and colleagues and friends. I zip my coat and lift my face to the cold. I breathe deep in the clean air, the stars bright. How nice it must be not to know.

I am listening to a panel on the philosophical tenets of Maitripa's *Amanasikara Cycle* by a thick German professor in a thick German accent. Colette is after him. I am in a middle seat. The dutiful advisee. Present, but not occupying prime audience real estate. I know my place.

German finishes. A sputtering of applause. Questions are reserved for the end, the moderator reminds us, as if anyone has anything to say. Colette stands. Someone young and nervous adjusts the mike, and Colette makes the joke she always makes about being short. I laugh the way I always laugh when the woman who controls my future makes a joke.

"In this paper, I will examine . . ." She speaks, and I zone out, my eyes on the photo of the tunnel wall. I've heard everything a dozen times. I stare at the most recent name. Martin Johnson.

". . . a three-part analysis of justifications of violence across the Buddhist canon."

I look up.

"While this is a bold approach, rooted in comparative study—"

I lean forward.

"—the triad of need, want, and moral imperative contrasts strongly with assumptions of nonviolence in modern understandings of the tradition. Rather than stemming from textual analysis, in fact, these assumptions align with Orientalist underpinnings—"

I cross my legs over my bag, the good one I save for conferences. The leather is fake, but it doesn't smell of weed, and I've never thrown up in it. It holds a pen, a notebook, and the manila envelope. I close the photo of the tunnel wall and open my email, pages and pages from years ago.

Sarah—

The writing isn't bad, but this approach is problematic. Broad-based analyses of general themes across an entire tradition are too ambitious at your level. I am concerned that you don't understand this.

I scroll.

Good afternoon, Colette,

Thank you for your email. I have given it some thought, and I hope you might see my perspective. My hope is, perhaps, to try something new. I recognize this lens is outside of our discipline. However, please see below the highlighted section of the paper in which I outline which textual sources I will rely on, as well as my list of secondary sources to support my argument. I look forward to your thoughts.

Kind regards,
Sarah

Scroll.

It is unusual to cross such boundaries. Please send me a full outline of your argument, including your conclusions and translations, so I can gauge its value.

I stop scrolling.

Colette lifts her head in the presenter's pyramid. Paper. Left corner of the audience. Right corner of the audience. Paper. She does not look at me. She continues. Justifications of violence. Need. Want. Moral Imperative. The audience murmurs. Shocking and innovative. Subversive. Genius.

Colette is a full Professor, not Assistant or Associate. Thirty years on staff. Nathan and I looked up her salary one night on the public records of the UCs: $275,000, plus $50,000 in benefits. Her salary increased more quickly than usual because of her extensive publication record for the first twenty years of her career. Extraordinary, the Dean said at a public forum I attended in my first year. I've never seen so many ideas come from one person. We're all waiting for your next book, he said, smiling. In the seven years I've been here, there have been no more books.

Paragraphs from my introduction. Witty anecdotes from my footnotes. One smug correction of a citation. The audience is captivated. It is an unusual subject matter. Only a scholar with decades of experience could attempt such a thing.

I don't stay for questions. I don't look at her when I leave. Her voice continues behind me, smaller and softer and lighter than mine. Charming, she told me once. I needed to work on my charm. I step into the hallway. People are beginning to mill, sneaking out of one presentation to get seats for another. Deep breaths and long swigs before they present research, their own or someone else's.

"Sarah!" Ann with no "e" moves through the throng. "Hey!"

I look for a place to hide.

"I'm so glad I finally caught you! I know we both have that interview today . . ." She walks toward me, parting the crowd like a woman coming to speak to the manager.

"What?" Colette's voice and my words ring in my ears. Ann with no "e"'s eyes bore into mine.

"Silly." She pats my arm. "For Iowa. You're at three-fifteen and I'm at four-thirty. Remember?"

"That's your interview today?"

"My second." Those teeth. "I was wondering if you wanted to do some preparation."

"I've done my preparation." I look at my phone. "In fact—"

"Of course." She takes a step forward. "Me too, but"—she leans closer—"what about the theorists?"

"Theorists?"

"In the discipline."

I wait.

"The theorists in the discipline," she says again.

"What about them?"

"I need to know who they are." The same smile. I open my mouth, but she plows ahead. "It probably doesn't matter. The chair of the department is Gio's former advisee." She gives a modest shrug.

Giovanni. Her adviser. I have never worked with him, because he is in the History Department, like her. He secured her five years of funding even though university policy limits it to four. He gives her $500 for every conference out of his own pocket, because he knows how expensive they are. It's so great, she told me one year. I put all of my stipends into my 403(b). Unless I'm too tired to teach, then I take the semester off.

Behind us, Colette's voice. She has told one of my jokes. Everyone is laughing.

"Just a quick rundown."

Behind the closed door, applause. Colette has finished. Colette is a triumph.

"A rundown?"

"The major players," she says, still smiling, but impatient. Why am I so difficult? "There can't be that many."

I stare at her teeth. "In our department, we take a required two-year course on theory before we even—"

"Well, I don't need everyone, silly! Just, you know, the most important ones."

More applause behind the door. Subversive. Genius.

"If you want a professorship in a discipline, you should pursue a Ph.D. in that discipline."

"Why would that mat—"

"Good luck."

The doors open, pushing us apart.

———

I am in a folding chair. The door opens. They call me in. I enter. I sit on another folding chair. The bed beside me. Hollywood doesn't conduct business in hotel rooms anymore, but academia never got that message. Then again, they've only got fifteen minutes. I assume Harvey Weinstein gave himself more time.

Two women sit in two chairs. A man reclines on the couch, one leg up. Behind me, hotel art. Behind him, a wall TV. A remote control. A piece of paper advertising HBO. In front of me, a small coffee table with a glass of the previous candidate's water. The outline of lips and saliva.

The women ask the questions I know they'll ask. I answer what I know I'll answer. The words are soft and dull, coming to my ears through a swarm of summer insects. The man does not ask a question. He does not lower his leg.

I want to be home. I want my father and my dog. I want my woods and my walks and my guns, the deer and the bears. I want the thick green book, the one the librarian had never heard of. When I was packing for college, after Mr. Todd drove me home from the funeral and Mrs. Sanghera promised to look after the house, I found the book in a trunk. A dusty government text from Quebec, soft with mold. I pulled apart the pages and found no trace of the stories my father spun.

They ask if I have any questions. I ask the question that is not a question, the question that proves I'm perfect. The women respond. The man yawns. Their words come to me through cotton balls. Their smiles waver like photos under water. I say something, they nod. Their words are slower than they should be, deeper than they should be. The man on the couch turns to me, his head round and bulbous, his eyes dim. He blinks.

How many of her students have finished in the last five years?

She was friendly in the beginning. Always asked what I was working on. Always asked to read a draft. Never responded. Never gave feedback. But had every copy of every paper, every article. Her eyes before anyone else's.

Through the haze and the fog and the dull, buzzing sound of the tenured professors in the hotel room, I know I cannot accuse her. $275,000 plus $50,000. I can't even afford a lawyer. Thirty years of scholarly excellence. Half a dozen books. So many great ideas. So many brilliant papers. Even if it's been close to a decade since the last one. Everyone has dry spells. And graduate students quit, right? That's why all of hers have left.

It occurs to me now, as long as I never finish, as long as I never get a job and climb the ranks and build my own publishing record, she is safe. It would be harder to defend herself against a peer. I wonder about my letter, or the casual asides. Professors talking with professors, asking for names rather than wading through nine hundred applications, when her safety depends on my failure.

But even without Colette, there are still nine hundred applicants. And in that nine hundred are the Flopsys and the Anns with no "e." Families with money, advisers with connections. Some shit always floats. Seven years—$165,000. My words from another's mouth. They stand. I stand. They shake my hand. I walk to the door. They sit. I leave.

I will never know if I could have scored on a level playing field. People like to say that competition, by definition, is unfair. Even without money or names or networks, some are smarter, work harder. Some are stronger, more resilient. Money doesn't matter, I hear. Connections open the door, but you have to walk through. It's always the people with money and connections who say this. If they had told me I couldn't win, if they had told me I didn't have a chance, I might have still decided to play. If they had said, This is visitors' night at a members-only club, I might have sat, knowing it would never be my seat. Learning for learning's sake.

Then again, if they had said that to me, they would have had to say it to themselves. They're not the smartest, the strongest, the hardest-working. They were born with their membership. They didn't earn shit.

Still, it would have been nice to have had a chance.

———◆———

The hallways are long. The carpets are plain. Someone else is sitting in the folding chair. I look up and see another folding chair. Another folding chair. Another folding chair. Down the hallway. Seated and waiting.

My fake-leather bag is light. The manila envelope with the statements, the documents, the letters are in the trash, dropped next to coffee cups with saliva and tissues with snot and all the other things we leave behind.

The weight on my back, the razors in my ass. Flopsy dripping down my neck. White men in rumpled suits mill between doorways. Conversations spill out of meeting rooms. The predator—the one I know, at least—remains hidden. The names in the tunnel. So many accidents, I overheard someone say, young people are so careless. Or maybe they knew they didn't have a chance, either. Maybe they were tired of wasting their time.

I reach the elevator and press the button.

> this conference sucks

I am in the room when the graces return. I look at the bedside lamp, digital numbers in red. It is six-forty-five.

"Oh Jesus," Amy says, hand on her throat when she sees me on the bed, silent in the dark. "You scared me."

"Hey, are you OK?" Sumi asks.

"Let's go out," I say.

"How did the paper go?" Mary asks.

"And the interview?"

"Let's go out."

Amy grins. "OK! Where to?"

"Wherever you want." I stand. "My treat." I pull my credit card and my room key out of my bag. I put them in my bra, beneath the clean button-down shirt, above the clean black pants. "Come on."

We're out the door and in a bar and laughing. I buy shots. I buy a bottle. We are laughing.

"This is so great!"

"I knew you were cool!"

"I'm coming to this conference every year!"

They dance and they drink, and the graces are beautiful and young and happy, and I drink, and there's nothing to smoke and nothing to snort, and Nathan is dead, and Flopsy's mother will get him a job, and Ann with no "e" doesn't need her stipend, and Colette is publishing my book, and Rapist is inviting the pretty young first-year out somewhere alone, and I drink.

I am dancing. A man puts his arms around me, and I pull his face toward mine. His tongue is aggressive, and I bite it. He pushes me away. I swallow copper. I am laughing.

We are outside. I have no jacket. One is throwing up. Another is holding her hair back, one hand against the brick side of a building to steady herself. A third is seated on the ground. The Uber is late, and we are laughing.

We are back at the hotel. One is holding the other. One has vomit down her front. One throws up in a plant at Reception. One yells out a name I don't know. They are laughing.

They go to the elevators. I find a bathroom in the lobby. I throw up red and yellow and chunks and foam. Something pink. Something orange. Ass up, face down, then standing at the sink, water on my face. No vomit on my shirt. No vomit in my hair. My eyes are red and I peed myself, but no man on my back. No razors in my ass. It's pretty good.

I pat my boobs. Credit card still there. Room key still there. First-years safe upstairs. I cup my hands beneath the faucet and breathe the water into my nose. I want to lie quiet on the bottom of the river that ran behind our house. I want to wait there, in the dark and the wet, until the ice comes and the snow falls, like Dad is buried, like the little black dog is buried. I want the deer and the birds and the bear to wander past. I want to dissolve in the mud and the rocks.

I dry my hands and walk out. Get to the elevator. Press the up arrow and lean against the wall behind me. The lights above the door flash, descend, count down. I'm sleepy. I could pass out, be found by a security guard, embarrass myself, and ruin my career prospects. I laugh, as if passing out is what I have to worry about. I burp. The countdown to "G," and the door dings. It opens. I push myself off the wall and slide inside. I press 8. The door closes.

Almost. A narrow hand and a blond head and a drunk man slips inside. Smooth and slow and quiet. The doors close.

I smile against the back wall of the elevator. I tilt my head and focus my eyes on his limp, light hair. I hiccup and swallow down whatever comes up.

"Hey, you."

He's drunk, too, I think. It's hard to tell with the lights bright and the elevator moving. He sways on his feet. My stomach rolls, and I think of Rapist's bed. I grin. "What's up?"

"Fuck you," Flopsy says, eyes forward.

I giggle. I hiccup.

He faces away from me. He slumps against the side of the elevator. He turns his head; his eyes narrow. I slide along the other side of the wall, brace myself against the cool, smooth metal and a poster advertising drinks at the hotel bar.

"I know what you've been up to." I lift my finger and wave it toward him. My voice is light and high and rhythmic. He looks at me, looks through me, drunk or high or something else. We stare, slumped against opposite sides of the elevator.

"Naughty, little Flopsy." I push myself upward. I reach my hand inside my bra. The numbers above the doors. The light hits 4.

"Fuck you," he says again. His eyelids dip.

I take one step. He turns away. I take another step. I cross the elevator. I am next to him. He faces forward. I stare at the dark hollows beneath his eyes. The light above the doors hits 5.

"I know what you did." It sounds like a line from a movie. One of the loud ones where men take off their shirts to save the President. I press my hand against the door. The metal is cold. Like Nathan, face-up in his bed. Like the table in the kill shed, blood pooling beneath my feet. My credit card and room key, now clutched in my hand, are warm, the edges sharp enough to do more damage than people realize.

"Fuck you."

"Is that what you want to do?" He's wearing one of his new button-down shirts. I guess he didn't change after his interview. Went out looking sharp. I look down but can't focus on his feet. I bet he's in his shiny new shoes. "Or do you want to do to me what you did to him?" I run one finger over the edge of the credit card, hard and sharp and thin.

"Get away from me."

He's serious now. His eyes still droop, but his voice is louder. Flopsy is in his new shoes and his new shirt. He had an interview and wants to be a big boy. I wonder if his mother is proud. I wonder if Rapist's mother is proud. I wonder about the mothers.

The 5 fades. The 6 lights up. I lean toward him. He shifts away, closer to the wall. He sags. Too drunk to stand. Too drunk to fight. The sharp outline of my credit card against my thumb, a slice to the jugular and he would bleed out in two minutes.

The 7 illuminates above the door. The buttons, smooth and white and round, are in front of us. One is red, the one you pull instead of push. For Emergency Use Only.

"Get away," he says, but he does not move. His breath is slow, he's sinking in on himself. He's playing dead. I am disappointed. Like the tourists after their trophy hunts, I wanted it to be fun.

I pull the red button.

He slides against the side of the elevator, staggers to the back.

Above us, around us, a siren goes off. An emergency sound. Because emergencies only happen when there's a siren.

The noise is piercing, and I wake up, sober up, whatever up, like I did in the bathroom. The elevator has stopped. Somewhere between seven and eight. I'm facing him. My back to the doors. He is in the corner. Behind him, his hands hold on to the metal bar.

"Come on." I take one step forward. The elevator moves slightly. We are swinging, suspended in a box, seven stories up. "Do to me what you did to him."

Flopsy slumps forward. Around us, the alarm rings.

"Tell me you did it."

Behind me, a voice from the row of buttons. Emergency Services. Are we OK?

The credit card cuts into the base of my thumb. I look for a sign. Guilt, perhaps, fear. Bravado. The alarm rings.

"Tell me." I don't know how loud I am. He flinches. He presses farther into the corner. The statements in the trash. The hotel art above the bed. My words from her lips.

I am in front of him. He puts his hands up, his sleeves pull back.

I grab one arm and he whimpers. He is cold and clammy. Veins darker and larger than they should be. His face, sunken eyes and sallow skin. I pull his arm closer. He staggers. A line of scabs and scars, from inner elbow to forearm, a bloom of bruise in the crease. I think of Jessica. I drop his arm.

He tugs on his sleeve. I step back. I tuck the credit card and room key inside my bra.

"I have money." He can barely get the words out; they lurch from his mouth, garbled and slow.

I stare at the track marks beneath his shirt. Flopsy wears long sleeves every day in Southern California. "What?"

"You can't do this," he mumbles. "I'm gonna report this."

"Are you gonna report what was under your bed?"

Behind us, the voice continues. They're sending someone. Don't panic. The elevator begins to move.

Flopsy drops his head. He fumbles with his cuff. I grab his face, skin damp between my fingers. I squeeze. His cheeks cave inside my grip.

"Does your mother know?" I don't know why I ask, I don't know why I care. Maybe that's why she keeps an eye on him, maybe that's what she thinks needs to happen.

Step One: Employment.

Step Two: No more heroin.

Step Three: No more rape.

Maybe these are her priorities.

He doesn't pull away. Lips press out like a fish inside my grip. I push him against the wall. Nathan, our runs along the beach. The times he lifted me up and into my truck. Carried me half a mile, past the Prada and the diamonds and the homeless because I was tired. Flopsy begins to shake.

"I still shit my pants."

His mouth falls open, lower lip drooping across the crease between my thumb and forefinger.

"Because of your friend," I clarify.

Fish lips gape.

"You have money." I let go of his face. I wipe his sweat on my nice, black pants.

He slumps.

"You have family. Job prospects. Friends." I smooth my shirt front.

His eyelids drift down. His head dips forward. I grab his arm and press my fingers into the oozing crease of his elbow. He cries out and his knees buckle and he slides to the floor. I crouch in front of him, my fingers in the soft, wet slick of his body.

"But I'm angrier."

———

The graces are sleeping. Long limbs and wild hair. Lump left early.

I strip and step into the shower. I help myself to their cornucopia of cosmetics. My phone buzzes.

> Sorry, just saw this! Hope you're having fun!
> Can't wait to see you ☺

I scroll up. I texted Eric while I was out. Misspelled messages between ten and two. Jessica got one. Nathan got four.

> I miss you

> I mis you

> Nathan, were are yo/

> AJpd F

I turn off the bathroom light and weave around luggage in the dark. I slide into a bed and set my alarm and plug in my phone. I lie, surrounded by sleeping beauties, and stare at the ceiling. *Nathan* floats in front of me, his name dark and thick in a sea of white, surrounded by dead kids. Something scratches behind my eye, and I wonder about the names beneath the flickering light of the tunnel, if they knew they'd end up there, if they chose to end up there. I turn to my side. In her sleep, Amy shifts and spoons me.

Flopsy used to be nice, in his slow, dumb way. The vacant smile of a consequence-free life. Rapist was nice, too. He found me on campus, put his hand on my arm, asked what I was reading, where I was going. Those first few weeks, he checked in on me. But that was before they knew that I knew, before Nathan waited for me outside the administrative building and Title IX called them in for interviews. They were angry then, even though he was found not responsible, even though the police didn't bother with an investigation and the entire Religious Studies Department hid behind the convenient narrative of a crazy bitch. I always wanted to ask Rapist: Why now? Why get angry now? You've gotten away with it. If I pulled off a con like that, I'd be dancing naked in the streets and buying lottery tickets by the dozens.

I roll onto my back, Amy's soft snores behind me. For some people, winning isn't enough, because the trial itself is the crime. They don't think they've done anything wrong, and no one has the right to tell them otherwise. The villain is the accuser, because she dares to open her mouth. Accountability, equality, justice. There are people who don't understand these words. There are people who think anger belongs only to them.

T HE FLIGHT IS DELAYED. Hours in the Denver airport. Colette sits on one side of the gate area. I sit on the other. California welcomes us with ash and smoke.

I walk to my truck. I pay the $40 daily parking fee, T-shirt tucked over my face, and start the engine.

> I'm back

> That's great! I downloaded Terminator 2 ☺

I'm in his bed, I'm in his arms, he goes down on me again, I come again, and it's all the way I'm supposed to want it to be. He removes my hands from his cock and holds me to his chest. Soft fingers draw circles on my skin, like Dad drew pictures on my back when the storms came and the house shook and the thunder kept me awake. And when Dad was gone, and college was starting, and the little black dog was old and frail and the dorms didn't allow pets and even though Mrs. Sanghera offered I didn't want to and I didn't need to but it was the right thing to do. I took her behind the barn and her cloudy eyes looked at me, her hobbled legs and stiff hips followed me. I ran gentle circles along her back with my left hand and used one bullet with my right hand and dug a hole with both hands and buried her under the bush next to Dad and packed up the truck and locked up the house and said goodbye to all that.

"What are you thinking about?" he asks, his voice dreamy.

"Field-dressing a deer," I lie, because it's better than killing dogs.

He chuckles and pulls me close. "I don't know how to do that," he mumbles. His breathing slows. His temperature drops.

I turn to my side and close my eyes. Dog probably hasn't been let out for days. Eric sleeps, and I slide out of the bed. I shut the bedroom door behind me, change into my nice clothes from the not-nice interview, and step outside. I text Jessica.

How are you doing?

I don't know what to tell her. I found a needle in Nathan's arm. I found a needle under Flopsy's bed, but I found track marks on Flopsy's arm. Even if Flopsy wanted to shoot people up to kill them while he shot himself up for kicks, he couldn't climb through a window, let alone attack a grown man.

Maybe it was someone else, someone connected with their family, revenge for the millions dead from opioid addiction. Maybe they targeted the prodigal son who refused security, whose contact details are available on the department webpage, who was featured in a local newspaper article on student volunteers, with a note on his family name.

There is the other option, the one I ignored from the beginning. I don't want to think about Nathan killing himself. I don't want to think about the names in the tunnel, how many of them killed themselves. Why wouldn't they? Nathan asked. Six figures in debt for a degree in Communications from a state school before they're old enough to drink? Most of my students are studying Accounting, I said. Even more reason to kill themselves, he said.

I sit in the dark in my truck and scroll through my phone. Email informs me I have an overdue library book. If I wait until tomorrow, it's another $12, because my $20,000 a year in fees isn't enough. I start the engine and drive to campus.

It's past midnight, and the parking lot behind the Humanities building is empty. I pull into a professor's spot. I grab my bag, the overdue book inside, and walk into the tunnel. The overhead lights flicker and blink. The posters, the graffiti, the names.

I walk to the dead kids. The latest: Martin Johnson. I pull my shirt over my mouth and my phone out of my bag. I open my web browser and type his name. Hundreds of millions of pages. I add UCST. *"UCST student Martin Johnson allowed to compete in Olympics despite sexual assault allegations."* I remember this. Last year. There were protests across campus. Someone egged his car. The Dean/Provost/Whoever sent an email full of "c" words.

I take out a pen. I shake it, tilt it downward, and write "RAPIST" in big letters next to his name. I put the pen into my bag and rifle for the book, take two steps toward the end of the tunnel.

I turn back and face the wall. The strips of flickering lights make their insect sounds. The names jump and dance beneath the sporadic glow. Martin Johnson, rapist. Above him, Raymond Philips, rapist. To the left, last year's list, the name Chemistry wrote, rapist.

And Nathan. Rapist.

Four out of twenty-two. I count the names. Two are female. Four out of twenty men. Accused of rape and dead. KKKathy and her patterns.

I think of the hunter in the woods, the man I almost killed, who almost killed me. I was in a tree, seated on a platform Dad built, twelve feet up. Water in a bottle. Sandwich in a bag. I heard him before I saw him. I shifted at the waist, rifle at my shoulder, eye through the sight. The movements were soft, deliberate, not clunking and crunching like those of most men in woods. I almost pulled the trigger. I was tired and it was cold and I had three French essays to write for three seniors in the AP class. A man stepped out, no orange hat, no orange vest, covered in camouflage from boots to balaclava. I was surprised he knew how to walk in the woods like I knew how to walk in the woods. His gun aimed at my head, my gun aimed at his. We stared at each other, surprised by our surprise. I lowered mine and nodded. He lowered his and backtracked. That night, I told Dad I had seen a man in the woods. Well, there are plenty of hunters around here, he said. No, Dad. A man like me. A good hunter. Dad laughed and ruffled my hair. Impossible.

I take out my phone again. My fingers shake. I type a name from this year, Dereck Nodianos. No search results. Another, John Holzclaw. An Instagram of a teenage German kid. I scroll down. Nothing with UCST. Another, nothing. Another, a newspaper report on his death. A link to donations in lieu of flowers. A scholarship in his name. Another, another, another. But I know there's something there, the way I know when I'm in the woods. Before I see her, before I hear her, the crack of ice or brush beneath her hooves. There's no proof of her presence, but I know she's coming, my finger on the trigger. The day I saw the man, I was surprised by my surprise, surprised to spot another predator, surprised to spot one so close.

My battery blinks at me. I take another photo of the tunnel and drop my phone into my bag. I clutch the library book. Googling rapists only works if they're famous. Even publicly accessible sex-offender lists, searchable by ZIP code, only include individuals found guilty in a court of law. The internet does not show accusations by random coeds.

But Title IX is an office of record, and those are the records they keep.

———

It's quiet, and the lights in the library are dim. The building is closed for renovations for the next two years, but the bottom floor is open twice a week, for twenty-four hours, to encourage timely returns. Today is one of those days.

The muted lights from the six-story building show little movement. I step inside and walk toward the main kiosk. The information desk is manned by a skeleton crew, usually a chubby administrator and a desperate undergrad who slept through his morning shift but needs the hours to meet his work/study quota. Tonight, there is no one out front, but the blue glow of a computer screen from behind the reservation stacks hints at human presence.

My steps echo across the faux-tile flooring. To my left, screensavers blink. The university's logo wafts from side to side on the four computers, not updated in years, next to the printers, which have never been updated. I open my bag and pull out the offending volume. I didn't read it, but it's in my bibliography. Most bibliographies are composed of books the author hasn't read. I drop it into the late-night slot.

My steps are muted under the overhang of the second floor, plastic sheeting like ghosts above my head. I follow the edge of the empty information desks; the blue light fades from view. My feet reach the gray carpet at the end of the entrance area. I peer down both hallways. Next week is Thanksgiving, and most of the undergraduates have gone home early.

The lights are dim. A jingle to my right. The large, awkward shape of a janitor's cart. Blue bottles of cleaning fluid, and a roll of brown paper towels. Beneath them, a circle of keys the size of a dog collar. Freshman said her cousin was a janitor here. Freshman said her cousin had access to every room on campus.

KKKathy told me Title IX was for sex discrimination. I'm here to report a crime, I said, not refuse to bang a specific demographic.

A small, round woman in a khaki uniform steps out of a room, garbage bag in hand. She empties it into the large plastic bag in the cart and returns to the room.

KKKathy told me Title IX didn't investigate unless an investigation was opened. So—you don't do anything, I said. We hold on to the records, KKKathy said. We are an office of record.

Dead kids float in the milky tunnel. Twenty-two. Dead rapists. Four. But not everyone speaks of their rapes publicly. Not everyone writes in the tunnel. If someone files a complaint of sex discrimination at UCST, KKKathy holds on to it, doing nothing. KKKathy walks through the tunnel every day. KKKathy knows which names she recognizes.

Ahead of me is a fire escape the students keep on its latch, so the Community College kids can come in and make out with their State School hookups. Above me, plastic tarps creak. No footsteps. No students. To my right, less than twelve feet down the hallway, the janitor returns. She reaches for a spray bottle and the paper towels. She goes into another room.

I land on the ball of my toe, rolling my heel and bending at the knee. Move lightly, Dad said, keep your body loose and your steps soft. I reach the cart and slip my hand through the key ring. It's heavier than I thought. No sound from the end of the hallway. No person in either direction. Don't run, Dad said, only prey runs. I walk, knees soft, ankles soft, to the emergency exit, propped open. I slip out the door.

I press against the side of the library and fumble with my phone. I turn on the light and shine it above the key ring. There are only three keys with blue rubber coating at the base, two with yellow.

I drop the keys into my bag. The air is cool, but thick with ash. Denver's freshness has spoiled me, and I squint in the dark. I walk to the right of the skateboard paths; the grass absorbs my sound. Figures pass. A homeless couple share a cigarette on the lawn between the walkways, red tip bright.

There are minimal security cameras on campus, and most of them are in doorways. I walk casually, my nice interview shirt pulled up over my mouth and nose, my hand tucked against my bag. I reach the administrative building, the one we go to for exam results and rape reports, next to the canteen selling pizza and lattes. I take the wide, shallow steps two at a time. Several yards over, someone on a skateboard whizzes past. The door opens; I slip through. The lights are off, except for exit signs. They cast a shadow of red along the length of the hallway. To my right, an alarm system blinks green. Behind one of the office doors, the click of computer keys.

I walk into the red glow. The typing grows louder. I pass a door, a thin yellow line at the bottom. Inside, the typing continues, followed by a yawn and the creak of a chair. Room 201, Academic Coordinator. Probably a Ph.D. with no professorial prospects, who took a campus admin job to pay the bills and feel, just a bit, like they were doing what they were supposed to be doing. Feel like it wasn't all a waste. They're in their office after hours, trying to turn their dissertation into a book. They say they don't care about the academic job market, they don't care if the book gets published. They say it's a personal project.

The red gets brighter; the exit signs are closer together. I reach a hallway on my left. In the upper corner, a sign for the women's toilet, the white outline of a figure in a skirt, pink in the glow. This next hallway is dark. Red fades behind me. I walk toward the Title IX office, two doors down from the elevators. I hear laughter, back in the room where the typing was. A door opens and closes. The clink of a key chain and the squeak of comfortable shoes. They head out the way I came in.

The Title IX door is plain. No name of the individual inside. To my right, past the elevator doors, the end of the hall. Windows look out onto a grass patch between this building and the next. No lights outside. My breath is loud in my ears. If you can hear yourself breathe, they can hear you breathe. I open my lips, and exhale slowly through them.

I pull the keys out of my bag. It's too dark to distinguish between the blue and the yellow. I crouch, one hand under the door handle, and feel for the rubber bottoms. I lift one and insert it into the door. It won't go in.

I pull my phone out of my bag and turn on the flashlight. Anyone looking through the window could see me, the unmistakable bob of light. I find a blue one. I flip my phone on the ground, flashlight down, and reach up to the keyhole again.

To my right, a hum. I push the blue bottom in, but can't turn it. "Pigfuckers," I mutter, louder than I should. The hum increases. I lift my phone to find the next blue key. The weight of the ring almost makes me drop it.

To my right, the elevator dings.

Mouth open, breath slow. I slide my left hand to the bottom of my phone and turn off the flashlight. My right hand shakes as I bring it up to the keyhole.

The elevator doors open. Heels. Two steps. One step. A woman says something. A bag shifts from one arm to the other.

I press the key into the keyhole. Slowly, my breath light and slow, as if I was in a tree and she was in my sightline, I turn the key to the right and move the doorknob to the left. I press the door forward and take two squatted steps inside. As the *clip-clip* of the shoes comes closer, I pivot on one foot. I press the door into the frame and let the handle slide upward, locking into position. It makes the smallest clicking sound. The *clip-clip* stops, a pause on the other side of the door. She continues. Down the hall, past the mailroom. A zipper opens, a key chain jangles, a door opens and closes.

I stand. Pitch-black, no windows. Confidentiality, KKKathy said when I asked. I turn on my phone. My hands are shaking, and I have to press the screen three times to turn on the flashlight.

Just like I remember. Desktop computer, shiny new Mac. Photos of kids and family, matching Hitler haircuts. A framed certificate on the wall. I didn't bother to look closely before and I don't look now, but I am curious how, precisely, one becomes certified in recording rape accusations. Is that a degree program? Fantastic career prospects.

I open my photos and zoom in on the tunnel. The first name this year, Adam Nungesser. Behind me, the filing cabinets. Three of them, side by side, as big as bodyguards. I hold my phone forward and pull out the middle drawer of the first one, looking for "N"s. Inside, manila folders lined like soldiers, some so thin they look empty, others bulging with papers, paper clips, receipts, Post-its. I skim my fingers over the tops. I overheard someone say a woman filed a complaint when he complimented her hair. Someone else mentioned he had to report when he wore a T-shirt a colleague found offensive. I don't know if I believe these statements, if they are half-truths or whole truths, lies told under the cover of politically correct absurdity or liberal overreactions. I wonder if the record-keeping of minutiae helps the university feel in control, so when the next Eliot Rogers or Brock Turner enrolls, doing what they do, administrators have something to point to, a pile of documentation that says: We're doing our due diligence. We reported the T-shirt.

I pull one file up, a thin one, containing only two sheets of paper. "*Case Number 8976*," it reads at the top.

Complainant states respondent grabbed her by the shoulder and forcibly kissed her against her will at a party. No onlookers witnessed the events. Complainant states she pulled away, and respondent followed, pushing her and grabbing her breasts. Complainant states she . . .

I put it back.

Case Number 7653
Complainant states she . . .

I shut the drawer, only remembering at the very end to be gentle. I open the middle drawer of the next cabinet. I pull out a big file, one with loose pieces and paper clips and handwritten notes coming out the sides.

Case Number 3490
Complainant's mother . . .

I shove the cabinet shut. The noise echoes in the tiny room. My phone flashes a warning—10-percent battery. The gossip in my department, who I told versus who found out. What happened versus what everyone thinks happened. Odd, that the only anonymity around rape would be in Title IX records.

I turn and shine my light on the eighties desktop phone with the pull-out drawer. I walk behind the desk. I feel the ledge under the phone and slide it toward me. In tidy handwriting, a series of numbers and letters. I press the screen button and the power button. The computer hums to life.

An empty box for a password. I enter the first on the list. A loud noise as the desktop screen appears, and I glance at the door. No sound outside. I click on the internet icon, and it opens to the university homepage log-in. ID and password. I look at the list of numbers and letters. What the hell is her name? I type Kathy with three "K"s. Surprisingly, that doesn't work.

I open a new tab and look up the university Title IX webpage. Her email address under contacts—ktaylor23@ucst.edu. I click back to the university log-in page and enter the next password. Error. Next password. Error. There are two more passwords. If I enter an incorrect one a third time, the system will lock me out and send an email to ktaylor23@ucst.edu that someone is trying to break into her office.

I enter the second-to-last password. The webpage opens. I click through tabs on the left. Insurance. 403(b). Payroll. I click on Title IX, and a database opens. I click on "year" and open this year's reports. I scroll down. I scroll down. I scroll down. Jesus. We're ten weeks into the school year and these are just the people who reported—306 so far. I scroll back to the top and open the first one. Names. I exit and open last year's list. 1,336. Names. The year before. The year before. I scroll down. Only four years digitized.

More tabs. Next year's report for the Dean. A series of reports for Title IX employees. Details on previous litigation brought against Title IX offices, men suing women they raped and the campus they raped them on. Email templates. "Resources for Impact Parties," a note from Student Affairs, a Dear Student letter from the VP of Counseling Services, complete with a signature designed to look real.

My phone beeps, the dull monotone of a dying battery. The tunnel names disappear and the screen goes blank. I stuff it between my legs. The computer hums. There were 306 complaints this year, 1,336 last year, 1,289 the year before, 1,212 the year before. Who knows how many more there are. Most reports are recorded behind closed eyes, and held in a different kind of database.

Another beep, and I cross my legs. I slide ktaylor23's passwords back beneath her retro phone. I stare at the computer. What will happen to all this when they upgrade their system? I look at the filing cabinets. It feels wrong, to hide these histories from the world. A tree falls in the woods. An office of record.

I root through my bag and pull out the USB stick I keep in the side pocket, next to the lip balm and the Altoids tin of weed. Nathan made fun of me for keeping a USB stick. *Just use the cloud. That's only for naked pictures,* I said. I reach below the desk and feel for the small, rectangular opening. I open this year's Title IX reports. Select "All." Save As. The USB box lights up, and a bar appears. Last year. The year before. The year before.

The computer begins humming. I glance at the door. Between my legs, my phone beeps.

The bars reach 100 percent. I stuff the USB stick down my bra and reach for my bag. I log out of the university webpage. I turn off the screen. Behind the door, another door opens, closes. *Clip-clip.* The computer hums. My phone beeps between my thighs. *If you can hear yourself, they can hear you.*

Clip-clip down the hallway. The elevator pings. The elevator closes.

I drop my phone into my bag. I open the door. I don't turn off the computer. Powering down makes noise. Ktaylor23 will think she forgot to turn off her computer yesterday. Or she'll file a report, police will arrive, fingerprints will be dusted and cameras will be studied, and Colette's plagiarism won't be the only thing between me and a future in my field.

I walk through the dark hallway, turn down the other hallway, long and red, where the exit signs lead to the big black doors of the entrance. The typing room is silent. I squeak in my shoes, noisy in my breath, and push open the double doors. The air is thick and dry. I cough, no T-shirt over my face, down the wide steps, across the quad, to the library. I reach the emergency exit in the back, still propped open. I toss the keys inside.

I walk through the tunnel to my truck and reach inside the rear wheelhouse to grab the spare keys. I plug my phone into my charger. Two missed calls from Eric.

Where did you go?

Is everything ok?

Couldn't sleep

Sorry

I start the engine. I start the wipers. Ash across the front window, almost like snow.

CLASS IS QUICK. The students are looking forward to Thanksgiving break. One says she doesn't believe Buddhists kill people. Another points to the Rohingya conflict in Myanmar. A third asks when the papers will be returned to us. A fourth asks about the grading rubric. I remind them it's only a paper, it's only an elective. Three in front, the ones I know have multiple jobs, hyperventilate. "Don't forget"—I smile—"I'm happy to write recommendations. And not just for graduate programs. Internships, jobs, anything. Come talk. We'll find you something." Afterward, while the others pack, one of the three comes up to me and asks for an extension. His younger sister killed herself. Different campus, though. No tunnel.

I sit in my office and text Jessica. She doesn't respond. Eric texts. I don't respond. He calls. I don't pick up. I open my laptop and plug in the USB stick. Vegan sits at one of the desks, fake yogurt on his lips and an Animal Warfare slogan across his chest. New shoes. I open this year's Title IX reports. I read the first, the second, the third, one filed yesterday. A senior was walking home and someone tried to pull her into the bushes. I guess that does happen.

Another. "I heard someone crying, but was pretty drunk. I went home around 10, maybe 11. I'm not sure. I don't know what happened, but she seemed really flirty with him. I thought he was hitting on someone else, but I guess that didn't happen. I know she was upset, afterward. I heard from [redacted] that she said she was in pain. I don't really know."

Another. "I was there. They were close all night. She was all over him. She was laughing and he was laughing. It was a good time had by all. She kept refilling his drinks. She said she wanted to stay over. She brought him to the bedroom. It sounded consensual."

Another. "She followed me around the house. She invited herself into my room. She was all over me. I rarely make love outside of a relationship, and it had been a really long time since I had sex, but I had heard from others that she was really promiscuous, so I figured a one-night stand would be OK."

Another. "I am still in shock. I am sorry she has the mental troubles she has, but that is no excuse for accusing me of such a crime. I am seriously considering bringing a legal case against her."

They blur together. Not once, in the rapists' response, do they admit culpability or uncertainty or even the possibility of wrongdoing. Their innocence and confusion, their futures at stake.

"How could she think that?"

"I can't believe this."

"This could ruin my whole life."

"I'm suing."

I open the previous year's files. The statements, the interviews. *What she said* versus *what he did*. Two hundredth, six hundredth, 1,336th. What a mess. It is so much easier if we don't believe the women.

"Shit baggers."

Vegan glares and makes a big show of adjusting his noise-canceling headphones. I wait two beats, then say "Sorry!" loudly enough for him to spill his hippie snacks.

I zoom in on the twenty-two names in the tunnel. I tear out the front page of a Norman Mailer book left on the desk and write them on the back. I circle the four I know have accusations against them and write a question mark next to the others. I cross off the names of the two women, then, on second thought, write a question mark next to them too. #feminism.

I open the search function for the PDFs. I start with the circled names. One letter at a time, I enter Raymond's name. The rainbow whirls. His name appears, highlighted in yellow, at the top of a report from last year, just before summer. The 1,221st.

"I'm surprised she thinks it wasn't consensual. She never told me no. I thought she wanted it." Fridays at Four, the woman who survived Raymond. Blood on the walls, she said. I read the words of a violent man who will never be violent again. Found facedown on the beach, she said. I tap my fingers against the desk.

Hollywood tells us that killing rapists restores order. Mathematically, this implies that killing rapists is a good thing. Rather than two wrongs making a right, it is one wrong, counterbalanced by a right, that brings us back to neutral. But movies are made by movie people, and movie people know so little about the world, or at least surviving it. Erasing Raymond does not erase his actions. According to them, she should be back to normal. A tidy net-zero. I draw a check mark across Raymond's name.

I type the next circled name, the Olympic hopeful. Three reports open. "Choking," "spitting," "vaginal and anal rape." Check mark.

The student from last year, the reason Chemistry attends Fridays at Four. Two files. Check mark.

I look up Nathan, even though my hands shake and my breath

catches and Vegan glares between his headphones. Nothing, at least not from Title IX, not from the last four years. But Jeff had his folder, and Jessica confirmed it. Check mark.

I look up the two women. No check marks.

I go down the list of this year's remaining sixteen dead kids, typing each name into the search box of each PDF.

"She's fucking crazy." Last year, 896th. Check mark.

No results found. No check mark.

"This is ridiculous." This year, 42nd. Check mark.

"It was totally consensual." Two years ago, 1,131st. Check mark.

I zoom in on my tunnel photo. There's another name, faded at the top of the list. I almost can't read it. Steve Parkerson.

The computer is slow; the rainbow ball whirls. It stops. Nothing from this year. Two Stevens, but no Steve Parkerson.

I search the year before. I search the earliest year I have. The rainbow whirls. David S. Parkerson. "He climbed on top of me. I couldn't get him off." Four years ago. I google his name. Dead this past summer, one week after graduation; 608th.

Check mark.

———◆———

I'm outside the Humanities building, my laptop in my bag, hanging off one shoulder. If I had a cigarette, this is when I would smoke it. I bounce my hands against my thighs.

"Hey." Eric walks out from the tunnel.

I lift my head toward his. It's afternoon. I've spent the past three hours glued to my computer in the graduate-student office, ignoring the coughs and "Excuse me"s. Someone stood in front of me, asking how much longer I'd be at the desk. I stared at the screen. Cross-referencing names in the tunnel to Title IX reports. Local obituaries, church services for mourning families, and newspaper articles to Title IX reports.

Twelve men who have been accused of rape have turned up dead this academic year. Including the kidnapper who was in the paper a few weeks ago, the guy who locked a sixteen-year-old in a shed and raped her hourly until the Feds traced her phone. His trial was canceled when he died in October, out on a $2 million bail. Police suspected suicide.

"Are you all right?" He pulls back. His smile fades. "You said you were on campus, but I couldn't get through to your phone."

"It's dead."

"What's going on?"

"I don't know." I hop from one foot to the other, really wishing I had a cigarette. Or booze. Or K. Anything, really. Now is a good time for anything.

"Hey." He puts both hands on my arms, rubbing me from shoulder to elbow. "What is it?"

I stop. He's a good man, a kind man. Hair of an eighties icon, eyes of a Disney prince. He investigates things for a living. "I think I found something."

"OK." A quick scan of my body. It's paternal, the look of someone checking for injuries.

"Twenty-two students have died at UCST since graduation last summer."

His eyebrows lift. He continues to rub my shoulders. "That's awful."

"Maybe it isn't."

"What?"

I grab his upper arm and pull him away from the door. We stand at the corner of the building, faded concrete between bike racks. Ash swirls around us. Gravel beneath our feet. "Twelve of them were accused of rape."

He stares.

"Twelve." I tap my hands against my thighs. "Out of twenty-two. All accused of rape. All dead."

"OK."

"Different causes." One foot to the other. "Overdose. Alcohol. Hypothermia."

"How do you know this?"

I stop. He's leaning back, just slightly, creating distance between us. "I found their obituaries."

He nods slowly. "How do you know they were accused of assault?"

I run my tongue over my front teeth. "I read their Title IX reports."

"How in the world did you—"

"That doesn't matter." I wave my hand. "What matters is . . ." I'm not sure where I'm going with this. It's too wild. A misandrist fantasy. The Handman's Tale. "I think someone is killing them," I say. "I think someone is killing rapists."

Eric opens his mouth. He says nothing.

"I mean, twelve dead students? And they all have that in common?" I lift my hands out to my sides. "And that big case? The kidnapper? He's dead, too. So, actually, it's eleven students and one barista. That's—"

"How did you get hold of the Title IX reports?"

I press my lips together.

"Title IX reports are not publicly accessible."

I look down at my feet.

"Sarah." A statement this time, like my father when he found cigarettes hidden behind a tree stump.

"Come here." I reach for his hand. It is limp within mine. I pull him away from the bike racks toward the tunnel. Around us, students laugh and flirt and chat. I bring him to the opening. I point to the wall. "Look."

"What am I looking at?"

"The names." I turn, but the wall is white. Sometime this afternoon, while I was buried in contraband narrative, Uniform and his bucket came through. "Wait, I'll show you." I pull out my phone. The screen flashes black. Battery at 0 percent. Fuck.

"What am I looking at?" he asks again.

"The names. The students write the names here. It's a list of everyone who's died. And people write comments on them, like 'I miss you' or 'I love you,' and this year there were a lot of 'rapist' comments, so I wondered—"

"Sarah."

I grab his upper arms with my hands. "Don't you get it? Someone is—"

Eric pulls back, stronger than I expected. "This university has over thirty thousand students. Every year there are accidents and deaths and, yes, instances of sexual assault."

"This is different. This is good news! This means . . ." I trail off. I don't know why it's good news. I don't know why it is helpful. But I know Flopsy hides in elevators and Colette will never let me graduate. I know my job will go to an Ann with no "e." I know Rapist will continue to rape. But this is something. This I can focus on. I can distract myself from my dead friend, my dead future, my debt, my fear, my rage.

There is another part of me. Something thick and sharp and red. The part that makes my hands shake. The part that throws my aim off. That part doesn't need distraction. That part is happy.

"I can't imagine what you've been through." His words are careful, like a fox leaving its burrow. "With your assault, and the department's response, and your friend's death. I can't imagine how hard it's been."

I blink.

"You need to see someone."

My breath leaves me in a rush, a huff of surprise and indignation.

"I don't know if you actually stole private files, or if you just think you stole private files, but this is not OK." His jaw is tight.

I reach into my bag and pull out the USB stick. I shove it at him.

"The names are on this." I grab my water bottle and open it, fingers fumbling. I pour it against the wall. I rub with my palms. "The dead names are listed here. They just cover them up every couple of weeks." I empty the bottle. I drop it and use both hands to rub off the paint. The names remain hidden; water runs white down my arms, drips onto my jeans and shoes.

Eric puts both hands on my shoulders and turns me away from the wall. "Jesus, Sarah. What are you thinking? That you're on the trail of a vigilante serial killer?" He drops the USB stick to the ground. "If that has what you say it has on it, it's evidence of a crime."

Water and paint drip from me. "Eric—"

He pushes me away. "Get some help."

———

My voice drones on about the Eightfold Path, the Four Noble Truths, the Ten Directions. I sound like the people I promised myself I'd never be. I can't even pretend this is interesting to me, let alone make it interesting to college kids who think they invented sex and beer. Their eyes are bleary. It's almost Thanksgiving, but they have essays due. Someone yawns. Another shuffles her feet. Two are staring at their laptops and don't think I can see the earbuds beneath their hair. I stop.

"You know none of this matters, right?"

Someone in the back, some kid whose name I can't remember because he only shows up half the time, looks up.

"How many of you are in this class because you chose it?"

They look among themselves.

I put down my notes. I look at my shirt. Same one I wore yesterday. I slept next to Dog, curled on the floor between the garage and the box, all the doors and windows open. Eric's voice in my head. I need to see someone. "And how many of you are here because you need a Humanities credit? Or because it fits with your schedule? Or because you refuse to attend class before ten in the morning? Or because you heard it was easy? Or because you're loading up on whatever you can to graduate early?"

A student raises his hand.

"Well, at least you're honest."

More shuffling. More looking. A student removes an earbud. Just one.

"Are the rest of you even interested?"

Silence.

The answer, of course, is no. Or, more accurately, not anymore. Some of them were, maybe, but they're not now. How could they be? Colette and I have sucked the joy out of this subject and reduced the magic and mystery of a worldview that has enchanted billions for thousands of years to a series of lists, names, and dates. Religion becomes history, history becomes statistics, statistics become accounting, and accounting becomes the day job they have no interest in, but have to pursue to pay off their debt.

"I don't give a shit, either."

The typing stops. All the earbuds are out. A baseball player along the back wall—Jay or Dave, I can't remember which section this is—smirks. His buddy looks at him for confirmation. Is she joking? One girl in the corner nudges another. Are we allowed to say "shit"? A freshman watches me from the front row, eyes wide. She's trying to understand.

"Let me tell you what's going to happen to your essays." I step in front of the table. "You're going to spend however long you spend on them. Some of you, it'll be days, maybe a week. For others, it's an evening. A few frantic hours on Wikipedia the night before. Maybe twenty minutes with AI. You hand them in. I ignore them for a week."

Baseball continues to smirk.

"I'm going to ignore them because they're stupid." Baseball's face falls. "You're not stupid." Baseball lights up. "Your work is stupid. And boring. Because you don't care and you don't try."

Freshman gapes.

"The university's policy of three weeks to get papers back to students isn't because it takes three weeks to read papers. It's because it takes two weeks and six days to bring ourselves to approach the enormous pile of shit that is your work." I put the last word into air quotes with my forefingers.

Brunette in the middle row is staring at me. Curly behind her chews her gum more slowly. Baseball is back to smiling, and I wonder if he was hit on the head during practice.

"So . . . two weeks and six days go by, and I finally bring myself to approach your steaming mass of excrement, because the smell is so intense I can't have it in my apartment anymore. And those papers that you spent however long on, hours or days or a week, I read in ten minutes." I hold up my hands and spread my fingers. "If I like it. Otherwise, I read the first sentence of the first paragraph, because, from those twelve words, I know whether or not it sucks."

Curly stops chewing. She turns to the Chinese student to her left. He looks around at the white kids.

"And it doesn't really matter what you write anyway, because I already know the name at the top of the paper. If I recognize the name, it means you actually come to class and occasionally open your mouth, so I give more of a shit. If I don't recognize your name, which is eighty percent of you, that means you don't talk, you don't do the reading, you don't even show up. And maybe that's because Daddy is paying your bills, so, if you flunk out, no big deal. Or maybe it's because you're working three jobs and what's the point when the planet will be blown up before you retire, as if you'll be able to do that. It doesn't matter, because I have to grade and Colette's lectures are shit and her reading assignments are ridiculous, so of course you don't understand everything, so of course your papers are shit, so of course I grade based on whether or not I recognize your name."

Baseball's friend brings out his phone and places it on his desk. He is recording.

"And why would I spend hours reading your papers? None of you like your grades unless you get A's, and even then, there's always someone who wants an A-plus. So you bitch and moan about how unfair I am, how unfair it all is, and it is unfair, but so's everything else, and every once in a while you should ask yourself if you did any real work." I walk to the edge of the whiteboard. "Or you'll come to my office hours. Not you guys who work three jobs, because you don't have the time, but the rest of you will show me your paper, with nothing to support your whining except for the personal belief that you deserve a higher grade because you feel you deserve everything, and that, my dears, that moment right there, in front of you, is the first motherfucking time that I will read more than the first line of your first paragraph."

Baseball's friend pushes his phone closer to the edge of the desk. I walk through the rows and pick it up. I speak into it.

"And you'll complain some more, and maybe even go to the professor, because you think she gives a shit. She won't listen, but you'll find her office, because it's not tucked away in some bumblefuck extension. But that doesn't matter, either, because she only comes to work twice a week, and when she does, it's sure as shit not to listen to an eighteen-year-old complain that his four pages of AI editing didn't light the TA's ass on fire. She doesn't care about you, but she doesn't know how to tell you that, because she hasn't spoken to someone under thirty since she was under thirty, and anyone under thirty who speaks to her does it with their nose so far up her ass she thinks their words are coming out of her own throat."

The room is silent. For the first time, no one is looking at their phone.

"Happy Thanksgiving. I'm not reading any papers this quarter."
I'm at the door, my hand on the handle, before I realize I've grabbed
my bag and headed toward the hallway. The students remain in their
chairs. "You all get A's."

———◆———

Everyone is texting. Calling. Emailing, I assume, but I don't look
at my computer. I don't need to upload the A's until the end of the
course, and it's Thanksgiving week, so most people have canceled
their classes anyway. I'm serious about giving them all A's. Why not?
Nothing means anything, so they may as well pass.

Colette has left a voice message. Apparently, the video is online
and trending—TA Rampage. Someone went through and bleeped
out the swearing. Someone set it to music, and it's a hit on social
media. This is the first time Colette has called me in two years. I
had no idea the way to get through to her was to go viral on TikTok.

Jessica has managed to get her phone back, or is out of rehab, or
made up that whole I Can't Look At My Phone thing, because she's
called twice and texted three times. All about Nathan. All about
sorry.

I don't pick up. Not for Colette. Not for Jessica. Not for any
students or faculty or administrators.

I swallow something. I snort something. I leave a voicemail for
Eric. "I know about Nathan." My words are slurred and the ceiling
spins. "He's one of the twelve." I begin to sing. "Somebody's out
there, sitting in a tree. K-I-L-L-I-N-G."

I drift off, pass out. The beep wakes me. I call back. "Do you
remember when I was lying in your bed and you didn't have a hard-
on and you asked me what I was thinking about, and I said field-
dressing a deer?" I must be sweating now. Or maybe it is raining,
there's a single cloud overhead, I'm like a cartoon character who

received bad news. The rain is hot and wet on my face, dripping from the sides of my eyes into the pillow. "It's never deer."

I lower my voice and hold the phone to my mouth; breath fogs the screen. "It's Flopsy. It's Rapist. It's all the Title IX boys. The celebrities and the politicians. Strung up by their ankles. Peel back their skin. Stack their pieces in the freezer and make soup from their bones. That's what I was thinking about. That's what I'm always thinking about."

The smoke is thicker now. My eyes burn. I turn my head, press the phone between my mouth and the pillow, and reach for another small paper packet. "Maybe somebody did kill Nathan. Maybe somebody is killing all of them." I swallow whatever I find. "If so, good job."

I throw the phone across the room.

———

Elaine slides a note under the door. It's not the first of the month, but if I'm going somewhere for the holiday, can I be sure to leave my check for December?

Dog lies next to me. The sun passes up one side of the mountain and down the other. Chickens make noise. Elaine knocks, timid and rhythmic. Empress screams from the balcony, screams at her to do her job and get the check and what the hell is wrong with that dumb girl anyway?

I lie in bed. The sheets stick to the sweat on my skin. Ash wafts through the shut door, the shut window, the closed blinds. At some point, the pills are gone and the powder is left. I don't have the energy to snort. Everything is shut, locked down, covered up, but everything comes in.

Eric hasn't responded. I guess he's wishing he followed the smart-man motto: Don't stick your dick in crazy. I am looking at

Nathan's phone, at the goats on the farm, somewhere up north. They're small and cute and bounce straight up in the air. I reread my text chain with Nathan. I go on Reddit. r/mybestfriendisdeadbutI foundouthesarapist. AITA?

I scroll through Nathan's messages. A photo he sent me, two years ago. Sober, if you can believe it, on the grass outside the mission downtown. Heads together, looking up. I remember this. He called me the day before, told me he had a surprise. I was sharing a house with five other graduate students, somewhere in the Riviera, one bathroom, $1,600 per bedroom.

He had a car that day. Maybe from his sister. He drove us downtown. We ate tacos, drank watermelon juice, and painted each other's toenails. The sun shone, and neither of us spoke about our research, our teaching, our writing. We weren't on the job market then. The tremors of hopelessness had reached us, but, like everyone in a Ph.D. program, we assumed we were smarter and harder-working than everyone else. We assumed smartness and hard work mattered.

He was telling me about a friend from his Italian years, an old monk who had just sent his first-ever email. We've exchanged letters for over a decade, I can't imagine him on a computer, Nathan said, laughing. It's nice to have an old friend. Keeps things in perspective.

I don't have any other friends, I muttered, my feet in his lap.

I don't believe that, he said. I pushed myself up, tipping the juice and spilling a taco across my thighs. I used to, but when you go years not returning anyone's phone calls or emails, they stop reaching out.

Have you tried reconnecting?

What am I supposed to do? Send a group email to everyone I used to know and explain what happened?

He began rubbing my feet. Would that be so crazy?

I closed my eyes and lay back down, the sun warm against my lids. Who wants to read that shit?

I felt his lips on my instep. People who loved you, he murmured against my skin. People who still love you. They will want to know what happened.

The screen fades, and our faces dull. I tap; his smile brightens next to mine.

Accusation of rape, age 17, by L. Martin, age 16, settled out of court—removed from record

I must have been asleep, because now I'm awake. Nathan's phone battery beeps next to me. The moon is climbing down, but no sunlight yet. I stand up, and the world tilts. I open the garage door. Dog walks out. Ash, insects, the distant call of early birds flow in. I listen to Dog's urine and sit on the edge of the bed. I plug in Nathan's phone.

L. Martin. Sixteen years old when she accused him of rape. Who knows how old she was when he did it. Allegedly.

L. Martin.

I scratch my eyes with my palms and blink in the dark. Ecstasy has left me thirsty, and Molly gives me the shakes. Dog shuffles and snuffles and stretches. I refill her water and leave it next to a bowl of food I must have filled at some point. I yawn. The air is thick and heavy and tastes of soot. I strip and step into the shower, door open, Dog outside. I have to wash my hair three times to get a lather. I scrub myself raw with a pair of pink exfoliating gloves that were here when I moved in. The water runs brown beneath me. I step out and brush my teeth.

L. Martin.

I sit on the edge of the bed, toothbrush in my mouth, and look up L. Martin on Nathan's phone. This is where a tenured professorship would be helpful. I could pay a graduate student to scroll. It's an exercise in futility, but they'd do it for their hourly wage and ability to put Research Assistant on their CV. Line. I scroll through a handful of the 1.9 billion L. Martins of the world. Men and women, celebrities and sponsored posts.

I stop brushing. The toothbrush dangles in my mouth. A drop of white falls to my thigh. The stillness in the woods. The cat scratches at the door. I swipe to his bank account. ID. Password. $25,000 a month to LMC LLC. A banker's check, the pixelated screenshot appears when I click on the details tab. Probably a financial services firm, Jessica said. Trust fund of $10 million in assets, Jeff wrote. A fixed percentage a year, one-quarter to one-half a percent. I look at the numbers: $25,000 a month is $300,000 a year, 3 percent of his trust amount. Much too high, according to Jessica.

Mint drips down my throat. I type "L Martin, LMC LLC" into my phone. Tens of thousands of pages appear. A rapper. A Korean freighting company. Someone making jewelry. I click on the next page. Social media feeds. The next page. An Instagram feed: 654 Followers, 235 Following. 134 Posts.

The sound, in the back of my mind, when the leaves are moving and I see them before they see me. I click the link. Nathan's Instagram opens. The only account he follows. I scroll through the posts of small goats on a small farm. Some dancing. Some sleeping. All owned by Lara Martin-Chase.

A TEN-HOUR DRIVE GOES pretty fast when you think you're about to meet the woman your best friend raped as a kid. Even faster when you think this same woman has been receiving monthly checks for more money than you make in a year, and you can't help but think, Huh, when a rapist pays his victim five figures a month and she doesn't tell anybody about the rape, that sure sounds like blackmail. And you drive even faster when, cross-referencing your thoughts with your own rape experience, you wonder if those five figures lost their shine somewhere along the line, because some things money can't buy, and now that your best friend/her rapist is dead and his contact information, including his address, is publicly accessible, it wouldn't be too hard to track him down, climb through his window when he's too baked to move, and shoot him up with enough heroin to take out a University of Spoiled Children freshman. So you spit out your toothpaste, pack your bag, bring in the dog, and fill three bowls with food and four bowls with water in the garage. You stick a check to Elaine's door and gas up the truck, and the sun's barely up, but you've been on the road for two hours already and no one is calling because it's a holiday weekend and they're probably still asleep.

And if, halfway up the 5, you think you're crazy and desperate and remember your almost boyfriend telling you you're nuts and remember thinking there could be a rapist-murdering serial killer on the loose (and how, honestly, you were pretty OK with that) because you thought you spotted a data pattern and you're good with data patterns because you're an advanced researcher, but, actually, it's just your friend who's the rapist, the friend you thought you knew so well, the friend you thought you had all the data on, but actually didn't know shit about. And the campus has thirty thousand students, and everyone does drugs and everyone gets raped and, though randomness is technically a pattern, random information is not a data set.

So—you pull into a Denny's outside the Bay and pee in a bathroom with no toilet paper and order a coffee and plug in your phone and call the number on the website linked to the Instagram page of the woman you're stalking, the one that lists her home address because the goat farm has a goat shop that's open ten to four, and you don't know why but you disguise your voice, so when a man picks up you fake an accent and say you vant to buy zome zoap, but you're old-fashioned and don't trust ze internet and could you just zend zem a check? And he laughs and says he understands and, sure, a check is fine. Would you like to put the order in now? he asks, and you say, No, no, I'm still deciding, but to whom do I write ze check? To Lara Martin? And he says, it's Lara Martin-Chase now, but you know what, could you write it to LMC LLC, because that's the business name and it makes tax organizing easier? That's zo veird, you say, because you grew up in L.A. and went to a private school with a Lara Martin, and you thought you recognized her picture. And he says, wow, maybe, she did grow up in L.A. and went to a

private school, not like him, and he laughs and you laugh and your
voice cracks and you say zat's great, sanks, and your hands are shaking so hard you have to press your phone twice to hang up.

So you fill up on gas and get back into the truck and feel a little
less crazy and a little more sad, and you keep driving. The sun is up,
the traffic in minimal, and the farther away you drive, the clearer
everything gets, and you don't know why until you realize there is
less ash in this air and you can see the blue above and the green
around and the hills aren't brown anymore, they're actually green,
and you wonder, briefly, if Lara Martin-Chase—who lives in the
North, where the air is clear and the hills are green, with a husband
and some goats and $25,000 a month, who maybe, just maybe, did
something to her rapist/your best friend and got away with it—is
living a damn good life. And you wonder if you are jealous.

The road winds between cows and trees and green. I roll down
my window, and smell sea and dirt and clean, clear sky. Hand-
painted signs for parking appear on my left. I come to a stop sign,
and a wobbly arrow, bright pink against a blue background, points
me to the right. The road narrows; pavement turns to gravel, turns
to dirt. The signs continue, each depicting a cartoon goat that man-
ages to stand sideways and smile at the observer. I've known a few
goats. They never did that.

I reach a sign that reads "PARKING," with a small heart above
the "I," even though it's a capital letter, so I'm not sure what that's
about. I pull past a mailbox; the trees swing wide, and a Victorian
house on a swell of green appears before me. Around it, thick trees
and lilac bushes. Rose vines crawl toward windows, and a glimmer
of ocean winks at the horizon. I park in a gravel lot and cut the
engine. I climb down. The sound of a dog, the scent of flowers, farm
sounds and farm smells. I read an article about stuffed animals with
electronic beating hearts that yuppies buy for puppies. I want to lie
on this earth and press my body against the familiar rhythm.

"I'm so glad you came!"

I turn toward the voice. A tall woman, in jeans and a T-shirt, hair pulled back and eyes bright, walks toward me. "It means I won the bet!"

"Excuse me?"

"My husband said no one would come the day before Thanksgiving. I said, there's always someone doing last-minute shopping"— she grins—"even for goat-milk soap. Hi, I'm Lara." She holds out a hand.

"Hi." I hold mine out, realize it has the keys in it, fumble and drop them. She picks them up and puts them into my palm.

"What's your name, honey?"

"Jessica." I don't know why I say it. Maybe it's the size of the house, or the clean air, or the expensive view, and I can only think of one person who would feel comfortable in a place like this, despite the barn smells. Or maybe I don't want anyone to know I'm here. Maybe I just want to be someone else for a while, somewhere else, and pretend I live a different sort of life.

"Hi, Jessica." She looks behind me. "Great truck."

"Thanks."

"I love a truck. Why people buy sports cars I'll never understand." She gestures for me to follow her. We walk up the gravel past a pair of redwoods, the scents of lilacs and rosebuds and goats and dogs and horses and cows. My eyes fill.

"Where are you coming in from?" She talks over her shoulder as she unlocks a barn door, slides it open. She turns and smiles and reaches one arm for a light switch, and I follow her into a four-stall barn. It's decorated to look like a shop, but the smells are right, pitchforks and brooms lean against the wall, water buckets are stacked in the corner. "Come on in."

"It's a barn," I say, like a tourist who does not know what a barn is.

She laughs, walks around, and turns on another light. A bookshelf lights up, with soaps and bath bombs and body butters. In the center of the aisle, where the animals would be tied to lead lines for tacking up, brushing down, or a soft goodbye before the hole out back, is a round table with brown bags and a sign reading "Soap Ends."

"We've got a few barns, so I figured, why build something?" She pulls up a stool and sits next to the soap bookcase. "We're both home with the animals most of the day, so when people swing by, we just bring them here. Sometimes I hang out and read." She points to the stall behind her. I walk over and peer between the bars. Another bookcase, smaller, with glass doors to keep the dust out, a wicker chair with a quilt and a footstool. On the floor, a round, padded dog bed. Damn.

"Is there anything in particular you wanted to see?" She gestures to the table in the center of the aisle. "We've got soap ends this week."

"I'm just looking." Why start telling the truth now? "I'm on vacation."

"Oh, great! Are you up for Thanksgiving?" She points a finger at me. "Are you Luke's sister? He said she was coming up."

"No." I shake my head. "I just wanted some fresh air."

"Of course." She puts both heels of her paddock boots on the bar at the base of the stool. "Those fires are still roaring. Man"—she shakes her head—"we had some a few years ago. So scary. We never had that as a kid."

"You grew up around here?" I pick up a bag of soap ends and pretend to examine it.

"L.A., but I left in high school and never looked back. Those are fifteen dollars per bag."

I nod and unravel the top, pretending to smell. "Your family didn't like L.A.?"

She laughs. "Not exactly."

I do sniff now. Fresh lilac greets me. I want to say, "I hope nothing bad happened," or "So—tell me about the time you got raped as a kid," but she seems nice, and, Jesus, even I have trouble with that question.

"I'll take these." I hold up a bag of soap ends.

She smiles and reaches for a bath bomb behind her. "I'll throw in this for free."

I realize I've left my wallet in the truck. She says it's no problem and we walk out of the store barn. There are two other barns, bigger and brighter, with smells and sounds I know.

"Lara!" someone calls behind us, footsteps on the gravel. I turn, and the greenest eyes beneath the darkest hair crinkle. He introduces himself. Ben, the husband. Instagram does not do justice to this man. "Your mom called. Apparently, Frank is on a new diet and can't eat pumpkin." He holds a phone. "And your sister wants you to call her back, because traffic is terrible, so they're going to stop along the way so the kids don't get tired, but she's worried the turkey will overheat in the hotel room."

Lara rolls her eyes and looks at me. "Why my sister felt the need to bring the turkey this year, from L.A. no less . . ." She turns to Ben. "Sabotage. That's what this is."

"I'll call her." He kisses her cheek. "And I've already started the apple pie." He walks back to the house, phone tucked between his chiseled jaw and sculpted shoulder.

"Well, it looks like I need a turkey. Did you have plans for today?"

"Not really."

"Want a tour? I can show you downtown." She puts her hand on my shoulder. "I don't know what your family's like, but mine is nuts, and when you have the big house, you're always the host."

I don't tell her my family is dead. I don't ask about Nathan or how she's so happy or would she be this way if she wasn't getting a payout or does she know that he's dead and did she have anything to do with it. I say, "Great."

"I'll drive." She pulls a key fob from her pocket and nods toward my bag of soap. "Have that for free. It's the least I can do to thank you for saving my sanity."

I put the soap into my truck and grab my bag and lock the door, and I am in her truck, dark blue, F-450 diesel dually. The A/C works, and the seats heat up, and we drive into a downtown that is cute and elegant and warm. She honks at a crosswalk and an old man smiles. She rolls down her window and shouts to a woman with three small kids about book club next week.

We go to a bookstore, and the bell jingles when we open the door. I have missed that sound and haven't heard it in years. A guy with a nose ring and girl with a neck tattoo greet us. Lara introduces me as Jessica from L.A. and Nose Ring rolls his eyes. "Don't mind him." Neck Tattoo grins. "He's from Portland, and no one hates L.A. more than Portlanders."

"Wanna bet?" I ask and point to myself, and Lara laughs and Neck Tattoo laughs and even Nose Ring laughs. He tells me I have to try the local creamery. He hands me a punch card. If we order two ice-cream cones, he'll be up to a dozen and he'll get one free, so just take this and go next door, and then bring it back, OK?

And we do eat ice cream—actual ice cream, not frozen yogurt. I have missed this taste and haven't had it in years. Lara points out the local shops and apologizes that so many are closed for the holiday. She tells me to come back next week, or around Christmas, because they light up the street and it's so cute and the ice-cream shop does their limited-edition peppermint and the bookstore has a Santa and the fancy restaurant that the L.A. people love has a secret menu they don't show to tourists, but if I let her know I'm coming, she'll get me in. The oysters are to die for.

And we walk to a butcher, an actual butcher. I have missed this smell, the fresh meat and the hanging flesh, no plastic in sight, and haven't had it in years. Lara introduces me as her friend Jessica, and the butcher, who is short and fat, asks me how I like it here. I tell him I grew up near a farm and miss it. I don't know why I say it, but Lara smiles and puts her hand on my shoulder. Short Fat makes a joke about Lara's L.A. sister, and Lara nods and says, Of course you were right, and he says it's fine, he knew he'd be right because didn't this happen last year? There's a turkey in the back, and it's fresh. No need to defrost.

And he goes in the back and brings out the bird, and it's a solid twenty pounds and wrapped in white paper, like it should be, inside a trash bag for leaks. I pick it up and say, No, no, I got it, and we bring it back to the truck, and Lara asks if there's anything else I want to see. Before I can answer, she mentions the coast, and how beautiful it is, and she knows a great drive, so we take a back route so close to the water I worry we'll fall in. I stare at the sand, and no matter how closely I look, I can't see any oil. The ocean rolls and recoils beneath crests of white, and the sky is blue. Lara is telling me about the annual sheep-and-wool festival, how desperate she is to win, because, you know, Ben says the ewes don't care, but she's entered them four years in a row now and they've never won and she's worried it's affecting their self-esteem.

"Where are you staying?" she asks as we pull into her driveway.

I have forgotten I don't live here and this is not my life. "I haven't booked anything yet."

Her eyebrows go up. "It's a holiday weekend. You might be out of luck."

She's right, of course, and I should probably continue this lie and come up with something other than I'm an idiot who decided to spend Thanksgiving in a tourist town without a hotel reservation, but, as much as I am enjoying pretending to be Jessica from L.A. on vacation, I don't feel like spinning any more webs. I shrug.

"Let me see if we can do something."

She cuts the engine, and we both climb out. I reach for the turkey and follow her past the trees and the lilacs and the shop barn into the house. They have a mudroom, which I've never seen in California, because Californians like to pretend they have no mud, despite the landslides. We kick off our shoes, and Ben comes into the small room with the coats and the boots and the bag of dog food and takes the turkey out of my hands. He laughs and says he knew she'd do this, so he's already made room in the fridge. We walk into the kitchen, with its wooden table and wooden chairs, and everything smells like sugar and spice, and Lara asks if her sister really isn't going to make it tonight. Ben says yes, and hoists the turkey onto his shoulder, lifting his shirt and exposing a sliver of stomach so perfect I can't tell if it's an abdominal muscle or a slab of marble carved by Jesus Christ himself.

Lara turns to me. "I was going to put them up in the guesthouse, but it looks like they won't be here. You want it? It's technically an Airbnb, when family isn't in it."

"Oh."

"It's small, but you can see the goats from the porch and the sunset in the evening."

"I don't want to put you out."

"You'd have to pay, of course." She turns to Ben. "We've got plenty of food, right?"

He nods, closing the fridge. "Plenty. Extra green beans, in case Frank says he doesn't eat sweet potatoes, either."

"Mom's boyfriend. Always on a diet." She shakes her head.

"Diabetes is not a diet, sweetheart."

"L.A. diabetes is like . . ."

"L.A. sober?" I smile.

"Exactly!" Lara grins. "Why don't you stay tonight, and have Thanksgiving with us tomorrow? Unless you have plans?"

"I don't have plans."

"Then, come on!" She squeezes my upper arm. "Don't be alone on a holiday."

"We'd love to have you." Ben smiles. "Don't feel awkward. Lara collects strays. That's how she found me."

"It's true." She moves to the sink and fills two glasses with water. "Sweet little tech bro, until I scooped him up and brought him back here." She takes a sip and hands me one. The water is drawn from a well. Not a hint of chlorine. It's been years.

It's getting late, and the sun's going down. They ask if I'm hungry, and I say I'm just tired. Ben heats up a bowl of last night's coq au vin anyway, and Lara walks me to my truck. I grab my nearly empty duffel and hold my goat-milk soap ends. We walk to the guesthouse. It is light and bright, with a porch on the front and a garden in the back, and I can see the goats and the cows from the window next to a table with a chess set and a bookcase. I ask if I can help put the animals away, and she says not to worry about it, but they'll be up early tomorrow if I want to join. She points out the kettle and the tea bags and instant coffee and fresh towels on the bed and flowers next to the window. She laughs and says she really goes all out when her sister is coming, because, you know, city living is hard. When she gets a break and can come up here, Lara likes to make it nice for her.

And the sun goes down and the windows stay open and outside are crickets and late birds and early bats. I shower with the soap ends; the scent of lilac fills my nose. I use the small bottles of nice things on the sink and put on a clean shirt from my dead friend/her rapist and wrap myself in the quilt at the bottom of the bed. I sit on the Adirondack chair on the porch and listen to the murmurs and munches from the barns. The air is clear and the stars are out and, somewhere in one of the big trees, an owl makes noise.

———◆———

I am up early and in the barn. Lara says, Hello, Jessica. She has to say it twice, because I forget that I lied to her, that I am lying to her.

Ben hands me a coffee and begins mucking stalls. We lead cows to fields and goats to paddocks. She points out the well and the hose, and I fill water buckets while she puts hay on the four-by-four and delivers bales like packages. She asks what I want to do today, and I say I'm happy to help. She says Ben is the cook, so we should just stay out of the way. The kids will be here soon, so get ready.

And the kids arrive, and the sister and the brother-in-law, and they are loud and friendly and funny. No one asks, Who the hell is she? Everyone laughs and says, Lara collects strays. The hot turkey in the back of the car smells bad, and Sister apologizes. Lara says she knew that was a bad idea, and who wants to eat an L.A. turkey anyway. The kids run around, and I walk them to the goat paddock and teach them to hold their hands flat, so no one thinks a finger is a carrot. The air is clean, and I have missed this, the color green, the color blue. I haven't had this sight in years. The kids want to climb trees, so I climb trees. Sister wants to know what I do, so I tell the story of Buddha on the boat, the question of justified violence and my three-part analysis. She nods and asks questions, and, for a moment, I remember it is interesting. The kids ask if I'm from around here and I say, No, I'm from Maine. Where is that? they ask. I describe snow and lakes and bears, a bit like this, but everything is on the other side. Even the bears, the little one asks, the bears are upside down? Of course, I say. Maine bears are famous for being upside down.

Food is ready in the afternoon. The animals get treats of apples and bran, because it's their holiday, too. We sit around the big table. The walls are lined in books, and Ben was right, Frank doesn't eat sweet potatoes, so we pass him the green beans. The turkey is delicious, and Brother-in-Law laughs when Sister asks if he wants to carve it. He points to Ben and says, I know what I don't know. The kids scream a little and kick a little, and Sister refills the wineglasses. It is loud and lovely, and I am glad I am Jessica today.

Brother-in-Law clears the table and stacks the dishes. Frank and Mom sit outside, and the kids run around on the lawn. Sister dries while I wash. Lara puts the dishes away. There's water and wine and more pie, if anyone is still hungry. Frank, despite his L.A. diabetes, comes back for a second slice.

"You guys are in with the kids tonight," Lara says to Sister. "Jessica is in the guest house."

"Is the blow-up in the closet?"

I wipe my hands on a towel with an embroidered goat on the bottom. "I don't want you to sleep on a blow-up. I can—"

"Don't worry." Sister hands the final plate to Lara. "We're not the ones on the blow-up." Outside, the children scream. One comes running in and grabs my leg. The other follows, shouting he didn't do it. They play hide-and-seek behind me; little hands hug my hips until Sister says it's time for baths and herds them upstairs.

Mom and Frank are tired, say they'll watch some TV in the guest room. Ben and Brother-in-Law are talking about recipes and sports and home repair. I go with Lara to the barn, and we bring everyone back inside, feed and water and clean stalls, empty wheelbarrows onto the manure pile. One of the dogs follows us. He sniffs my crotch and rolls on his back.

"Mind if I hang out?" Lara asks as we exit the barn, lights off and animals happy. I shake my head and plug in the kettle in the guesthouse and find two mugs, put a teabag in each and pour the hot water in, bring them outside, and put them on the Adirondack table between the Adirondack chairs.

"I hope you've enjoyed yourself." Lara takes a cup and looks out over the fields. The hint of ocean is dark now, no oil rigs pinning it down. The trees around us are too big to sway, and even though it's dark the owl isn't out, but small black things dip and dart in the sky. How long it's been since I've seen bats.

"My name's not Jessica." I don't have to say it. I could keep it to myself and drive back into the flames. Lara would never know, but while I am up here, in the clean air with the nice people, I want to feel clean, too.

Her eyebrows lift above her cup.

"It's Sarah."

"Hi, Sarah."

We sit in the quiet. The light from inside the guesthouse shines behind us while the big house glows. In an upstairs window, Brother-in-Law chases a child. Downstairs, Frank eats another piece of pie.

"Let me know what I owe you for staying here." The bats dart and dip.

She sips her tea.

"It's been really great."

She nods.

I grip the mug between my hands. "Don't you want to know why I lied?"

She puts her mug on the table. "You seem nice. People are complicated."

"God, you really have your shit together."

She laughs and stands, grabs the quilt off the back of her chair, and unfolds it, tucking the sides beneath her and wrapping it around her legs.

"I'm friends with Nathan."

She reaches for her tea. "Who's Nathan?"

The owl is here. He makes his hooting sound.

"Nathan from L.A. Nathan from when you were sixteen."

"Oh."

"Do you remember him?"

She laughs again, smaller, that laugh all women do, exasperated but well trained. "Well, if you're thinking of the Nathan I'm thinking of, then yeah, I remember him."

"Is it—" I start again. "Are you—" Fuck. "What do you think about him?"

She looks into the dark. Above us, the owl. Above us, the bats. The nickers and the murmurs and the grunts from the barn. Inside the big house, a child laughs. Lara turns her lips down, the thinking frown. "I don't."

"Don't what?"

"I don't think about him. Not anymore."

"Is this the Nathan who . . ." and I don't want to say it, because it's a terrible subject and a nice night and none of my business anyway. But mostly because I don't want it to be my business. I don't want it to be real. I want women to be liars and men to be victims and Nathan to be alive and preparing a court case of defamation in which I'll testify. No way, no way, there's just no way. He's such a great guy.

She looks at me, eyes soft, the face of someone who has done the group therapy, the one-on-one therapy, the journaling, the crying, and come out the other side. "I was raped by a guy named Nathan when I was a kid." She taps her foot beneath the quilt. "Is that the friend you're talking about?"

I nod.

"Tough news to hear." She sips her tea. "Did you want to know something about it?"

"Did you sign an NDA? Back then?"

"I think so. I mean, I was only sixteen, so I think my parents signed it. But that kept it out of court, and there was some money." She takes a sip. "Is that why you're here?"

"He's dead."

She nods.

"You knew?"

She nods.

I run my finger around the rim of my mug. "Were you black-mailing him?"

She laughs, a real one, and shakes her head.

"Twenty-five thousand a month. Every month." I watch her face. "A banker's check from Nathan to LMC LLC."

She puts the tea on the table, so softly the cup makes no sound, the liquid does not move. She looks at me, decides something, and clears her throat. "About seven years ago, a check came in the mail. It was addressed to me, to my maiden name, which was weird, because I have a pretty small social circle and Ben and I got married when we were, like, twenty-two, so no one calls me Lara Martin. My bank didn't know who it was from, but I held on to it, because, I don't know. Drug money? Wrong person? I mean, you don't just get twenty-five thousand dollars in the mail."

I shiver, and she stands, shuffles inside her quilt to a tack box on the edge of the porch, and opens it. She pulls out another blanket and shuffles back. She hands it to me.

"The next month, another check came. I held on to that one, too. When the third check came, Ben suggested I reach out to the bank. We were worried someone wasn't getting what they needed, and we didn't want to get sued or something." She watches me tuck the blanket around myself. "No one could tell me anything about it. I spoke with some manager, who put me on the phone with a financial planner, and then they transferred me to someone else. It was a week before I talked to, God, I think the guy called from Switzerland.

"He asked me to confirm my childhood address, asked a couple of questions about my younger years, and then said, yup, this is you. I was like, but who is it from? I mean, I grew up a little fancy, but there are some pretty big divides within the one percent." She picks up her tea. "Not all of us have Swiss guys handling our checking accounts."

I think of Ann with no "e," her free ride and ophthalmologist. I think of Jessica, who could probably buy the field of ophthalmology and rename it Pegasus Shit if she felt like it.

"So I told the Swiss guy I didn't want the money unless I knew what was going on, and he said he'd have to get back to me. One week later, I got a letter in the mail: 'Lara, I'm sorry. Nathan.'

"The letter included a return address. I wrote back, reminded him of the NDA, asked what are you doing? He said he was trying to make it right, whatever that means. I wrote back again, said I'm not interested in appeasing your conscience. He said, it's not about my conscience. He hoped the money could help me know that he knew he did a terrible thing. And all on paper. Stationery. His name and address on the letter, handwriting and fingerprints. I don't know. It was like he wanted the clearest possible paper trail."

"Sounds like he was buying his way out of guilt," I say.

"Maybe. My last letter to him, I wrote: What if I don't want the money? Are you going to force it on me? Force something on me again?" She closes her eyes.

"What did he say?"

"His last letter was a blank check, a copy of the NDA, voided by some attorney, and a typed letter from another lawyer laying out all the ways to work around a statute of limitations." She taps one palm against the quilt. "So I cashed the checks, and they kept coming, and a few weeks ago someone called me, maybe that Swiss guy, and said Nathan was deceased but a trust had been set up years earlier and the money would continue."

The owl hoots.

"Do you feel guilty?"

"Guilty?" She turns to me, eyes wide. "Why?"

"Does taking the money set a precedent? That rich guys can buy their way out of trouble."

"Oh, I think that precedent's been around for a while." She grins. "Rapists admitting their guilt, sentencing themselves, if you will, in a world that doesn't, is a pretty good precedent, in my opinion. I guess he could have given it to a charity, but I'm not sure how giving it to women he didn't rape is any better than giving it to the one he did. I view it as reparations, not . . ."

"Indulgences."

"What?"

"Historically, most religious traditions have a financial means by which sins can be purified. Buying your way out of hell, so to speak." Nathan's dissertation.

"Huh."

"Nathan and I were in the same Ph.D. program."

"He was your friend?"

I nod.

"And he never . . ."

I shake my head. I want to say, of course not, but I can't.

"Maybe he, I don't know, got cured or something." She sips her tea. "Why are you here? Are you checking up on the money?"

I shake my head.

"Are you, I mean, did you want proof?"

"Jesus, no."

She waits.

"It happened to me, and Nathan saved my life."

"Wow."

"I mean, he didn't, like, pull the guy off me or anything, but afterward, for the last three years, he was the only person who believed me, the only person who looked after me."

"I'm glad you had that," she says, after a beat. "I'm glad you both had that."

I bear down and feel the slats of the wood on the undersides of my thighs. "It's just so hard to believe, you know."

"I know." She shrugs. "I couldn't believe it, either, and I'm the one he did it to."

The owl hoots. She watches me, like I am watching her. Her

words are as delicate and precise as a cat on a barn beam. "Do you want to talk about it?"

I shake my head.

"Do you want details? Would that—"

"No."

"Well, do you mind if I say something?"

"Go for it."

"When it happened to me, it was like a bomb went off. My whole world turned upside down. I flunked out, and ended up at some hippie school for delinquents in Maui, which I realize doesn't exactly sound like torture, but come on, why should I be the one to move? And it's not like they make special schools for rape survivors."

"Imagine the enrollment numbers."

"No one from my old school spoke to me again. Someone egged our house. My father was fired, because his boss worked for Nathan's parents. We moved. My parents got divorced. Dad died a few years later, and I always wondered if the stress of that time had something to do with it. Nathan was fine. No consequences. Of course, no one would talk to me, so it's not like I could keep tabs on him."

She shrugs. "I remember someone telling me, when I was twenty-five or something and still so messed up, 'It doesn't have to fuck you over.'

"Look." She puts her hand on my Adirondack armrest. "I know that doesn't sound profound, and I didn't get it at the time, but I think, deep down, after it happens you just can't imagine ever feeling normal again. Whether you act out or hide away, the real question is, how do you get back to who you are? I think what that woman meant was, you can get back. You can return to who you were."

"I don't know." My voice is small. Smaller than it is in class with the men, smaller than in the hotel-room interview, smaller than in the woods.

She grabs my hand. "I always read this stuff about making lemons out of lemonade, what doesn't kill you makes you stronger, all that crap. What they're saying is, nothing will ever be the same again, so make the best of it. But I think a terrible thing can just be a terrible thing. You can change and grow, if you want, but you don't have to. Instead, you can find your way back to yourself."

I grip her hand. My throat is tight and there is no ash to blame.

"Nathan was a bump in my road. He got me off track for, like, a decade, but I got myself back. You can get yourself back."

We sit in silence. I mention Maine, and she says she used to go skiing in Vermont. I mention lobster, and she says I need to come back for the oyster festival. A coyote howls. She folds the quilt and puts it on the arm of her chair. She picks up the mugs and says good night. I stay outside and listen to the night sounds. I think of Nathan, floating in a sea of milk.

In the morning, Ben puts coffee in a thermos and tells me to take it with me. Sister and Brother-in-Law each give me a hug and say they are so glad I wandered through the other day. Kids scream and shout, and one plants his face in my crotch. Ben sends me off with a sandwich made of turkey and stuffing and slips me the last slice of apple pie. Lara walks me to my truck. I tell her I'll Venmo her. She laughs, and I know she'll never ask for the money.

She hugs me. We are the same height. Don't feel bad, she says, her arms around me, don't feel bad for being his friend. I put my arms around her. We are the same width. I'm glad she says it, because I do feel bad. I feel bad he did what he did. I feel bad I loved him, I still love him. I feel bad she saw this side of him, but maybe we all have terrible sides, and I feel bad for thinking this, as if the ubiquity of the crime renders it less horrifying. I have missed this, the touch of a friend, and haven't felt it in weeks.

I take the 101 south and pull over somewhere. Ocean to my right. Mountains to my left. The air is still clear and the traffic is still light. I eat apple pie with my fingers, the scent of lilac goat-milk soap on my skin. Surfers and sunbathers frolic along a rocky coast beneath me. I called myself Jessica because I wanted to pretend I had a different life. I think of Lara. Her house filled with books. Her barn full of animals. Family and friends and food. I pull onto the highway and drive toward the smoke and the ash and Flopsy and Rapist. With every mile, I wonder how I will find my way back to myself.

THE STUDENTS TWITCH in their chairs, avoiding my face. Most showed up, impressive since I uploaded their A's this weekend, back in the box, Dog under my feet. I uploaded A's for everything, the papers, participation, final class grade. I destroyed the curve, which Colette may or may not care about, because she may or may not pay attention.

It's gray again. The air is thick. Fire containment went down while I was away. The wind kicked up last night, and even the cool kids have T-shirts over their faces, masks and glasses. They squint at me from the back of the room. There are no windows in this building, but the smell and the soot come through the walls.

Someone's phone vibrates. I open my mouth, but three more go off.

"Hey." I hold the chalk up like a pointer stick.

Cindy stares at her phone. "It's an alert."

One of the seniors says, "We need to evacuate."

I put the chalk on the ledge and reach for my bag. Sure enough, a notification hovers on my home screen.

> **Emergency Alert**
> Wildfire east of 101, north of Ventura.
> Evacuations occurring. Watch news or call 211.

"Look!" A student in the front row turns his laptop to face the center of the room. I come out from behind the table and stand next to someone in a bikini top. On-screen, a video of flames jumping across the 101, fireballs flying from the mountainside toward the ocean.

"I surf on that beach."

"That's, like, two exits from here."

"Whoa!" Another holds up her iPad. Video footage of Oprah's neighborhood, designer windows and $40 cocktails up in flames.

"I had ice cream there last week."

Earbud looks around. "Should we—"

Our phones go off. Beeps, rings, vibrations.

> **Emergency Alert**
> EVACUATION ORDER along Santa Rosa Way
> and Harbor Avenue

"That's where we are, right?"

"We're right in the middle of that."

"Are you sure?"

"Santa Rosa is the post office, dude."

"Harbor Ave is the north of campus."

"OK, guys." I lift my hands. "Let's—"

Noise erupts in the hallway. Doors slam. The kid in the corner opens the door and is pushed back by someone striding past.

"All right, we're leaving." I grab my bag.

Students scramble. Someone trips over a skateboard. Swearing. Sweating. Younger and more fearful than I've ever seen them. A generation of nonchalance slides off their shoulders like shale down a mountainside.

"It's going to be OK," I say to Cindy, who is standing next to her desk, backpack slung over one shoulder, laptop under her arm. She does not move.

Students begin pushing. There are no alarms, no overhead siren or campus broadcast system. Everything is word of mouth. More phones buzz. Someone in the back speaks into their watch. "Mom, can you come get me?"

"Where do we go?"

"Looks like they're opening up an evac center downtown. The buses are picking people up."

"Fuck that. I'm heading home."

"Can I catch a lift?"

The classroom empties in less than a minute. Even Cindy, her eyes wide. The noise outside the door continues. People running, pushing, shouting. Someone speeds past, phone held up to their face as a moving image talks back. The smell is stronger. I find my keys at the bottom of my bag and shut the door.

There are only four classrooms in the annex. Everyone on this floor has left. I take a right through the glass doors into the main area of the building, where young bodies usually drape over furniture, pairs in a single seat, discussions and giggles between bubble tea and internet memes.

I first walked in here with Nathan. We drank coffee and discussed Weber. I made a joke about Americans wearing pajamas in public, and he told me he saw a student in a bathing suit. I said I didn't believe him. The two of us, wide-eyed in this brave new world of West Coast fashion and teenage confidence. It is empty now. A tissue on one chair. A spilled cup in front of a sofa. College interrupted.

I walk toward the doors. The glass windows are dark. People scurry past, shirts over noses, sweatshirts backward, hoodies over mouths. Two professors stand near the doorway. They shake their heads. "I guess we're rescheduling exams."

The ash blasts my face, stings my eyes, and is much worse than an hour ago, when I pulled into the parking lot. I scurry, too, keys in hand, and dodge skateboards, bicycles, running freshmen. The sky is orange, the air bright and black. To one side, the mountain range is a jagged line against a lighter hue, a canvas of Halloween. To the other, the sea is dark and matte and still. The oil rigs like scarecrows at the edge of a field.

People are screaming now. Cars honk and rape whistles blare, and inside the tunnel someone falls. I hoist her up. She spits blood on the pavement. The line to the bus is long. Students grab electric scooters, pile into back seats. Some just run.

I reach my truck and only notice the thickness of the ash when I touch the door handle. Up close, the mountain ranges dance with flames. Somewhere, a siren goes off, and the highway is jammed going north. Honking and swearing. Engines overheat. No texts from Elaine, so I assume she and Empress are on the road. I join the swarm of vehicles, the ash so thick and air so orange I can't see more than the bumper of the car in front of me.

It's not the first time we've received emergency evacuation notices. I guess I've been here longer than I want to admit, since I respond to the threat of burning alive with West Coast indifference. We crawl forward. Someone honks and drives past me on the right, the scrape of their car loud against mine. I wrench my steering wheel, pull out of the gridlock. Another honk, more swearing. The truck is slanted, the shoulder not wide enough for all four tires. I press the gas and try to see through my windshield. There's an exit, cars backed up on that as well, and I swerve right, still on the shoulder, still driving too fast. Middle fingers and "Fuck you"s. I ignore a red light and turn onto a side street, another side street that gets me north to the back roads I discovered once, when I was too drunk to manage the freeway, that lead to the box.

It's two hours before I reach the town with the retired lawyers and actors and second-rate wineries. I'm at the base of the gated community, my hand out to enter the numbers on the keypad, when I see Eric's car. He mouths something and steps forward into the orange haze.

"Hey." I look past him toward the highway, but can't see anything. I hear the shouting, the honking. My T-shirt still pulled over my nose.

"I figured I'd find you here." He coughs.

He opens his mouth and I shake my head. I think of Lara and Ben and wonder if, someday, I can have that, but that day is not today. He holds up a hand and walks around the front of the truck, tracing the hood as if to keep his balance, or not get lost in the haze. He pulls on the passenger-door handle. I lean across and pull up the small nub. He climbs in. I roll up my window.

"They've evacuated this area."

"I'm just making sure they got the dog."

"OK. Can we—"

"Eric." I shake my head. "I need to get the dog, then I need to leave." I gesture to the world around us. "You need to leave, too, in case that wasn't obvious."

"I want to help."

I close my eyes and lean against the headrest. The gun rack pokes my scalp. I forget, for a moment, that the world is on fire, and breathe deeply. I cough and spit, saliva down my top and across my pants.

"Here." He hands me a bottle of water, one of those little ones that fancy Uber drivers keep in the back seat. "Drink it. This smoke is really bad for you."

I take two sips. It tastes like shit.

"All of it."

"No."

"You're exhausted. Just drink the water."

"No."

"If you're going to rescue a dog, drive back through all that"—he points to the highway—"you should at least be hydrated."

I roll my eyes and finish the water. I hand the empty bottle back to him. I put both hands on the steering wheel. He reaches forward and touches my keys in the ignition. He points to the Kesha key chain.

"It was a gift." I don't need to say from whom.

We sit in orange and gray. A siren wails. Another. Through the windshield, the world is dust.

"I got your voicemail."

I laugh. Ash fills my mouth and coats my tongue. It's funny, actually, that I was so off base. I thought the mystery was a homicide, like in the movies. The bitter cop and his sassy sidekick. It would all get tied up in the end. That's the shocking secret, I guess. Drug user dies of overdose. Careless students die careless deaths. Twenty-two out of thirty thousand. Twelve out of twenty-two. The obviousness of it all. Like flipping a coin. "I know what you're going to say."

"What am I going to say?" Soft syllables float from his lips to my ears, like the nights when we lay together, his fingers drawing circles across my back.

"What you already said. Get help."

"That's what I'm going to say?"

"Of course. That's what everyone says." I cough and reach for the water bottle. It's empty.

He's watching me now, eyes tracking my movements. For a minute, I think of the man in the woods, gun aimed at my head. I don't want advice. It tends to come from people like Feminist Carl, and I don't throw out the welcome mat for them. The women in Fridays at Four don't offer advice. They know it doesn't help. Lara tried. It doesn't have to fuck you over, she said, but I'm not sure I believe her. My eyes are heavy.

"What if I don't say that?" His thumb traces slow circles around the open water bottle.

"What else is there to say?"

"Traditional therapy doesn't work."

"True." I yawn, trying to keep it shallow, so I don't breathe in more than I have to.

"There are other kinds of therapy."

I open my mouth to tell him I need to leave, to check on Dog, to head north. There's no hope, Eric. There's nothing here for you. I yawn again, chin to chest, eyes closed.

"What if I told you I know a different kind of therapy?"

"Trust me," I murmur. "I've tried it."

"Not this."

"Eric—"

"Consider it a gift."

My skin feels warm, my limbs feel heavy. My shoulders fall away from my neck. Nathan's laugh, k-holes and mushrooms and E. I yawn again, my breath so shallow I barely register the ash. I reach a hand toward the ignition. It stays by my side.

His eyes are close, but they're blurring now. His whole face is blurring. I open my mouth to tell him, It's nothing you did, I'm sorry that I hurt you. All the things women say so men won't kill them. What I really want to say is, Fairy tales are bullshit. Some of us can't be rescued.

"You're going to love it." His eyes are on me, I think, but my eyes are closed. It's hard to tell. Be still, Dad said, be still when they see you.

"It's over," I murmur, or think I murmur, but the gun rack moves, the whole seat moves. I'm sliding down, toward the floor, toward the ceiling. The air pushes down and the cushion pushes up. My skin weighs against my bones.

I hear something, his chuckle perhaps. A scratch of metal against plastic. A door opening. A blast of heat. The words *"not yet"* whispered above me, floating down as the cool, torn fabric of the seat presses against my cheek.

He is on the other side of me now, my body sliding away. I open my mouth to ask why, why is he above me, why is he driving, but I

'M AT HOME. The view across the mountains is what I remember. Fog rolls in from the coast and fades as I drive north into the woods. I need to keep my eyes open, scan the sides of the road for moose, but my eyes are closed. Someone is driving me. The movement is smooth. It rocks me like the boats with the lobsters and the cousins. My head lolls and I am lying down. I jostle and wonder where we are going, if it's time to help Mrs. Sanghera with her barn or chop wood or pack guns, but there's that smell. It doesn't belong here. It crawls inside my nose, and I try to shake my head. Something is holding it in place. We are not in the woods and there are no animals, only that terrible smell. I cough, and a voice, gentle and soft, drifts down. Dad, his steady hand on mine when my fingers are stiff from breaking ice on water buckets in the morning when the sky was still dark and I went to bed hungry but didn't say anything because he went to bed hungry, too, or when my face got tight from the words of the tourists when they saw the quiet girl with the torn jeans and the faded shirt and wondered what someone like me was doing in a place like that, a place like where I was born. I don't know why Dad is here, why that smell is here. It sounds like Dad, but he couldn't possibly

———◆———

Movement again. Something burning. Something tilting. The earth shifts beneath me, my stomach rolls. I don't remember going to bed. My head pounds, and I wonder if Nathan and I drank more than we had planned. That smell, the one that doesn't belong. Nathan is in his bed, Dad next to him. The little black dog between them. Eyes open, eyes on the ceiling. They're not asleep and the smell is everywhere and no one is moving and I don't know how to wake them. There are hands beneath my shoulders, beneath my knees, and I try to struggle, but I know the scent below the smell. I press my face against the chest. The voice again, deep and calm, designed to soothe wild animals and nervous children. It can't be Dad and it can't be Nathan, because they're in the room and I can't wake them and they don't move. The steady voice presses me against a familiar scent. Movement rocks me, shorter and sharper than the lobster boats, absent the salt and the wind, and I know someone is carrying me, their steps uneven. It is dark again.

———◆———

I'm lying down, something cool and damp against my forehead. Still the coughing, cloying stench. I can't see anything. The mountain range is gone, but I think of cooking, venison stew, dog curled on the rug, wood stacked next to the fire.

The smells are all wrong. The smoke is too thick, too dry, without the hint of chicory and cherry. No crunch of leaves or snow. The meat is too fresh, the tang sharp like a kill shed, not a kitchen. But the heat is there, warmth from the stove, warmth from the fire. Sweat blooms across me. I try to lift my hand, but it won't come up.

I cough, and the voice comes. A soft hand against my head. It tilts me to one side and slips a straw between my lips.

"Drink this." Deep and smooth and calm. An excellent barn voice.

My lips are dry, and I sip. A thimbleful of water reaches my throat.

"Rest."

A kiss.

"It's almost time."

My eyes open.

I am not at home. There are no mountains. There is no stove. The smoke is from the air, not a chimney. The smell remains.

My eyes are dry, and my throat burns. I don't feel my usual post-blackout panic. The frantic check of my body, the search for blood or bruises or semen. Making sure I have my underwear on. Kegels to test for tearing. I don't even feel the hangover, although I've woken up drunk enough times not to trust a pleasant early morning. A giggle rises in my throat. Perhaps I'm finally over it.

My eyes adjust to the light. A hanging bulb behind my head. I tilt backward, expose my throat, and watch the golden halo. It's so pretty, the way the light catches the ash in the room, the way it floats around me, and reflects off the particles like whatever that is in a snow globe.

I bring my chin down. There is a wall in front of me. Wood paneling, but not paneling. Just wood. The inside of a garden shed. My head slides to the left. A small table, a washcloth, a bottle of water.

My body is thick and slow, pressed down by gravity and held up by whatever is beneath me. I feel the edges of the k-hole. I reach for the bottle with heavy arms. The movement stirs my stomach, and I am throwing up. There's a bucket next to the table. The vomit is viscous and thick. Small, sticky pieces lodge in my throat.

I reach for the washcloth and wipe my face. I lean back against the chair. It squeaks under my movement and I look down. It is a lawn chair, designed for middle-aged women in middle-class pools. My head pounds, and I press it against the frame. Behind me, a door opens, followed by a rush of that terrible smell. I twist my head, but all I see is the bulb and its radiant light. Eric steps forth, a golden glow above his head.

"Oh no," he whispers. His voice sounds so much like my father's. "I was worried you'd be sick." He reaches for the washcloth and refolds it, pressing it to my face. "I was hoping you'd sleep through it."

I open my mouth, but the only sound is my coughing, the stench of the outside swirling in. I lean to the side and throw up again.

"Here." He bends to one knee, the golden glow around him. He brings the bucket to my face. I gag, the dry heaves when there's nothing left but the body doesn't know that yet. I lean back against the chair. He lifts an opened water bottle, holds the straw to my lips.

"What's going on?" I ignore the straw.

"You'll feel better soon. Do you want to try going back to sleep?" He presses a hand to my forehead. "It might help to sleep through the side effects."

"What side effects? Where am I?"

"The ketamine hasn't left your system yet. It will wear off quickly though." He tucks a strand of hair behind my ear.

I jerk my head away. "You drugged me?"

"Only a little." The ash lands on his shoulders like fairy dust. "I told you. I want to help."

"How is this helping me?" The plastic creaks beneath me. My

arms are tired, but my words come more easily. Only a little, he said. I flex my fingers.

"I wanted to—"

"Fuck you!" I reach a hand up, slower than I want, but manage to slap him. It's pathetic, a slumping wallop, but his eyes widen. Well, at least I've offended him.

He puts the bottle back on the table and remains on one knee. He lifts the washcloth and hands it to me. I throw it at him.

"You know I'd never hurt you," he says, a wounded note in his voice. As if I'm the one who drugged him, kidnapped him, and stuffed him into a garden shed.

I look around the space, my neck stronger, my head moving more easily. "Where are we?" Nausea rolls through me. I lift my hand to my mouth. It moves faster this time.

"I know what you need, Sarah." He's still on one knee. "Your research. The three parts. When you left me that voicemail, I knew you understood."

He picks a new bottle of water off the floor, makes a big show of the unopened cap, and hands it to me. I shake my head. "I didn't want you to feel any guilt, so I brought you here, asleep. And when you are done, you can go back to sleep. Like a dream."

"Ketamine?" I don't tell him I know all about ketamine.

"A small dose, just enough to free you."

"Nothing else?"

He shakes his head. The Rick Astley face, the gentle eyes. He offers me the water again and I take it. I test my strength; the plastic crinkles under my grip. I move my shoulders. The sound of cars, faint and so quiet a city person wouldn't notice. Somewhere outside is the highway.

"I didn't—"

"I know what you need. I know what you want." He touches my cheek, the fingers as gentle on my skin as his mouth was that night. "We both know it's right."

I lean forward and bring myself upright. To my right, a folding table with something zippered on top. Shelves line the wall. I feel a slight breeze behind me. The door? I turn my head to the left. The far side of the shed is dark. Eric stands, his face gilded by the yellow bulb. Something large on the floor, toward the back of the room. Beside it, a drain.

I breathe deeper. The metal smell, like when I used to roll coins around in my mouth, wondering why my father kept them in a jar on the top of the pantry, why he hoarded them like candy when they tasted so bitter. Fresh hunt.

"The ketamine will relax you, but I'm here to assist."

I test my grip on the armrest. I lift each leg, just an inch. I recite the Four Noble Truths in my head.

"How are you feeling?" he asks.

"Loopy," I say, not quite a lie.

I turn my head to my right, to the item on the folding table. It is black, a thick file in a fabric casing. Zipper on one side, canvas handle on the other.

"I wasn't sure which brand you prefer." He walks behind me and picks up the folder. "This has the best reviews. I got a few extra pieces." He hands me the zippered folder, and reaches for another case on the table, also black. Long and narrow, solid plastic. He pulls out an eight-inch bone saw. I know the brand. It is stainless steel with a vibrant green handle, designed to fit between your middle and ring fingers. Unlike a saw designed for cutting wood, it requires the dexterity of your wrist to angle around tendons, ligaments, and other pieces that hold living things together. The tip is blunt so it doesn't puncture organs and spoil the meat. It's so easy to ruin a kill.

"It came with this, but I don't know what it does," Eric says. He places the saw in my lap and holds up a tool that looks like a cross between scissors and a wrench.

"Rib spreaders," I say. He beams. I feel like I'm passing a test.

I unzip the folder, my hands not entirely steady. A field-dressing kit. Complete with gut hook knife, which looks exactly like, and does exactly what, it sounds like, boning blade, caper, and skinner. Gloves for the squeamish.

People who survive terrible things often say it was unbelievable. An out-of-body experience. I clutch the zippered folder, feeling very much in my body. "What are you going to do with these?"

There are no windows. The cars, if they were cars, are gone now. Heat radiates through the sides of the shed. I shift in my chair and press one hand to my jeans. No wallet in my back pocket. No keys in my front. I don't see my bag.

"Sweet girl." He folds the field kit in my lap, lays the rib spreaders and bone saw on top, stacked like Christmas presents. "These are for you."

I blink.

"I use needles. Or alcohol, funneled into them once they're already drunk. But you"—he shakes his head, his gaze adoring—"I have so much to learn from you."

"What do you want me to do?"

"It's not about what I want. This is about what you want. Field-dressing a deer." He looks giddy. "Or dismembering. I'm not sure on the difference, but you can teach me."

He walks to the left side of the cabin, disappears into the dark. "I brought you both," he says. I shift in my seat, hoist my weight onto my elbows, and swing my legs to the side. I am facing the far side of the shed, but I see nothing. To my left, the door he came through. Underneath it, a bright yellow line. Daylight.

He is moving something heavy and slow. The waft of pennies is stronger. It reaches me through the smoke, the meat is so fresh. He pulls the kill behind him, his body blocking my view.

"You can start with this one. I got it ready for you while you were asleep." He reappears, smile bright beneath the light. He reaches out a hand. "I'd love to watch."

The light overhead shines just far enough that I can almost see an outline. She's already been skinned, it looks like, but it's hard to tell in the dark. The cavity is open, genitals are removed, guts taken out. I ignore his hand and lean forward. The bone saw bites into my stomach.

Her fat content must be high, or maybe she just looks whiter than usual from here. The shape is unclear. If it is a deer, the legs are spread wide. It might be a boar, if they have those around here. Stripped of skin and upside down, all meat looks the same.

I stand, and he walks me two steps forward. We move under the light. Particles sparkle and twirl. The walls are clearer now. Pin-pricks of light visible between the boards. The floor is red. I look at him, and he shrugs. "I didn't bring any buckets, because I figured you wouldn't want to save anything." What an odd thought. Not wanting to save the meat. I follow the line of the legs. In the dark, the shadows are the wrong shape, hocks pointed toward me when they should be pointed away. I tilt my head up to the hoof or severed limb or

A human foot.

I'm stumbling, the red still wet. I'm in his arms, his voice in my ear, the soothing sounds of a farmer to his calf. He moves us away from the hanging thing, the meat with the human foot, past the tools across the floor. We sit, on the other side of the shed, on the plastic chair. I am on his lap.

"It's OK, Sarah." He slides my hair across one shoulder. His mouth is warm on my skin, the slightest press of teeth. "He's yours."

"How?" is all I can manage.

"However you want." He misunderstands the question. He lifts me up and next to him on the plastic. He stands and walks behind the hanging man. Metal scrapes against concrete. The smell gets stronger. The man comes closer. The red climbs over the head, bent too far to one side. No antlers to stabilize it against the floor. A slit in the throat, and the blood has dried down the sides of his face, across cheeks and open eyes, into hair. The chin, mouth, and nose are clean and pale. There is something familiar, eyes staring, mouth shouting.

Flopsy.

"Why him?"

"Because you told me." Eric comes out from behind, reaches a finger under my chin. He kisses the tip of my nose. I stare at Flopsy's open eyes. Lights off. Eric walks back to the body, pushes playfully against the hip. It swings, movement restricted by the broken neck wedged against the floor.

"This one is for dismembering." He looks up, worried. "I hope you don't mind. I just really wanted to try it. And you've done it so many times. You can dress the other one."

"Other one?"

He moves toward the door and reaches a duffel bag the size of a hay bale. He drags it with both hands to the center of the room. He kicks it. Something moves inside. He picks up the bone saw, the rib spreaders, and the dressing kit and places them next to me on the plastic chair. He kneels at my feet. "You study and I do. This time, you do and I study." He jerks his head behind him, toward the bag on the floor and the meat in the back. "These two didn't have much of a record. Thank goodness you told me." He rests his head in my lap. He closes his eyes.

My eyes are on the bag, my hands on his head. I realize I am stroking him. His soft curls stick to my palm.

"They so rarely get caught, and when they do, there's no punishment." He laughs against my legs, his breath warm on my crotch. "That's why I focus on schools."

He lifts his head. "I know you're sad about that one, but he got away with it, too, you know. He got away with it for years."

My hand stills.

"I would never have even known about him if it weren't for that article, that award he received. I saw his name, and figured he had to be an asshole with a family like that. I did some digging and, lo and behold, a report of assault allegations, hidden everywhere but in police records." He rubs a thumb across my lips. "It's usually too hard to get to people like that, but he was right down the road. No security. Not even a lock on the window. People like that get away with everything." He grins. "Not this time."

He leans down, hooks the end of the bag with the curved tip of the blade, and jerks. Inside, a movement, a gurgle. He rips the thick canvas open and pulls back the sides. Rapist, naked and curled, with a fresh slice along his hip and outer thigh.

"He's got enough Rohypnol in him to keep him quiet"—Eric looks at his watch—"but he'll still feel it."

"You roofied him?" I stare at the gutting knife. The other knives, shiny and sharp, wink next to me in the dark.

He points the knife at me. "Fair's fair, right?"

"He didn't roofie me."

"That doesn't matter." He kicks Rapist in the back. Eyelids flutter. Eric doesn't notice. "You need to do this."

I shake my head. A look I haven't seen before crosses Eric's face. He taps the knife against his palm. A drop of blood appears on the pad below his thumb. "You want to."

I don't move.

"You know it's the only way to stop him." The knife taps more quickly. "You know he needs to be stopped."

The woman who left the department. The master's student in the strappy top. The first year at the conference. Fridays at Four.

The knife stops. He moves in front of me. His body blocks the bulb. "You do understand, don't you? You understand what I'm doing?"

Behind him, Rapist's eyelids open.

I open my hand for his knife, but he holds it out of reach. I say the thing he wants me to say, not because he wants me to say it, but because it's true.

"I understand."

———

Eric grins and hands me the knife. He kisses me hard on the lips. "Where do we start?"

"I want to be alone." Rapist blinks. "I want to do this alone."

"But—"

I reach for his face, keep his eyes on me. "When it's over, I'll call you."

His brow furrows.

"Dismembering is a two-person job." I caress his cheek. "I'll need your help."

He kisses my hand, drops it, and walks to the door.

"Really alone," I say, seated beneath the pile of knives. I wag my finger. "No cheating."

He looks wistful. "I'll go for a walk, but I would prefer—"

"I know. But this one is mine."

He gives me a look, something romantic and committed, and opens the door. Light and ash swirl behind him. I glimpse my truck, parked less than ten feet away. An expanse of burnt field and orange sky. He shuts the door.

Rapist blinks. I think of an old comedy sketch, someone pinching his fingers in front of a camera, squishing the heads of people in the distance. I squish Rapist's head with my fingers.

I stand. Knives clatter to the floor. I kneel next to Rapist. I shove his shoulder. He flops open, shucked. His thighs drape and his head lolls. The femoral artery. Surprisingly little mass holds legs to a body. Like tearing off a drumstick. The throat, classic but messy. His chest is bare, but chests are tricky. Hit a rib and all you do is wound them, but if you aim correctly and pierce the lungs or heart, they're clean. The blood stays inside.

Wildlife doesn't let you get this close. Killing with a knife is a farming technique for the docile and domesticated. Mrs. Sanghera used knives. Straight across the throat. I am used to distance. Bullets and arrows. Of course I've used knives, but field-dressing cools down the meat. It doesn't stop the heart.

I could paunch his gut. Let him bleed out. That's a rookie mistake, behind the ribs instead of in front. You have to chase them down, and if you hit the intestinal tract you've contaminated the meat. I haven't made that mistake since I was a kid, but Rapist won't run. I tap the gut hook against his penis. Castration is another tool of farmers. When it's not done properly, they bleed out in minutes. I press the knife below his eye. He twitches. Can't cut around the anus yet.

Maybe this is what he feels when he does what he does. It's not the need or the want. It's the easy power of an unfair fight. Maybe he plans. I bring my thumb and forefinger in front of my eyes again and squish his head. Maybe he doesn't plan at all, just helps himself when he knows he can get away with it. Contrary to nature documentaries with thrilling soundtracks, predators are opportunists, not strategists.

Maybe I do need it. The movies are right. Bad thing happens. Kill bad guy. Feel better. A tragedy is an unfinished comedy. I need to finish it.

Maybe it is the best way to stop him. It's hard to prove it happened, harder to prove it will happen again, but some things you don't risk. Slaughter an uninfected herd to prevent an outbreak down the road.

Or maybe I just want to, and I have more in common with the tourists than I think.

I stand. My back is stiff from the chair. My stomach rolls from the drugs and the stink of the meat. I squat twice and stretch my arms overhead. My legs are strong.

I scan the shed. The wall filled with shelves is empty. I pat my pockets again. No keys. I walk to the door, twist the handle, and breathe through my mouth. Footprints in the ash lead around the back. I step out, the door open, and look to the right. I take two steps. Three steps. Mouth open. Breath silent. Ahead, the earth drops off. Behind, mountains rise and flames lick the sky.

I reach the side of my truck, and above the back tire. I slip my spare keys, perpetually unnoticed by Californians, off the hook and slide toward the driver's-side door. It creaks, the way old doors do. I grip the steering wheel. I lift one leg.

Fuck.

I look over the bed toward the shed.

Goddamn it.

Soft knees, soft ankles. Rapist, fully prostrate, moans. The blood from his hip oozes.

I crouch over him. His eyelids flutter. His mouth opens. I don't know what he's feeling. I've never tried roofies. I approach most recreational chemicals from a position of equity, but I do have a bias against that particular drug. Seems a bit unfair, really. Roofies don't rape people. Rapists rape people. Sounds like a bumper sticker.

"I'm going to get you to my truck." On the other side of the shed, Eric shuffles, waits for me to call him. "It would be *nice* if you could *help*." He blinks again. Another moan. I put my hand over his mouth. "Shut up, motherfucker." I grip my keys between my teeth.

Use your legs, Dad said when we were throwing hay bales with Mr. Todd. Bend with your knees, Dad said when I forgot the sled and we were in the woods with a kill and took turns carrying her, 160 pounds of doe across our backs. I drop to one knee. Rapist doesn't move. I drape his arm above me. I slide my hands around his waist and hoist him up and over my shoulder.

I stand up. He gags above me. I grip his ass with one hand, his hip against my head. Four fingers on front. One thumb in back. I stagger to the door. I shuffle sideways across the metal entrance and pause. No Eric.

I'm at the truck. I tilt sideways. I press the backs of his legs against the faded paint, and let him slide down the metal. He's taller than me; his feet hit the ground with his chest pressed against my face. I lean against him, my body against his naked front, and bring both arms beneath his ass, grip under and around, and lift him on his back onto the driver's seat. He whimpers, my hands on his wound. I shove. One foot catches on the step, and I loop it over my arm and swing both his legs in, under the steering wheel, over the stick shift, until he is curled, fetal again, on the passenger side. I grip the wheel and hoist myself, but my hands slip. I grab the wheel again.

"Hey!" The voice not far behind me. I don't look back. "Sarah!"

I heave myself up. I am turning the key when Eric reaches the door, tears at me through the open window. I fumble with the stick, and Eric darts backward. I let go of the clutch, kick the gas through the floor, and leap forward; Eric is climbing into the bed. I'm out, faster than I thought this old thing could go, tires spinning, dust flying.

Through the rearview mirror, I see a boot kicking the rear windshield. It cracks the glass. The gun rack whacks the back of my head. Rapist makes a noise. Maybe he is crying. Eric screams my name, the gravel spins, tires screech, and my hands, covered in the blood of bad men, slip across the wheel.

We're over the edge of the hill. The ground disappears and highway rushes toward us, perpendicular with the ocean behind it. I slam on the brakes, but we fall, smoke from the fires, smoke from the engine, Eric in the bed. Glass shatters, and pain blossoms when his foot makes contact with my skull. Rapist cries or whines or screams, but the wind and the engine and the tires drown it out.

We slam against pavement. My nose cracks against the wheel.

We jump and bounce, and Eric's foot is inside the truck. I try to stay on the road, but red creeps in from the sides of my eyes, and the wheels slip out beneath me, highway slips out beneath me, and everything is gray and orange until the world smashes again.

Water rushes in where there was a windshield. I slide toward Rapist, the truck lilting to the right, ocean pouring in across the dashboard. The driver's seat is dry, rising up and overhead. Hot, wet skin, passive and unconscious next to me, slips away as the passenger side tilts down. I grip his hair as his face submerges and pull him upward. We tilt together, the truck shifting farther, nose down, passenger side beneath us. I pull again, soaking wet and slippery, bending him at the waist, and drag him toward the steering wheel. His back against the roof, his hips past Eric's foot. His hair comes loose in my hand and I grab again, under his shoulders this time, and pull until something pops behind my eye, but we are up, my feet against the passenger window. I pull us through the driver's-side window, everything sinking, and reach for the outside of the truck.

He is wet and heavy, with eyes lolled back and mouth agape. Water rushes up to my waist. I slide us along the outside of the truck, gripping him, gripping the edge of the bed, until my feet find the rear tire and I clutch him with one hand, the tailgate with the other. The cabin is submerged, but the textured bed beneath my arm is rough to secure farm equipment, not smooth to protect antiques. Rapist moans and coughs, seawater and saliva across my face. I am standing, feet on the driver's-side back tire, clutching the tailgate. The water is to my shoulders, and Rapist is lighter, floating within my embrace. The sky orange and gray, blurry with shades of red and black, and I don't think my eyes are working, but it's darker behind us, rocks against the surf. Overhead, someone waves and shouts from the highway. I open my mouth and something comes out, but it's only water, from the ocean, from me.

Sirens and noise and cars and lights. A rush of people on the road, twenty feet up. A shattered barricade. A cyclist stares down, a minivan pulls over. More sirens and more lights above us. Beneath us, foot stuck in a tangle of broken glass, eyes open, lungs filled, is Eric.

I hold Rapist against my truck, the tailgate above the waves. The water is steady now, lapping as oceans do, just below my chin. His cheek reaches my shoulder. I prop it against my head, his mouth above the water, my arm around him. I don't let go.

YOU WAKE UP. WATCH THE CEILING. GO BACK TO SLEEP. Someone pokes you. Someone prods you. Go back to sleep. Weird sounds, weird smells, you don't know where you are, and everything hurts. You close your eyes. Back to sleep.

Waking up in a hospital is a lot like waking up with a hangover. It lasts longer, and you're dressed in paper, even in Southern California, where you'd think they could do better.

My face hurts and my lungs burn and, judging from the train of men and women in blue pajamas with clipboards who avoid eye contact, I've looked better. I see a phone, a puzzle book, a laptop. I've never been laid up in a hospital. I thought I was supposed to get flowers and teddy bears and chocolates.

The police have been in and out. They took a statement. They came back, took another statement. Old Cop was there, every time someone else came in. Stood against the wall, watching me. It seems like the whole department is walking through this room, everyone except for Eric.

No one says anything about Eric.

Or Rapist. A doctor came in and smiled at me, the way Colette smiled when I won the CAORC Multi-Country Research Fellowship, the smile they give when you are worth their time. He explained the red button, the one with the drugs. The blue one lifts and lowers the bed, so I can sit up or lie down without having to sit up or lie down. I haven't pressed the red button yet.

"Good morning." Another one comes in. Scrubs look like pajamas. Maybe with the medical-school debt they can't afford real clothes? He helps himself to my arm, plays with fluids and needles. He writes things on his notepad. I press the blue button.

"How are we feeling?" He tucks the pen behind his ear.

"Amazing."

He grins, teeth so white they're blue, and I remember I'm in L.A. I saw the hospital name on the thing on my wrist. Some big place with a VIP wing for liposuction and helicopters, and a regular wing for me. His hair is thick; his shoulders are broad. This guy gets laid.

"You're quite the hero." He smiles again. Fucking angelic.

"Awesome."

"It's an incredible story."

"Fantastic."

"Unbelievable, really"—the smile, the eyes—"considering he gave you enough ketamine to take down a horse." The teeth sparkle. "You must have quite a tolerance."

Ah. Hot doctor. Thinking his pretty face will make me confess my illegal drug use. Hot, dumb doctor.

"Golly."

"I can't believe you were able to carry a grown man, operate a motor vehicle, and pull both of you out of a sinking truck with all that in your system."

"Adrenaline."

He looks at me.

I look at him.

"Anyway," he says, "maybe they'll make a movie out of it."

I lift my left hand. Three missing fingernails. "How long have I been here?"

"A few days. You have a visitor. You up for talking some more?"

I try to nod, but I've got a cushion neck brace on. "Sure."

He opens the door. I look to my left, to a tray of food. I stretch the hand with the missing fingernails and nudge off the lid. A Jell-O pudding cup. The Cosby special.

"Hi." Jessica, in her designer jeans and torture heels, a bag so big she could carry herself in it. Frederick follows. He stands in the back.

"Hey." I push the pudding to the other side of the tray. My right arm is bandaged, forearm small and hand bulbous, wrapped in gauze. It looks like a penis. I smile at Frederick. "Hello, you."

"How are you?" She walks slowly, picks her way across the linoleum like she doesn't know how it works. She slides the chair in the corner toward the bed and sits. Crosses and uncrosses her legs. Holds the bag in her lap, puts it on the floor, brings it back to her lap.

I lower the bedsheet and lift the paper gown. Last night, while I played with the blue button, I inspected myself. I have a thick, jagged line from my hip to my knee, a track of stitches that would make Frankenstein wince. From the windshield, a nurse told me. I'll tell people it was a shark, I said. She thought that was funny.

I peel back the gauze.

"Jesus, Sarah."

"Worse than this?" I wave my bandaged fist toward my bandaged face.

"You look like every kid I went to high school with."

I lay the gauze back down and fish the red button out from the side of the bed. "They gave me drugs."

"Those don't really work. PCA pumps lessen the workload of

nurses, but the contents are tightly controlled." She sighs. "It's such a bummer."

I drop the white tube with the red top, less impressed with my restraint. "I'm peeing into a bag."

"Well, that's good, right? So you can rest?"

"There's a stick in my crotch."

"I've had worse things in my crotch."

My lips crack and something pulls inside my mouth. "Did you just make a joke about your vagina?"

"You're rubbing off on me." She gestures to the side table. "I got you a phone and a laptop. Jeff found your Dropbox account and your Verizon, so they should be good to go."

"How—"

"You shared them with Nathan." She looks down. "Family plan."

I swallow.

"I know I already said I'm sorry." She speaks quickly, hands on her lap, eyes on her hands. "You don't understand where Nathan and I come from. He could have gotten away with it. I mean, he could have kept getting away with it. You wouldn't believe the things people do when they know they can. And, trust me, we can."

"I believe it."

"We thought he was nuts when he ran off to that monastery and then he came back and gave away all his money and started dressing, well, like you." She looks up. "No offense."

"It's fine."

"I think he was trying to be better."

"Maybe that's why he was friends with me. Rescue a fucked-up woman as penance for fucking up a woman." I reach for the sippy cup.

"He loved you, Sarah." Jessica lifts the cup and holds it to my lips. She smiles. "Plus, you don't exactly seem like someone who needs to be rescued."

I grin again and my lip splits wider, more pennies across my tongue. "How are you doing?"

She blushes. "I got a job."

My eyebrows go up. It hurts my face, and it's probably rude to look so surprised.

"Drawing. It's a small anime studio. I think they're hoping I'll buy the place." She shrugs. "Maybe I will."

"That's great. Are you, you know, you good?" I gesture to her arms, the track marks hidden under her cashmere poncho blanket thing.

She sits back down. "Considering the past month, I figured it would be better to get ahead of things, so I checked myself in."

My head begins to throb, and I would love to press the red button. I toss it off the side of the bed. "That's great."

"I guess it's time to start taking care of myself. No one else is going to do it."

"I'm here. Frederick, too." I tilt my head in his direction and try to wink, but my eyes are swollen and my cheeks are pressed so high from the neck brace that I doubt he notices. "We'll work together."

She smiles. That soft shimmer, the Hollywood look, which, I think, is actually Jessica being Jessica, even if some dude with an expensive camera decided to pretend he invented it. "You should be able to log into your work." She points to the computer. "I don't know how long they're going to keep you here, so I figured you might need that."

I press the blue button and slide backward. "Thank you." I close my eyes and hear her above me, a whiff of expensive perfume as she tucks the stiff white blanket across my chest. She shuffles, picks up the bag. I hear the door open.

"She's OK, by the way."

"Who?"

"L. Martin. I don't know if that matters to you, but she's OK."

"It matters."

To: Colette Frankenson <cfrankenson@ucst.edu>; Ralph Black <rblack@ucst.edu>; Jeffrey Lurkstenstein <jlurkstenstein@ucst.edu>
CC: registrar@ucst.edu
Fr: Sarah Common <scommon@ucst.edu>
Re: Dissertation Submission

Dear Dissertation Committee,
Attached is a copy of my dissertation.

Regards,
Sarah Common

Figured you'd need this. I'd love to visit Maine.
—J
P.S.—Frederick says hi.

The keys in my pocket, a beautiful cherry-red pickup outside the garage. Dog sniffs the new tires. Under my arm, Jessica's framed drawing of my other truck. RIP.

Elaine offers me half my security deposit. "It's such a shame you can't stay on the West Coast." I laugh.

There are clothes, shoes, sheets by the curb. Last night, I brought two boxes of library books to campus. I walked through the tunnel and noticed someone rewriting the names on the wall. Therapist 2.

I finger the key. I could take everything with me. It's a double cab, extra-long bed. Jessica went all out. Lara would love it. Instead, I announced free stuff online and across campus, with the address and both security codes. People have been driving through all day. Empress is thrilled.

Dog cries while I pack. They always know when you're leaving. I lift my carry-on and new computer into the back seat. The stitches pull beneath my clothes, but a nurse rewrapped my right hand so I can at least use the thumb. Another box of books on the floor. Two pots and some olive oil from the one time I went to a farmers' market, back when I thought that's where farmers were. The sky is gray, but containment is at 45 percent. Campus is closed until after the winter break. Exams have been moved to January. I emailed the students: Don't worry about grades. Take care of yourselves. I'm here if you need me.

Another car pulls up. I wave with one hand, double-check the contents of my bag with the other. I move to the bench outside the garage. Dog flops on the ground, her chin on my foot. Old Cop steps out of the car. He's in jeans and a T-shirt that reads "Grandpa." He walks to the bench. He sits down.

I riffle through my bag. Wallet. Tissues. Lip balm. Keys in my pocket. The pills and powders are flushed. Passport. Phone. Nathan's journal.

In front of us, the billionaire's fields. While I was in the hospital, the cattle were rounded up for the slaughterhouses. The hills are bare.

"Why?" he asks, staring straight ahead. I know this voice. His world is different now. He wants it to go back to the way it was. He wants what happened not to have happened. He does not yet understand this can never be.

"Why what?"

"Why did you save him?"

"I only had time to save one."

The fields are brown and dry and empty. "Why save either?"

One cow, in the distance, crests the mountain. She begins to graze. I shrug.

"I would have thought—"

"I don't care what you thought."

He shuffles his shoes in the sand beneath our feet.

"Are you glad you did it?"

"No."

"Do you regret it?"

"No."

He leans forward, lets his breath out like he's been holding it a long time. "I can't believe it."

"Sometimes people do things we can't believe." The cow wanders along the crest. There's always one, the estate manager told me with a smile, his teeth missing, his eyes bright, one that escapes the cull.

"I feel like an idiot."

"Well, at least you didn't sleep with him." Dog gazes at me with forgiving eyes. I scratch her head.

"I'm sorry." He clears his throat. He looks at me. He's not talking about Eric anymore.

"OK."

"It's just—"

"Nope."

He closes his mouth.

I send him off with Heidegger and a fry pan. He says it would be better if I didn't leave the state until the investigation is finished. I say I'm a regional hero and I'll do what I want. Old Cop drives away, over hills and around bends. On the top of the mountain, at the edge of the sky, the cow lifts her face to the sun.

Rapist was lying in the hospital bed. Still is, as far as I know. They put him into an induced coma. Apparently, Rohypnol + blood loss + fluid in his lungs and, despite my best efforts, significant blunt force trauma = some pretty bad shit. Don't worry, one of the nurses said when I went to look at him. His vitals are great. He'll get out of this just fine. I nodded and asked to be alone. Of course. When we wake him, we'll be sure to tell him who saved him. He needs to know!

Yes, I said. He needs to know.

There were fewer tubes than I expected. Only a few going into one arm, the crease of a narrow elbow, another coming out the top of his right hand, just above his long digits. The bruises on my hip, four purple marks in a half-moon, the thumb an exclamation point along my back. Most people would describe his hands as delicate.

I saw a movie once where the bad guy killed someone with an empty needle, something about air bubbles in the bloodstream. I looked at my IV, wheeled in beside me, the needles in my arms. I could have pulled one out and sucked some air into it. No one would suspect me. An injection would have been poetic, much more so than Rohypnol or dismemberment. I would be inside him this time.

I didn't kill him in the shed. I didn't kill him in the hospital, but I did stand there, propped against the IV pole. I stared down at the unconscious man. He was naked. Limp dick between still thighs, face-up, in a paper dress. We were alone in his room. Behind the door, people walked and talked and laughed, but we both knew what you could get away with in a quiet room with people down the hall. I leaned down and asked him if he could hear me, if he remembered. I asked if he knew what had happened to Flopsy, if he understood why Eric did it. The machines beeped. The bags dripped. He did not speak. I leaned closer, bruised and bloodied face against his.

I told him I was going to tell him a secret, something I would never tell anyone. I told him I was going to tell him something no one would ever believe. I'm such a great girl.

I told him how long I waited, one hand on the wheel, before I went back and carried him out. How long I sat, the knife beneath his eyelids. I told him how steady my hands were. I didn't need to. I didn't want to. But it may have been the right thing to do.

I leaned closer, my teeth above his jugular, my eyes on the slow pulse of his throat. My fingers found their way to his neck, and the ease of it, the thousand tiny voices telling me how good it would feel, how natural, and I wondered if this was why Jessica struggled as she did, if addiction was a voice telling you who you are. I stepped back and opened the door. Outside, nurses and doctors and family members. Statistically, he'll do it again. He'll get away with it again. This is who he is. My fingers twitched.

The truck is packed. Empress stays in her tower. She will snoop through the empty studio when I'm gone, looking for something to write about in her weekly column. I leave the USB stick next to the bed. Elaine went into town. She will clean after I leave. She will put another advertisement online. She will cater to the tantrums of the woman with the silver hair who sleeps in a separate bed, on a separate floor. It's amazing how some people love some people.

Are you heading back home? a nurse asked me while I filled out the discharge paperwork. I am, I said, I am going home. People who love you, they will want to know what happened, Nathan said. Cardamom and sunsets.

Dog lifts her head. She pads to the garage and nudges the bag of food. The dust from Old Cop has faded. His confusion, like Eric's, his face in the rearview mirror. His foot caught when we went over the barricade, when I pulled Rapist past him and he watched beneath the water, eyes open with rage and shock. In the end, his world didn't make sense, either.

I turn to the dog food. One of the few things the freebie crowd hasn't taken.

Nathan never asked me why I studied violence. He probably thought it had something to do with violation, that I was processing, as so many do, mistaking scholarship for therapy. But I chose my subject matter before I met Rapist and Flopsy and Colette, before I joined Fridays at Four. I studied violence because the world is violent, because I know violence. I studied violence because I am violent.

There was a day when my truck was in the shop. Sometime in

our first year. I was waiting at a bus stop downtown. Before the fires, before the rape, when the air was clean and the nights were soft. Nathan, back when he had a car, pulled over.

Just enough room for a damsel in distress, he shouted. I laughed and hopped in. We bought caramels. We discussed readings. Back then, we took classes instead of taught them, we thought we had a chance. He told me about his sister and his monk life. I told him about the little black dog, my father and my childhood, growing up a woodland creature in a dark, deep forest.

It sounds hard, he said, but kind of wonderful.

Gas is topped off and the back seat is full. Some clothes, some books, music from a dead man's apartment. I turn on Tracey Chapman and pull Nathan's journal out of my bag. I put it on the dashboard. It's amazing how some people love some people.

The passenger side has space. Just enough room for a damsel in distress.

I steal the dog.

ACKNOWLEDGMENTS

Someone told me they see acknowledgments as the history of the book, how it came to be.

This book came to be through my brilliant agent, Catherine Cho of Paper Literary. Catherine responded to a cold query with no relevant publications, no M.F.A., no insider connections. Catherine read the book in one day, offered that same day, tied herself to an unknown, with no track record, no sales record, before any competing offers. Her brilliant editorial eye, and that of Melissa Pimentel, have been immeasurably helpful.

This book came to be through my wonderful editors, Vanessa Haughton and Jennifer Barth at Knopf, who improved the manuscript by leaps and bounds, and Ella Gordon and Areen Ali at Wildfire. All have graced me with their insight, professionalism, support, and humor. Publishers of the works most meaningful in my life, these imprints humble me with their association.

This book came to be through my teachers, fellow writers, supporters, and friends. Henriette Lazaridis and the delusions of grandeur, Michelle Hoover and my favorite year. Rachel Howard, Lori Ostlund, Valerie Fioravanti, the writers of Sacramento, Danielle, Naomi, Gab. Morning café and retreats in Bourne. Everyone who read, responded, offered feedback and encouragement, I thank you.

This book came to be through my family. How lucky I have been.

This book came to be through my students.

This book came to be through my animals.

This book came to be through the man on my back. I have carried you a long time. I set you down now.

This book came to be through everyone who knew about the man on my back. I have carried you, too. It is time for you to carry yourselves.

This book came to be through two friends in particular. Without them, there would be no book, because without them, I would not be here. How do we thank those who keep us afloat? How can I pay back the gift of keeping me alive?

Her name is Sarah. His name is Nathan.

A NOTE ABOUT THE AUTHOR

CHRISTINE MURPHY has lived, worked, and traveled in over one hundred countries, including eleven months in a tent across the African continent and a year as a resident in a Buddhist nunnery in the Himalayas. A trained Buddhologist, Christine has a Ph.D. in Religious Studies. This is her first novel.